THE SILK SCARF

AUSTRALIAN AT HEART BOOK 3

FRANCES DALL'ALBA

Poinsettia
Publishing

Also By Frances Dall'Alba

<u>Australian At Heart Series</u>
Little Blue Box - Book 1
The Stone In The Road - Book 2
The Silk Scarf - Book 3
Rustic Denim Love – Book 4

<u>Sway Of The Stars Series</u>
The Shooting Star – Book 1
The Glittering Star – Book 2
The Giving Star – Book 3
The Priceless Star – Book 4

<u>Standalone Books</u>
Eight Seconds
Jack & Eva

For my dad, for providing nourishment for a healthy mind.
And for Lisa — my critique partner and friend. Still in this together.

Chapter 1

M elita Van Der Meeliko had to get her act together. *Take a deep breath, girl.*

Three years after that last kiss should have cured her of the crush she had on Luke Harvey, but his arrival only caused the swirling in her stomach to intensify. Nothing had changed.

The intersection on the Bruce Highway, which linked Brisbane to Cairns, looked no different to when she'd limped off the road with a flat tyre two months ago. *To South Johnstone*, read the lichen-encrusted sign on the side of the road, with cane fields stretching as far as the eye could see in one direction and banana farms in the other.

Melita got out of her car and waited for Luke to do the same. They'd driven from opposite directions, she forty kilometres from the Tully township, and Luke eighty kilometres from the Cairns airport.

When he got out and stretched his arms above his head, she held in a groan. His navy cotton shirt, pulling taut over his chest and shoulders, couldn't hide the result of hard physical work as a tradesman. His body was a work of art. His messy sandy-blond hair hadn't changed, but the smattering of stubble on his face had her licking her dry lips. She swallowed, hoping to calm her racing pulse.

Was he nervous about this meeting too? It had only been one kiss. One that she remembered whenever she closed her eyes at the end of a long day.

"Melita, wow, this is out in the sticks." He gave her a quick hug.

Taking a step back, she gulped in a lungful of air. If he agreed to do the renovations, how would being together work?

Her mouth opened and closed soundlessly until she ground her jaw and clenched her hands. *Get a grip.* "Hi, Luke, thanks for agreeing to come."

"Hey, you did all the organising. I just hopped on the plane."

Did she detect resentment in his voice? Was he annoyed that she'd paid for his flight and hire car? But since this was her project and she didn't want anyone else doing the renovations, of course his travel costs were hers to cover.

"Come and take a look inside," she said. "The settlement came through last week."

Luke raked a hand through his hair and glanced at the house. "Any idea how long it's been sitting empty?"

Melita walked towards the forlorn-looking building she'd stumbled across two months ago. "It was built during the 1930s and has been vacant for most of that time. That's all I know."

"Mmm."

Uncertainty assailed her, the same as it had when she'd first seen the house. It was old, really old, and Melita couldn't shake the feeling that there was a good reason it had been abandoned. But she came from money, so she understood that whoever built this house had clearly done so with a sense of design and an unrestricted budget.

The front door opened on a squeaky hinge. There'd been no keys to hand over; the real estate agent had apologised.

"What a waste for it to sit vacant for so long."

Melita shrugged. "It's perfect for what I want."

Luke's gaze met hers and held. "You think?"

She managed to ignore her rapidly beating heart. "I know it's in the middle of nowhere, Luke, but take a moment to listen to the traffic on the road. It never stops. This property is positioned on the only major highway running along the east coast of Australia. It's smack-bang between Port Douglas and the Whitsunday region." She turned away from his probing gaze and fingered a mouldy wall, leaving an obvious streak. "If you exclude the Sunshine Coast and Gold Coast, this stretch of highway is dotted with every other popular Queensland holiday destination. Not to mention a dozen spectacular waterfalls."

Luke chuckled as he turned on the spot. "You've done your research, hey?"

"I know my market."

"You're not worried about how isolated it is?"

Her shoulders lost their tension. Moving to Australia had taken her a long way from the rich Boston suburb where she'd grown up, but she'd never felt so at home. "No, I'm not. Every woman, man and child needs swimwear in the tropics. I want a signature business marker and a place where I can set up my manufacturing crew. You've heard my one thousand and one ideas before, but I always come back to this. A tea house and exclusive swimwear boutique, all in one place."

Before they'd shared that kiss, she and Luke had been friends. He'd taught her to drive and, as he'd been the first person to spend more than five minutes listening to her, she'd spilled all her ideas for the future.

Luke nodded and left her side to continue his inspection of the two-storey house.

If anything, Melita's resolve to succeed in this project had strengthened; two months had not dampened her enthusiasm. She'd looked past the ghastly yellow paint ingrained with black mould, the broken windows and the emptiness that tugged at her. Instead, an image swayed in the heat's haze, one that included a building with rendered round edges, high sides decorated with finials and a second storey with a stunning view of the ocean in the distance.

Ever since she'd secretly entered and won that swimwear design contest at fifteen, her passion had never waned. Small successes had only fuelled it further. This place would provide an outlet for her designs that were starting to find a foothold in the swimwear market.

A flurry of movement had her turning towards the staircase. Luke ambled down, looking up at the decorative cornice, a feature she wanted to keep. She fought the urge to touch him when he reached her side. Instead, she curled her fingers and waited for his appraisal of the house.

"It's surprisingly very solid," were his first words, and she released a huge sigh. "I want to hear all your plans, to gauge whether the renovation is feasible."

She tilted her face and managed a lop-sided smile. "I'd like a few walls knocked out to open up the café. That sort of thing."

Luke gave her a long, hard look, a hint of puzzlement in his eyes.

She sucked in a quick breath. Was he feeling something too?

"Are you sure about this, Mel?"

What did he mean? Was he referring to the project or them? They had parted with unresolved issues. "I am."

He nodded, his gaze never leaving hers.

Three years ago, her half-sister, Ella, had stormed into her life, turning it upside down for the better. Learning of Ella's existence had been the first bombshell to drop her way in her short twenty-four years. Ella was also Luke's half-sister, though he and Melita shared no blood ties. That had never been their issue.

She dragged her gaze from his so she didn't melt into a puddle at his feet. "I know it's a long way from home, but I'm going to set up base in Tully. You'll have the use of a rental property there for as long as the renovation takes."

She flicked her gaze back in his direction. His eyes were downcast as he rubbed his chin. She hoped he was considering taking on the project.

How would they cope being together all the time? She was desperate to keep emotions out of this arrangement because she'd never been able to gauge what had driven Luke away. That one kiss they'd shared on a stormy afternoon had left her wanting more, but she didn't blame Luke for walking away, whatever his reasons. Her own parents had been incapable of loving her. Had never shown her any affection or love. She'd reached adulthood believing there was something wrong with her.

She shrugged the thought away. All the more reason to succeed in her business venture; she could only blame herself if it went wrong. "I have a good vibe about this place, Luke. Will you help make my dream a reality? I wouldn't want anyone else doing the work."

A frown creased his brow.

In the past two months, she'd worked herself up. It was a few years since her mother's suicide had crippled her confidence. On all fours, she'd crawled back to some semblance of normality. Succeeding in business meant she could claim she'd recovered, rebuilt her confidence and achieved the dreams she'd tucked away long ago.

"It'll take weeks to get the plans and approvals through council and—" His voice snagged and he cleared his throat. "And what about working together?"

He reached out and brushed her cheek. Her breath hitched.

"We'll be around each other a lot. Consulting, discussing, planning." He hesitated before adding, "I'm not sure how it'll go."

She swallowed, resolved to get on with her business. "Me neither. But I need you here, Luke. I trust you."

He dropped his hand. "Even after what happened?"

"Nothing happened." *And it probably never will because I'm incapable of being loved,* she wanted to scream. *Not even my goddamned parents could love me.*

His odd expression brought back the tightness in her chest. She'd never understood his reasons for ending their friendship. That one kiss cancelled out all the good moments they'd shared, never to be repeated.

Still, she was tempted to reach up and kiss him. Remind him of how good things had been between them. But if she was the only one that felt that way, how would she ever recover from the shame? Better to renovate her property and succeed in business than embarrass herself by inflicting her love on someone who didn't want it.

His husky tone sent a shiver up her spine. "We were good friends once."

Melita could only nod. Couldn't swallow or speak. Luke was worth a thousand friends, and in reality, she didn't have too many.

His odd expression returned, along with a little smile. "So, what's the go here? My flight leaves in four hours and it's a two-hour drive back to the airport."

Resolving to keep it strictly business between them, she cleared her throat and tried hard to ignore his good looks. The years had only enhanced the width and breadth of his shoulders and the corded muscles in his arms. His torso oozed with strength. It was time to shake off her attraction or it'd taunt her forever. One project. Six months. Move on to the next. Business only.

"I didn't want to take up too much of your time," she said. "I'm in Brisbane again next week, but I wanted you to see the building for yourself, spend a couple of hours here, get a feel for it. And I wanted to show you what I have planned."

Luke nodded. Putting his hands on his hips, he took another look around. "It was only the cost of a flight and car hire, anyway. Not a big deal for you."

There it was again, that touch of resentment. Did Luke have an issue with her money? She clenched her jaw, the urge to grind her teeth as strong as ever. Her wealth hadn't been a problem when they'd been friends.

Leave it be, she scolded herself. Her money wasn't going anywhere. If he couldn't love her as she was, it was better they'd gone their separate ways.

"Let me show you what I want done. You can tell me if it's possible, or if I'm just dreaming."

Her words elicited a smile from Luke, which nearly undid all her good intentions.

"You're the biggest dreamer I know." His hands came up, daring her to defy his claim. "Just putting it out there."

For some absurd reason she began to laugh, and Luke, with his disarming smile, followed suit. They needed this if they were going to work together, being able to laugh at stupid jokes. It was what she missed so damn much about their friendship. Thankfully, their shared laughter speared the tension between them and scattered it around the room.

Could she pretend they were friends again?

Still chuckling, Luke meandered towards the only window in the downstairs room and stared through the grubby glass. "Ella phoned me last night and told me about Flynn."

Melita sobered up. "Shoot, that didn't take long. I haven't told anyone yet."

Luke turned and leaned against the sill. "When did you find out?"

"Two days ago. Dad travelled from Boston with Flynn." She was still processing the second bombshell to fall her way—the second biggest secret reveal of her life.

Even though he was a few feet away, Luke's concerned gaze touched her like hot burning tongs. "Are you okay about it?"

His concern disarmed her and she blinked rapidly.

"Aw, Mel." He closed the distance between them and took her in his arms. "Want to talk about it?"

She inhaled deeply, accepting his closeness. She'd missed this so much, being able to talk to Luke about anything. Three years was a long time to bottle things up, and the news she'd received had rattled her.

Luke took her hand. "We'll discuss the house soon. Come and tell me what's upsetting you." He led her outside and plonked himself under a tree in the backyard.

Letting her hand slip from his, she looked down at him. "Can you put me out of my misery first? Will you do the renovations?"

He patted the spot beside him. "Of course, and you can thank that cute Boston accent of yours."

Relief whooshed past her lungs and she smiled. "I think I've lost most of it. I'm speaking more like an Aussie every day."

Luke's eyebrows rose and he pulled a face. "Er ... I think you've still got a way to go."

She chuckled, enjoying the fleeting carefree moment.

"Now, tell me about this brother of yours. Will I like him?"

Dragged back to earth, she squared her shoulders and took a seat beside him, careful to keep her distance. "Thank you, Luke. You have no idea how much your help means to me." She leaned against the tree and allowed her body to relax.

Luke wasn't so cautious; he took her hand and held onto it.

Melita wasn't in any hurry to take it back. It was all the prompting she needed to bare her soul, to tell him what was twisting her in knots. "Five or so years ago, I would've welcomed the news I didn't belong to my family."

"Hey, you never told me things were that bad." Luke gave her hand a gentle squeeze.

She grimaced. "It wasn't something I wanted to share. Things weren't pretty in our monstrosity of a mansion. I never said anything, but I've never been able to shake off the hunch that somehow Dad was to blame for Mom's death."

"But didn't she commit suicide?"

Pain sliced across her chest and she reached up and rubbed against it. All these years later and it still hurt to think about that day. "I'm sure you remember how much of a bully Dad was from Ella's abduction court case."

Luke nodded.

"Hard to believe he's the same man, isn't it?"

Luke squeezed her hand again, giving her the strength to dredge it all up.

"He changed when Ella entered our lives. Coming face to face with his long-lost daughter was a huge wake-up call. Ella didn't care how much money he had and didn't spare him a thought when she dragged me and Patrick to Australia with her. But then you already know all this."

Luke released her hand and folded his arms behind his head. "Head-strong. Yup, that's our Ella. You should've tried growing up with her."

Melita managed a half-smile she wasn't feeling. He could always turn a serious conversation into a light one.

"And look at Patrick," she continued. When her brother had arrived in Brisbane, he'd agreed to check-in to a rehab clinic in the outback. "Within two years of cleaning himself up, he's happily married and successfully running his own cattle station."

"And then?"

"Just when I think my path is clear and things might go to plan, I ..."

"Find out about Flynn," Luke finished for her.

"My biological brother I never knew existed."

Luke shifted closer and she fell back against his shoulder. She tucked a tendril of hair behind her ear when a soft breeze twirled around the tree. "I was so mad with Dad. If Flynn hadn't come looking for me, I'm not sure I would've ever found out. It's not like Mom had never conceived a baby. Why would I ever think I wasn't hers?"

"So why were you adopted?"

"Mom had a miscarriage that sent her spiralling. It wasn't her first apparently. After my biological parents died in a car crash, dad heard about me through a work associate and basically used a lot of money to buy me. Thought it might help Mom heal, except in the end, it didn't do jack shit."

"Aw, Mel, that sounds awful. What about Flynn? How's he taking this?"

"Oh, Luke. It was all very civil. Flynn flew over from Boston with dad, and Patrick was there too. When I had a chance to calm down, Flynn looked tense and a little lost, like he really wanted a sister. That's when all my anger drained away."

Luke kneaded her arm and she dared to relax this close to him.

"He's two years older and grew up knowing he was adopted, with a little sister somewhere out there in the world."

"What's he like?"

She didn't hesitate to reply. They'd only met two days ago, but the thread that bound her and Flynn was real and tangible. "He's terrific, Luke, he really is. We have the same eye and hair colour. It was so weird. Within a few seconds of having Flynn sit across from me, a lot of questions I'd subconsciously asked over the years were answered."

"Like what?"

"My name, for starters. Who calls their child Melita, with a surname like mine? I don't mind it, but it is a mouthful."

Luke chuckled. "So Melita's your birth name?"

"Yes."

"And what does this brother of yours do?"

"All things marketing and web design."

"Oh, yeah?" Luke shifted away from the tree, forcing Melita to turn sideways. "Is he already employed by the very clever Melita Van Der Meeliko?"

Melita burst out laughing and nodded in reply. Flynn had indeed been briefed about her project and his enthusiasm for it was infectious.

Learning of Flynn's existence was timely. A wake-up call of her own. It was good to be reminded that family was important. She'd never been able to pinpoint the pivotal turning point when her father had changed, and she sometimes struggled with the intimacy he now showed. Confusion and hurt still knotted her chest when she was with her father. Why couldn't he have been a more caring parent when she and Patrick were kids and desperately needed his attention?

Luke rose and helped her up. "Okay, time to run through what you want done here." He said, flicking grass and twigs off the back of his shorts.

She sighed and checked the time on her phone, prepared to push the awkwardness with her father to the back of her mind. If she'd reacted differently to the news about Flynn, it might've fractured what was left of their family unit. It wasn't the first time they'd had to rebuild. She would do what was necessary to keep her father happy and take on the challenge of getting to know her new brother.

As for treating Luke as a friend ...

Okay, I can do this. Or fail trying.

Chapter 2

Luke fitted his mask to his face just as the last piece of wall crashed to the floor and a cloud of dust rose. He waited a few minutes for it to settle before giving a thumbs up to the demolition crew, indicating it was time to come in and clean up.

Nearly fifteen metres of internal wall had come down. Was it too much? None of it had been structural, but it still made him nervous. Though he'd been on the tools since he was sixteen there was still so much for him to learn. A mistake could cost him every cent he'd managed to save.

He spent a few minutes rolling up the barricade tape used to cordon off the area and carefully packed away his demolition saw. Then picking up his toolbox, he made his way to the other side of the building where a pile of his tools lay.

Discussions over the design of the tea house had been long and varied. Melita had some great ideas but was happy to put her faith in him. He needed to make her renovation dreams come true or it would keep him awake at night.

Or was something else eating at him?

Before he'd discovered Melita was adopted, sharing a half-sister with her had never been a problem. So, what was the problem now? Nearly six months had passed since he'd learned of her brother Flynn.

He removed his dust mask and hard hat, mussed up his hair and walked outside for a dose of fresh air. Sweaty, dusty and distracted was the norm for him lately. He couldn't be in the same room as Melita without his body reacting to her closeness. Nothing had changed.

She was due to arrive any minute. Having recently relocated to Tully, she'd set up a new workshop for all the staff who wanted to follow her from her small set-up in Brisbane. She'd borne all the costs of the move, of course—but then, money wasn't a concern for her.

Was this why he continued to hold back? There was no longer any reason, except for the money issue. The problem being, in his case, he'd skimped and saved every cent of his savings, while she had a shitload and her bank balance tripled every year. At least he earned his money.

No! Stop! That wasn't fair. It wasn't her fault her great-great-grandfather had set up trusts all those years ago, and from what Luke could tell, she didn't squander hers. She was money-smart and learning more every day. Her words. He just had to trust himself a little more and be confident his building abilities wouldn't waste her money on his mistakes.

He walked to his utility for his water cooler and swigged a couple of mouthfuls straight from its tap. Replenished and suddenly buoyed knowing he'd see Melita soon, his mouth turned up. He pictured her face when she saw the result of the demolition.

The bulk of the building's ground floor would be an open plan cafe. The second floor would house the boutique and changing rooms. The actual design and manufacture of her swimwear would happen in a new detached building at the rear of the large block. He'd be overseeing its completion too.

Leaning against his utility, he watched the demolition crew clean up, pushing aside his concerns about his lack of confidence, and his reasons for not sleeping well at night. Instead, he visualised Melita's small, slim body, perfectly moulded in all the right places, and the smattering of freckles on her nose, which he'd been wanting to kiss again for a hell of a long time. Well, he'd get to those after kissing her full on the mouth first. Then there were her unusual grey eyes with brown flecks that eyed him appreciatively each time she looked his way. He wasn't blind.

Stop it, fool!

He wasn't about to blow this amazing opportunity—a limitless budget and a great idea. And when this tea house took off, she wanted a second to follow. He could easily be employed by Melita Van Der Meeliko for years, meaning he might finally make his mark in the building industry as a specialist in eco-green smart buildings.

Ah, shit. If he couldn't get over the money issue, he should move on as he did three years ago.

But the need to wrap her body in his arms continued to linger.

Desperate.

Yep, that was a word floating around his head lately.

"Have you got time for a quick snack?"

She asked the same question every time she turned up. Today she carried a tea towel-covered woven basket.

Luke smiled, doing his best to ignore the terrible job her denim shorts were doing of hiding her shapely legs. She was the best promoter of her swimwear, hats and accessories, and was never too proud to wear and show them off.

He nodded. "Let me wash my hands."

He made his way to the backyard and the only working garden tap on the property, though it wouldn't do much for the dust in his hair or the thick layer on his high visibility work shirt. Next to Melita, he looked rough around the edges.

Surely, with Melita's upbringing and fortune, she would prefer someone more refined, well-articulated and educated. She oozed class, with the way her russet-brown hair was styled and her scarf wound loosely around her neck. As he was only a run-of-the-mill tradesman, she was *way* out of his league.

But that didn't stop him from wanting her.

Bending over, he splashed water on his face, then some on his head to dampen his hair and smooth it down.

He turned back and came up short.

Melita waited, towel in hand. "Need this?"

He chuckled. She understood him better than he did himself. "Thanks. I would've used my shirt, but that would be a waste of time."

She turned and headed for the front yard. "I know."

He swore she swung her hips, more so than usual, for his pleasure.

Swallowing a groan, he clenched his hands and followed her. Things would end badly between them one day, because friendship was not enough.

As they sat in a shaded spot on the lawn, he asked, "So what did you bring today? A thick slice of mud cake or a decent curry pie wouldn't go astray."

She frowned, making him laugh.

"Are you telling me I'm out of luck?"

"Luke Harvey, thank God I'm around to save you from yourself. I have a delicious wrap with chicken, salad and bean sprouts."

He feigned disappointment. "What sort of rabbit food is that? Did you at least throw in a beer?"

She pulled out two bottles of water with a smirk.

He loved the banter between them. She'd been surprising him during morning or afternoon smoko lately and he appreciated every visit she made to the site. Their first meetings and planning conversations had been awkward—until he'd saved them by telling bad jokes and making her laugh. For now, he would take anything he could.

When she reached into her woven basket, she added, "I did bring you a treat."

He quirked an eyebrow. "Oh, yeah?"

She pulled out a massive slice of chocolate cake and held it up out of reach. "Healthy food first."

He burst out laughing and, leaning forward, kissed her on the cheek. They both froze—he'd even surprised himself—and warily eyed each other. He could barely swallow as he lost himself in her eyes. This was the first move he'd made since agreeing to renovate the property.

"Hey, boss, better come and see this!"

One of the demolition crew had bellowed across the yard, jolting Luke out of his trance. He rose on unsteady legs and cursed his stupidity. *Good one, dopey.*

Looking down at Melita, he reached for her hand. "Want to see what the problem is?"

She nodded and put her hand in his. He liked its warmth.

Crazy, crazy fool.

A couple of the crew were lugging a metal box from the back room. Luke estimated it was about a metre long and half a metre wide. And it looked heavy.

"Found this under the rubble. Possibly in some hidey-hole between two walls."

Luke nodded. "Take it out onto the front lawn. I'll grab my cordless grinder and cut off the lock."

When he returned, the men were back inside and Melita was using her tea towel to clean the dust from the box. "I wonder if it contains photo albums or exciting memorabilia."

Luke cocked his head. "Why would you think that? Who'd go to the trouble of hiding photo albums in a wall? I'm thinking of calling the police. It's more likely to be wads of money, or guns and ammunition or something as dangerous. It might blow up in our faces."

Melita's eyes widened. "You think so?"

"I have no idea, but I bet there was a good reason it was hidden between two walls."

Luke switched on the grinder, the noise reverberating through the air.

"Stand back," he ordered as he pushed his safety glasses over his eyes. She stepped back a few metres while he made quick work of cutting the lock in half.

When he switched off the power tool, the unexpected stillness around them was ominous. His mouth was suddenly dry. He removed the broken lock and released the hasp and staple. He was about to lift the lid open when Melita reached out to stop him.

His gaze flicked up and collided with hers.

"If it's ammunition inside, you ... you get to choose what happens between us."

He didn't miss the catch in her voice. "What?"

She squeezed his hand. "If it's photos and stuff, I get to choose."

He balked. "No way, Mel, that's crazy. A woman like you can take your pick. Don't sell yourself short."

Her gaze didn't waver. "Open the box, Luke."

He shook his head vehemently, dust particles flying from his hair to float delicately between them.

"Please, Luke."

He swallowed. They'd survived being apart long enough; he'd lived a half-life for three and a half fucking years. Even learning about Melita's adoption, and having certainty that there were no family ties between them, hadn't propelled them to change the situation. Would he ever stop thinking she was too good for him?

"Okay," he whispered.

She pried one end of the box and he muscled in on the other, taking the bulk of the weight. The lid was heavy and its hinges squeaked as he opened it. They looked inside.

A piece of red silky fabric lay on top and it struck Luke that it was clean. Not a speck of dust. No evidence of moths eating away at it. In fact, it looked as though it'd been locked away only yesterday.

He picked at its edges and slowly pulled on it. When he'd tugged enough of the fabric away, the sun's strong rays latched onto the shiny gold bullions he'd revealed, causing him to squint in the brightness and Melita to raise her hand to shade her eyes.

There was no telling how long they squatted there, transfixed. All Luke knew was that his heart began pumping a hell of a lot faster.

"Do we call the police now?" Melita asked.

Dazed, he nodded. "What the hell kind of property did you buy, Mel?"

She stammered, sounding lost for words. "I-I have no idea."

"I think it's time we found out."

Chapter 3

"Don't ring the police."

They sat, spellbound, looking at the metal box jam-packed with neat rows of shiny gold bullion.

"Don't ring the police, yet," Melita repeated, not sure if she'd already spoken the words aloud.

Luke rolled onto his backside. "You sure?"

"I want to call Dad first."

Luke raised his knees, spreading his steel-capped boots wide, and rested his arms on top. "He'll be asleep. You might have to wait."

"No, this is urgent. He'll understand." She pulled at the scarf around her neck. "While I phone him, could you please close the box? I think we should keep it out of view in case any of the demolition crew comes over. We also need to come up with a story about what we found. We don't want anyone knowing what's inside yet."

He rose to his feet. "What do you want me to say?"

She extracted her phone from the basket and searched for her father's private mobile number. "That it contains albums and memorabilia."

Luke flipped the lid closed, causing the metal to vibrate. "Then you get to choose. Is that what you want?"

Melita looked up as the call connected. Her jaw dropped when Luke's meaning sunk in, but she didn't have time to reply.

Thomas picked up.

"Hey, Dad, it's Melita. Sorry to wake you, but I have a problem. "

After she ended the call, she phoned Patrick.

When she slipped her phone back inside the basket, Luke asked, "What did he say? Your dad, that is?"

Sitting cross-legged on the lawn, she pushed aside what Luke had said for now, confused with what he meant. Did he want to be the one to make the next move?

She pulled on her scarf again, annoyed for giving it such a hard workout. It couldn't be helped. There was a lot to sort out. She had to protect their find.

"Patrick is calling Mr Blundell, a solicitor in Innisfail he knows well. He'll explain our urgency, so hopefully Mr Blundell will be here soon. Once the bullion has been sighted, counted and documented, Mr Blundell has to escort us to the bank and have it secured in their safe."

Luke nodded.

"Dad will contact his Australian-based lawyers and organise to fly them up from Sydney. We may have to go to court. If Mr Blundell does all the preliminary preparation, dad's lawyers can take over when they arrive. Dad knows of similar cases in America that have been won by both sides, so it could go either way."

"So who gets to keep it?"

"Depends. It could be stolen property or the result of any number of crimes. There are a lot of reasons someone may have hidden it. That's why we need a solicitor first, before the police get involved. It may have been here since the 1930s, and ninety years is a very long time for there to be any easy leads as to how it got here."

"Except the last thing we need is a hold up on the renovations. Investigations can take ages," Luke put in.

"Oh." Why hadn't she thought of that?

She rested her elbows on her thighs and cradled her face. Her initial idea had been to find the previous owner of the house and return the gold bullion, but this wasn't a straightforward situation—if the house had sat vacant this long, they may never find an answer. The person or persons involved would be dead by now and she didn't doubt they'd been killed before their time. Otherwise, *someone* would've come back for the box. She didn't need to be a genius to understand that much.

⁂

After Luke closed the lid of the metal box for a second time, he let Melita deal with Mr Blundell while he went in search of his phone. An old memory crept up on him and he wondered if his grandfather, Jim, knew anything about the property. He'd told Luke stories about growing up in the cane fields of the north and how he'd spent his first working years cutting cane by hand. Luke couldn't remember where his grandfather had lived because the town names had meant nothing to him back then.

He took his phone from the safety box in his utility, knowing he may have to call a few times to allow his grandad to walk inside if he happened to be gardening. Living alone, his grandfather still maintained his independence. He'd learned to cook, clean and do laundry after Luke's precious nan passed away. Luke's mum had insisted Jim come to live with them after he was widowed. When he flatly refused, he was given an ultimatum—learn to look after himself or he'd have to live with them. Jim had raised a scornful look to his daughter-in-law, but in the end, it'd been the perfect threat. With a little help from Meals-on-Wheels and a weekly cleaner, he'd been living an independent life for ten years. Sure, he was getting a little slower and a little hard of hearing, but his brain was still sharp. And if this house had a history, he would know about it.

Jim picked up on the fifth ring.

"Hey, Grandad, it's Luke here."

"Luke? Everything okay, mate? Aren't you usually working at this time of day?"

Yep, still sharp. "I should be working, but we've got a situation here and I have a question to ask you."

Jim chuckled. "It's not a building question, is it? I was the most hopeless handyman. Thank God your father had natural ability."

Luke's muscles squeezed across his chest. The mention of his father still hurt. Nearly four years had passed since the workplace accident, but at least his grandfather had been there to get him through those tough years.

"No, nothing like that," Luke said. "You know how I told you I was doing a renovation job up north?"

"Yeah, and I offered to cook and clean for you so I could revisit the area. Have you changed your mind? I can still come up."

Luke chuckled. "I might take you up on the offer, Grandad. We've only just started knocking down walls, so I'm not sure how it's all going to pan out. I'll let you know soon. It would be great having you around, even if you could only manage a couple of weeks."

"How's the heat?"

"Disgustingly hot and humid, of course."

Jim bellowed with laughter. "You young ones. Too bloody soft. You should try cutting cane by hand in the middle of the day and *then* tell me how hot it is."

Luke smiled. They made them tough in those days.

"So, what's the question, my boy?"

He squatted beside a large tree and leaned against it. Melita and Mr Blundell were still busy taking photos and notes.

"The property I'm working on is located on the main road at the South Johnstone turn-off. Is it close to where you used to live?"

"South Johnstone? Um ... hang on a minute, do you mean the road leading to South Johnstone, or in South Johnstone itself?"

"The house is right on the Bruce Highway, opposite the turn-off that leads to South Johnstone."

"Oh, you mean the mafia house?"

"The what?"

"Back in my day that's what everyone called it. Let me guess, nobody told your young friend before she bought it?"

A shiver crawled down Luke's spine, despite the humid heat. "She was only told it was built in the 1930s and that it's been abandoned for most of the time since."

"And bloody rightly so. The miserly Italian who lived there was a real bastard, so the rumours went. Used to beat his wife, kept her locked upstairs, and for some reason the mafia paid him a visit one day and they left with one of his ears."

Luke squirmed at the image of someone having their ear hacked off.

"A real charmer he was. If the stories were true, it wasn't too many years after he built the house that he and a few others were murdered in it. All connected to the Black Hand, of course. Nasty stuff, but by the 1950s, when I was a young lad, most of the mafia mess in the north had been cleaned out."

Luke felt the blood drain from his face. He could barely hold the phone up to his ear. An old foe had seized him and rammed its way inside his head. His hand began to shake and the phone fell to his lap.

The black hand. For years, nightmares had shaken Luke to his core. Just three words from Jim was all it took to bring back the terrifying ordeal of that one night when he was ten years old, and a black-gloved hand of another sort had threatened to strangle him in his darkened bedroom. That was all he'd been able to tell the police.

It was hard to believe that one event had defined his life and still carried the power to affect him. He gnawed on his bottom lip, hoping to still the shaking. When he tried to swallow, he couldn't get past the memory of a gag being shoved in his mouth, of being unable to breathe. Of wishing for death. Even now his breathing sounded harsh and laboured.

He picked up the phone again, his knuckles white, and held it against his chest. Jim's voice was still audible. He did what he always did when those memories reared their ugly heads. He took deep, even breaths. Inhale, hold, count to five slowly, release. Do it again for good measure. And again.

When he felt ready to stand, he rose on unsteady legs and made his way to his utility. He managed to hold the phone up to his ear. Jim sounded excited as he prattled on, no doubt pleased he could impart so much information.

Luke caught sight of Melita and Mr Blundell in his periphery and was reminded of the reason he'd phoned his grandfather. As he got his breathing and heart rate under control, the implications for buying the house were starting to filter their way in. It was obvious this could hugely affect Melita's business and to fail before she'd even begun would crush her. She lived and breathed swimwear design. Had done so for all the years he'd known her.

He clenched his utility's rack for support and made a concerted effort to listen to what Jim was saying. "Are you sure, Grandad?" He hoped it was the right question to ask at that point in the conversation.

"There's only one turn-off to South Johnstone, right? It might be nearly forty years since I lived up that way, but I bet that section of highway hasn't changed much. You don't forget a house like that. Why do you think no one ever bought it? They couldn't give it away. There were a couple of kids who eventually inherited it when their mother died, but they didn't want a bar of it. It's sad, I know, but the murders affected them for the rest of their lives."

Luke raked a hand through his hair. "What happened to the wife?"

"The story was she refused to live there. She moved to Tully with the two kids. One son stayed on in Tully his whole life and had a daughter. I went to school with her. She suffered from polio as a youngster and wasn't too bad a kid, but even two generations later no one let her forget she belonged to the mafia house."

"Did everyone know it as the mafia house?"

"They probably still do. Ask any local in town."

I'll bet they do.

"So, no one mentioned it to your young friend before she brought it?"

"Nope. Zilch."

No wonder Melita didn't encounter any problems buying the place. Nobody had argued over her offer; she thought she'd got a bargain. Now he'd have to be the one to tell her its history. Gold bullions aside, the property was tainted with murder. A bloodstained history would lend a bad vibe to Melita's business—before she even opened.

"That's a shame. The real estate agent probably couldn't believe someone wanted to buy it."

"Thanks, Grandad. I better get back to work. Thanks for all the info. I'll let Melita know and phone you soon about heading up here for a visit."

"Thanks. It makes my day when you call."

"Aw, Grandad, you know I love talking to you. I'll call again soon, but I better go now."

"That's okay. You get back to work. Seeya mate."

"Bye, Grandad." Luke felt guilty for cutting the call short. His grandfather would never admit to it, but Luke knew he missed having company and was prone to bouts of loneliness. He made a mental note to spend more time with Jim when he returned home to Brisbane.

He put away his phone and found an old rag to wipe the sweat from his face—more likely caused from his sudden panic attack than physical exertion. He eyed Mr Blundell, who was still busy with his notes and camera, and almost hesitated, thinking maybe he should see how the demolition crew's clean-up was going.

But that would be avoiding the inevitable. Melita had to know.

He made his way to where she and Mr Blundell stood, near the metal box. Melita turned in his direction and gave him a beautiful, wide smile.

Shit. How is she going to react to the news?

Her smile dropped and concern laced her expression. "What's up?"

Mr Blundell looked up too.

Luke addressed him. "Excuse me, Mr Blundell."

"Call me John, please."

"Um ... okay. Could you do me a favour?"

John nodded.

"Can you tell me if this house has always been referred to by the locals as the mafia house?"

"The what?" Melita asked.

"Er ... yes, it has." John averted his gaze. "You haven't been told?"

Luke turned away from John and took Melita's hands in his. Squeezing them, he said, "My grandfather told me everyone in the area refers to this house as the mafia house. It was abandoned for all these years because the family that owned it couldn't even give it away. People were murdered in it."

Whether it was from the heat of the afternoon sun or the shock of the news, Melita swayed. So much so that he stepped closer to catch her—just in time before she fainted.

Chapter 4

"L uke, I'm fine."

"Sit! And don't say another word."

Melita huffed. "My fainting had nothing to do with what you told me."

"Then what *was* it about?"

He'd showered and cleaned himself up and smelled deliciously like freshly cut timber. He always did. She figured it was a scent so ingrained in his skin it didn't matter if he was working or not.

She didn't like having to pacify him. Her fainting had caused him to panic like she'd never seen before, but really, what was the big deal? She was far from dead and she did her best to convince him. "It was a combination of the heat and it being that time of the month. That's all, so stop getting so worked up."

His eyes widened comically.

"Did you roll your eyes at me?" She could've sworn that's what he'd just done.

"Are you serious?" All six foot of him leaned over her. His sandy-blond hair may've been washed, but it was messy as usual, just how she liked it. Combed hair on Luke made her squirm—it made him look as if he was trying too hard. The smattering of stubble on his bold face looked so damned sexy she forgot what they were arguing about.

"You forget I grew up with three sisters. It wasn't unheard of for that excuse to be used to get out of chores."

She giggled. His hazel eyes bored into hers in a not so friendly way, but they were surrounded by sun-browned skin and she could do nothing but melt under his gaze.

"Look, thanks for taking care of me tonight," she said. He'd insisted she come to the farmhouse where he was staying, the one she'd leased for the duration of the project so out-of-town contractors would have somewhere to say. "I was fine within five minutes of leaving the mafia house."

Irritation flickered across his face. "Don't call it that."

"Why not? While you and Mr Blundell were in the bank securing the gold, I decided I'd embrace its past and include the history in the renovations. I can't wait to get Flynn onto marketing the property, history all intact."

"Please don't tell me you're serious?" Luke raked both hands through his hair and plonked himself on the couch beside her.

"Deadly serious. Look, this happened nearly one hundred years ago. This history doesn't have to take up a significant portion of the boutique, but a small section with old photographs, the story of the gold bullion we found and anything else we can dig up will be a point of interest."

He frowned. "I'm not sure about all this."

"Listen to me."

Luke turned to face her.

"All my life I've lacked confidence in my ability to achieve things. I didn't think I was good for anything, that I suffered from some kind of defect." She paused and his gaze softened. "I have a good feeling about this. What did your grandfather say about the girl he went to school with?" Over dinner, Luke had talked her through what was said during the phone call. "The girl with polio, right?"

Luke nodded.

"Well, we're going to find her if she's still alive. She lived in her grandfather's shadow all her life and I want to make sure she's being cared for. She may not *want* to be involved in this project, but then again, she may. If she does, I'll spin a positive light on the house that the public will love. I'll create a display that promotes the property's history but also my support of a good cause. I'll donate, say, one dollar from every sale to medical research. People love that sort of stuff, and they'll realise that regardless of the house's history, we're going to do good things here."

By now Luke's jaw had dropped. "Did ... did you think of all this or have you been talking to Flynn while I was in the shower?"

She chuckled. Flynn was the only person she hadn't phoned that day, but his marketing spiels were having an effect on her. They got on *so* well, always laughing and talking over each other to make themselves heard. The development of her marketing strategy for the boutique-cum-tea house was well underway, with a thousand ideas to sift through and a hundred options to consider. The past six months had been crammed full of activity, excitement and decision-making, and Flynn had been right by her side. She couldn't believe her good fortune in connecting with her biological brother and couldn't wait to share the day's news with him.

But talking to Flynn would have to wait.

Now it was time to turn her attention to Luke. "No, I haven't. Not yet." If only she could spare five minutes to get her head in order. Time was whizzing by at such speed that she longed for a day where the biggest decision she had to make was what colour she should paint her nails. Every day she was making decisions with barely minutes to spare.

"Well, I'm not sure it's a good idea." Luke stretched his legs and let his head fall back against the couch. He looked tired, physically tired, from working in the humid heat, as he did most days. His eyes closed and she was desperate to know what thoughts were running through his head. Were they as tangled up as hers?

Every single time she was near Luke, her body was hyperaware of his closeness. She needed to know if she was capable of intimacy with a person. She couldn't remember the last time she'd hugged anyone besides her father, and that always made her uncomfortable. Did her inability to be loved leave her damaged in some way?

He sat only a metre away, but she couldn't quite coax herself to shuffle closer.

She counted to five to calm her nervous flutter and murmured, "I said you could choose what happens next if the box contained money or guns. It didn't hold albums or memorabilia."

His eyes snapped open. "I know."

"And we didn't have to lie to the demolition crew," she added.

"Not yet. When was John going to inform the police?"

"Not until Dad's lawyers have done their stuff."

He sat up and reached a hand towards her. "The gold is worth a lot of money. I'm worried about your safety."

His hand rested limply on the maroon vinyl between them, though it may as well have sat on the opposite side of a gulf. Was this his way of saying 'it's your move next'? She was nervous about them being together. Was it better to remain friends?

She had no clue what he was thinking and didn't doubt he was nervous as hell too. He'd always been wary of the social gap that existed between them. Resentful of her wealth. Time to squash it.

"Don't be," she said. "I'll probably donate the proceeds from the gold bullion to the Tully community. I'm not sure how we'd go about finding its rightful owner and it could do a lot of good for the local area." With a shrug she added, "I can't do anything with it yet."

Silence filled the space between them as she thought about how she'd never had a boyfriend before. For the past three and a half years, she'd only wanted Luke, and her chance to let him know was staring her right in the face.

"Are you okay, Mel?"

It was barely a whisper from Luke, but it asked a lot—a question she had no clue how to answer. He slid his hand closer and wound his fingers through hers. His warmth engulfed her and her emotions took over, threatening to spill.

"Hey." He tugged on her hand. When she didn't move, he said, "We still haven't worked out how to fix this, have we?"

She hung her head and nodded, not trusting herself to look at him or speak. Neither wanted to be the next to move. She sat mesmerised by his thumb, stroking her maddeningly, round and round, until one lone tear dropped on it.

"Aw, Mel." He pulled her towards him and lay on the couch, taking her, too, all the while, tenderly tucking her hair away from her face and cradling her against his chest.

❦

Luke closed his eyes and tightened his arm around Melita. She'd managed to curb her emotions and now lay quietly. He concentrated on the rise and fall of her chest against his and inhaled the fragrance wafting from her hair. Sunset frangipani. The backyard of the mafia house was littered with them and each tree was filled with hundreds of pretty flowers. Each one was an unusual colour combination of pink, orange and white, making for a spectacular sight when the sun began its afternoon descent. He could smell their overpowering fragrance on Melita. Maybe the perfume had infused her hair during the time she'd spent there today.

He lifted a work-roughened hand and continued to tuck hair away from her face. Lightly tanned from living in Australia, she'd lost the pale and delicate look he remembered from when she first arrived. It hadn't taken long for the freckles to appear, transforming her from a shy young adult into the gorgeous woman she was now.

And he wanted her.

His body reacted to her closeness, despite how tired he was. He'd normally be asleep by now. A refreshing shower and a full stomach was usually all it took. God alone knew how tired he was. The humidity this far north zapped his energy, making sleep the only antidote. In these conditions it was a constant job keeping up the fluids his body sweated out.

He grimaced, sleep not getting a look-in. His mind was far too alert and didn't give a damn about his tired body.

Finding the gold bullion worried him. It didn't matter how much it was worth, how long it'd been hidden, or who currently owned the property. None of that changed the fact that it was tainted—with blood, greed, murder, hacked-off ears, you name it. Coupled with the mention of 'the black hand' and it was the perfect bad omen. He couldn't rid himself of his fear. It was always there. No one could turn back the clock on the eight hours he'd been left gagged and blindfolded in his bedroom, with threats of strangulation or being shot if he made a single sound.

When his mother had found him the next morning, he'd been shaking and on his last breath. He'd barely been able to get air past the rag shoved inside his mouth, and a steady stream of tears had kept his nose blocked. There'd been evidence of the intruder, who'd come in through Luke's open window, but nothing had been taken. Luke's father had welded in a security grille that same day.

For a ten-year-old, he'd grown up fast that night and superstition had addled him ever since. The control it had over him was frustrating as hell. He made sure never to walk underneath a ladder, the same way he steered clear of black cats. He never opened an umbrella indoors, just as he always put his right foot down first when he rose from bed each day. These were a few of the rules he lived by—just because.

He couldn't reason why the recurring nightmares from that night always coincided with bad news. He'd suffered from nightmares the night before his father was killed in a work place accident. Those same nightmares had come to visit when his mother was arrested and extradited back to the States, and before his sister's cancer diagnosis. Though his mother had been acquitted and his sister was in remission the sting of the nightmares was hard to ignore.

Counselling had never been suggested. He'd never spoken of that night and was embarrassed by it all, but that didn't change how he felt about the gold bullion. It fit like a glove how the mere mention of those words by his grandfather had brought on a panic attack on the same day they'd found the loot. If bad luck wasn't lurking around the corner, then shoot him. He knew when bad luck was about to strike in his life.

Despite her wealth, which caused him to shudder whenever he thought about it, he cared too much for Melita to keep his fears to himself. How did he express his concerns without coming across as a lunatic?

Not wanting her because of her wealth was one thing. Not wanting something bad to befall her because of his history of bad luck was totally different.

Chapter 5

"What do you mean by that?" Melita couldn't help scowling at the real estate agent. "Are you sure she wants to remain anonymous?"

"Yes, I am. I'm sorry, but those are her wishes."

Flynn, who'd flown up to Cairns two days earlier, scraped his chair closer to Melita. He put a warning hand on her arm and squeezed gently. "Thanks for asking," he said to the agent. "It's just that we found personal property in the house and wanted her to know about it."

The real estate agent tapped the end of his pen on the desk. "I can assure you, bearing in mind its history, there would be nothing in the house she wants to keep."

"The history you didn't tell me about," Melita shot before Flynn squeezed her arm harder, then rose and tugged on her hand.

"Thanks for trying," he said. "We won't take up any more of your time."

Forced to follow Flynn outside, and with no further advancement, Melita was feeling far from friendly towards anyone in the local area. In the week since coming up with the idea of incorporating the property's history into the development of her boutique, she'd had zero luck locating the granddaughter with polio. Alive she was, but the locals wouldn't share any information with a stranger. No matter how much good Melita was doing for the local community, they remained tight-lipped. Awkward glances, knowing looks, as if she were stupid and couldn't tell they were keeping the woman's whereabouts close to their chest. Not even buying that eyesore of a property and turning it into something grand would make anyone slip her the details.

Her sullen mood followed her all the way back to the house she was renting for the duration of the project. Flynn drove without instigating conversation. He knew her too well. Knew he had to let her brood and stew until she came to her senses and let the matter drop.

But she couldn't.

Why didn't she do as Flynn suggested and sell the goddamned gold, then blow the money on holidays, jewellery, cars and whatever else she wanted? After all, she was sold a property so tainted that no one wanted to own up to it's past.

The news of the bullion's discovery hadn't gone public yet, though the police were aware of the find. Her father's lawyers had ensured that the gold would remain her property unless it was proven otherwise, and that had to occur within a certain time frame. Until then, its existence was not to be made public.

When it did, it would take a long and costly court case to prove anything and no one in this town had that sort of money. This was a pity, because she was more than keen to share it with them if they included her in their community.

Then there was Luke. In the week since she'd lain in his arms, nothing had gone right. Why had she left the safety of his embrace that night? They'd both nearly fallen asleep, and the flicker of panic on his face when she'd risen to leave—as if he'd been afraid he would never see her again—had surprised her.

When Flynn parked the car in the garage, she scrambled for her house keys then swung the car door open wide. She was on the verge of crying and didn't need Flynn to see her this way, but with so much happening with lawyers and police and her emotions going haywire every other minute, she lost control of her tears anyway. Despite her protests that it was better not to make a scene.

At the front door, her vision blurred and she struggled to insert the key into the lock. She was ready to slam her hand against the door's hard surface when Flynn came up beside her and took control of the key.

As he opened the door, he turned to look at her and swore. "Jesus, Mel, what's going on? Come here." He took her in his arms and steered her towards the white and airy lounge room.

Everything, she wanted to shout.

"This can't possibly be about not finding this woman."

Flynn was a no-nonsense sort of person. Get to the crux of the problem and solve it. That's where they differed. He shoved a handful of tissues her way and it was time to mop up the mess. Fast. Flynn would sort this out whether she liked it or not. It'd be better if she was in control—as well as she could be.

He disappeared for a second and reappeared with a glass of water. "Here, drink this, and then I'm getting to the bottom of this."

She managed a smile. They'd met barely six months ago, but she knew him so well. Every now and then it would strike her that he was her biological brother and she might've gone through many more years, or a lifetime, without ever knowing it. It was in moments like this that she thanked her lucky stars.

After putting her glass down, she sat back in the comfy grey lounge chair and eyed Flynn. Any second now he would ask the questions he wanted answered, so she may as well wait for them. He sat on the sturdy oak coffee table, his knees inches from hers.

"Okay, firstly, let's get the basics sorted. So far, you've been unable to learn the whereabouts of this woman, whose involvement you now believe is critical to the success of the property. Yes?"

"Yes."

"And she's alive?"

"Yes."

"So why all the girly emotions?"

Ugh! She picked up a cushion and threw it at him.

Flynn laughed, catching it at his chest. "Shoot, Sis, haven't you heard of private investigators? Do you need lessons on how to spend your millions?"

She frowned. Okay, so he had a point, because, no, she hadn't thought of that. But she wanted the community to back her *and* the project, not reject her from the start.

She told him so.

His eyes widened at her confession. "Mel, it's called marketing. Have I taught you nothing? When you sell the gold and start spending it in the local community, they're going to be licking your boots to get you onside. A new hospital, a revamped park, aged-care facilities, and we both know there are sections of the town the local council can't afford to fix after the last cyclone years ago."

She huffed and her shoulders sagged lower on the lounge. He was right, of course.

"So, what else is bothering you?"

She looked up. "What do you mean?"

"Do I need to spell it out?"

She had no idea what he was talking about and remained mute.

"What's happening between you and Luke?"

She groaned, shoving a cushion against her face to muffle the sound before mumbling, "Nothing."

"Nothing, huh?" He tugged at the cushion and pried it from her face.

She let it fall to her lap. "Can I ask you a question?"

His eyebrows rose. "If you want."

She knotted her hands, taking the corner of the cushion with them. She'd never openly spoken of this fear, so she baulked. "Um ... what sort of childhood did you have?"

"What do you mean?"

She worried over a bead with her finger, smoothing its surface. "I mean, were you hugged a lot and made to feel loved?"

Gone was his rigid stance. His eyes softened and he tried to speak, but when his words wouldn't come, his shoulders slumped. What she was trying to explain must've been written all over her face, because realisation dawned on his.

"I wasn't hugged or told I was loved," she said. "From what I remember, my mother was depressed all the time. My father, I hardly saw. I'm a freak, Flynn. I used to think there was something wrong with me."

"Oh, Mel." He rose from the coffee table and, sitting beside her, put his arms around her and rocked her gently.

She was going for broke now. Why stop? It was time to unleash everything that was stomping on her heart.

"I don't know if I'm capable of being close to a person. Can you believe I've never had a serious boyfriend? From the first day I met Luke, I've never wanted anyone else. I don't know how to be in a relationship. I never had one with my parents, or even Patrick. We were all so distant in that monstrosity of a house that we easily co-existed without having to see each other. I'll admit things with Patrick are a lot better since we came to Australia, but I'm nervous about trying anything with Luke. His family are so warm and loving, and I'm the little bar fridge in the corner. Cold. Ice cold."

When he chuckled, resentment speared her chest. "What's so funny?"

He pulled back to look her square in the face. "You are. You're funny, cute, adorable and totally in love with Luke. So big brother is going to come to the rescue and teach you a few things."

She doubted the problem could be resolved and grumbled, "Yeah?"

"Yeah," he repeated in an Aussie drawl. "As you know, I was an only child in a very doting family and I got lots of hugs every day. Until I protested as a teenager and forced them to back off for a bit."

Melita giggled at the image he painted. She was yet to meet his parents but would the moment she returned to Boston.

"So, rule number one is, every time we see each other, we have to hug, squeeze, hold for five seconds and then release."

His carefree chuckling set something off inside of her and she found herself laughing freely with him. He pulled her up and forced her to practise a few times. Hug, squeeze, hold, release. They were laughing so much that tears streamed down her cheeks. She collapsed onto the lounge, grabbing more tissues.

All the while, Flynn continued with the lesson. "After you and I have practised, you can practise on Luke. The same rules, except make the hold only a second or two at first. You might come on too strong if you try holding on for five seconds."

She didn't know why this was so funny—it was probably the saddest topic they could be discussing—but she laughed some more and wiped her eyes.

She stopped short when she remembered something. "I think Luke's grandfather has come to stay with him for a few weeks. I don't know how I'll feel hugging Luke in front of him."

Flynn stopped laughing and sat up straight, his faced angled. She could hear the cogs turning in his head.

"Is this the same grandfather who used to live up here and went to school with polio girl?"

"Yeah," she said slowly, and all the while some trigger was trying to go off.

"Good grief, don't you see?"

"What?" As usual she had no idea where this was leading.

"Girl, we have our private investigator! He's the man to ask where to find her. Oh. My. God. Why didn't you tell me sooner that he'd come to stay with Luke?"

She shrugged. Yeah, why hadn't she thought of it sooner? Somehow, she'd missed *that* clue.

Chapter 6

Luke locked up his utility and did a final check for tools that might've been left behind, either in the yard or the building. You took your chances, because you could bet your last dollar, if you accidentally missed a tool, a bunch of kids or experienced thieves would turn up to take advantage of your one lousy mistake.

He shook his head, knowing full well how costly it could be. He'd been stung a few years back when his cordless drill had disappeared. The next morning, with a sickening feeling in his gut, he'd realised he'd forgotten to pack it away. That mistake cost him his next week's wage.

He scanned the yard as he circuited the house, then he did a thorough scout of all the rooms. The property wasn't anywhere near lock-up stage yet, but in the ten days since the walls had fallen, it already looked remarkably different.

He stopped for a moment, in the quiet of the coming dusk, to look at the progress they'd made. The rendered walls, while in good condition, were being sheeted over up to the old and delicate cornice. It curled and swirled around the edges of the ceiling with an impressive floral design. Back in those days, only someone with a shitload of money could've afforded such a costly feature. It added a special touch that nothing new could imitate.

Satisfied he'd packed up everything, it was time to turn in for the day and enjoy his grandfather's company and cooking. Nothing to complain about there. At his utility, he checked his phone—something he always did before driving off. A blinking light alerted him to messages received. His mother and sisters were always messaging him. 'Keeping him in the loop' was their excuse. He smiled. His phone was a time-waster, but he didn't mind being smothered by his sisters. They felt it was important, so who was he to spoil their fun?

A message from Melita wouldn't have gone astray. Had she dropped off the face of the earth? Yeah, she'd made a few rushed calls, but there'd been no site visits lately, no afternoon or morning smoko—nothing. Probably better this way. The thought of needing to compete with her wealth left him in a sweat.

He ignored the messages from his family for now and read Jim's message asking him to call before he came home. His grandfather was very tech savvy for an old man and knew his way around Facebook, Instagram and a whole stack of internet sites he'd been taught to use. 'Social gatherings' he called the classes he'd enrolled in to learn how to stay up-to-date. Luke had laughed at the time and the memory still brought a smile to his face.

He returned the call. "Grandad, it's Luke. Do you need me to pick up something before I come home?"

"Luke, is that you?"

Luke excused his grandfather's poor hearing and inability to seeing the caller ID clearly. "Yeah, Grandad. Did you need me to pick up something before I come home?"

"No, no, not at all. I just got a visit from that Flynn fellow. Your young friend was caught up in a road accident and"—Luke's heart thumped painfully—"she's okay, but they took her to the Tully hospital. Flynn wanted you to know."

He swallowed, fear threatening to engulf his senses. *Easy, boy. Deep breaths, slowly now.*

"I told Flynn I'd send you there as soon as you finished work. I'll have your dinner waiting for you when you get home."

"Thanks, Grandad. I'll let you know when I'm leaving the hospital. I'll get over there right away."

She was okay for now, but next time his bad luck affected her anything could happen. He had to tell her. It would be wise for her to stay well clear of him if she wanted to survive to see the completion of her first project. Her money didn't need to come into their relationship status. His bad luck would sort it out first.

Luke halted at the door of the hospital room and looked in. The smell of disinfectant irritated his nose, igniting the memory of his sister Victoria, sick in hospital during the worst of her cancer treatment. They'd taken it in turns to sit with her and the smell had never left him.

Guilt rested heavily against his chest. Most weekends he'd stayed the entire time, only going home to sleep. He'd never told anyone, but he blamed himself, of course. If only he hadn't had the panic attack the day before. If, if, if. He even tortured himself with thoughts of why he hadn't fought off the intruder. He should have kicked and screamed the house down until his parents had woken up. Why had he submitted to the intruder's demands without making a peep?

He knew he couldn't turn back the clock, but bloody hell he wished he could've done things differently. Maybe then the nightmares would have left him alone all these years. Maybe bad luck never would have infiltrated his family. Once or twice the word 'curse' had crept into his vocabulary. Another reason he'd ended things with Melita three years ago.

Keeping her overnight for observations, the nurse told him when he got to the hospital. A nasty bump to the head was their main concern. Melita looked pale and her eyes were closed. Something clamped tighter around his chest. This was his doing. Something intangible had reached out with its tentacles to prey on Melita. The signs were all there. The memory of the black hand coming towards his face and mouth, the panic attack, Melita's accident. It all tallied up. Again. *Shit!*

He pulled up a chair and sat beside the bed.

"Hey, Mel," he whispered. The nurse said it was okay to wake her. Flynn had left only minutes earlier and was due back in about an hour. Luke had a lot to explain in that time.

Her eyes flicked open slowly and her smile blossomed across her face when she recognised him. "Hey, Luke."

Her voice sounded scratchy, making Luke doubt how much he should say while she lay on a hospital bed.

She cleared her throat. "Can you come closer?"

He slid the chair closer to the bed.

Her smile wavered and she looked nervous. "No, I mean lean over me."

"You want me to stand up, kinda thing?"

She nodded.

He slid the chair back and placed his hands either side of her face. He couldn't help brushing her hair off her cheek and tucking it behind her ear first. A simple touch, but with everything spinning around in his head, it was enough to leave his hand shaking. Could he live without touching her again? Should he just shut up and live with his fears? Bad luck or wealth, what did it matter? He should make the most of the time left to them before bad luck ruined everything?

While all this was going through his head, he hadn't noticed that she'd wound her arms around his neck. But then they tightened and he heard her count to five. He looked into her uncertain depths and knew something was off.

Ignoring that he was still dressed in his work clothes, caked in dust and gyprock powder and not to mention dried-up sweat, he twisted and lay on the bed with her.

"Mel, what's up?"

Had the bump to her head been a serious one?

Tears pooled in her eyes and she began to sniffle. "I'm sorry I haven't been around the last week."

So, there was a reason?

"It's me, Luke, I'm the problem. I want to tell you about my crappy childhood and that I don't know if I'm capable of intimacy with anyone. I had no one to love me when I was growing up. I think there's something wrong with me."

He took one of her hands and squeezed it. He had no idea what she was going on about. One minute she's in a car accident and gets a bump to the head, the next she's going back to her childhood. There didn't seem to be an obvious link.

She looked back at him and he wiped away a lone tear dripping down her cheek.

"I was in a foul mood after not getting any closer to finding the polio girl and—"

He smiled, trying to make light of what sounded like a serious conversation. "I've never seen you in a foul mood. I don't believe you."

She smiled back and his heart opened wide, squashing some of the things he should be telling her.

"Flynn couldn't believe something like that would upset me so much either. Of course, he knew there was more to it and pried it from me."

Luke lowered his head and his scruffy hair touched her pale cheeks. Their breath mingled. "Mel, what the hell are you talking about and why were you counting to five?"

She turned to look out the window, where dusk was settling, then she grimaced and shifted away.

"Mel, I need to know what you mean." He cradled her cheek with his roughened hand and turned her to face him.

"Luke, I'm going to sound like an idiot, but the truth is I've never known how to be intimate with anyone. My parents never hugged me, never told me they loved me. I've never had a real boyfriend and I didn't have a childhood like yours. I see what your sisters are like around you. It's nothing for them to hug you and plant a kiss on your cheek any day of the week." She cast her eyes down and her fingers knotted together where they rested on her stomach. "I told Flynn all this and ..."

"And?" Luke prompted.

She glanced up. "And I know this sounds stupid, but he told me I should start practising. I promised Flynn that I would the next time I saw you. That was one of the reasons I was on my way to the worksite today."

Wow! How had he never guessed this was going on in her head? Was this why she'd been holding back since learning of her adoption? *Shit.* Why hadn't he pried further? If only he'd known what to pry about! He held her gaze and was quickly losing himself in the brown flecks mixed with grey. "How did he want you to practise?"

She chuckled wryly. "Hug, hold, count to five, release and repeat." She blushed, embarrassed by her admission. "Except I'm not supposed to hold to five the first few times, otherwise you'll think I'm coming on too strong."

Relief swept through him, and he leaned his weight over her, regardless of how grubby and sweaty he was. He didn't mean to groan, but the sound vibrated around them as her fingers tangled in his ratty hair. Hell, he'd hug, hold, count to five and never release Flynn, just to thank him for getting Melita to open up.

She was giggling against his sweaty hair and he lifted his face in case she was gagging. "I need a shower, don't I? I smell bad."

Her tears pooled again.

"Ah, did I say the wrong thing?"

A few tears loosened and tricked down the sides of her face. "You smell like forest timber and I love it."

He frowned. She wasn't making sense. "I think that bump to the head is seriously affecting you."

She shook her head, all while smiling and sniffling and blinking away tears. Like she'd won the lottery and wasn't giving it up.

How could he tell her that the accident was his bad luck rubbing off on her? Finding the gold, his panic attack, her accident, all wrapped up into one neat package. He couldn't burst her bubble. She would retreat and never have the guts to be intimate again. She'd associate any attempt at intimacy with his rejection if he told her it was safer to stay the hell away from him.

"What's wrong, Luke?" Her smile was gone and her jaw trembled.

His thoughts must've been thickly plastered across his face, so he tried for jovial and shimmied a smile back into place. "Nothing. How about practising one more time before I leave?"

God, how he wanted to kiss her goodnight—but that would be leading her on. He couldn't. He still had to tell her. When her arms tightened around him, the least he could do was hold her for more than the count of five—or at least until the moisture in his eyes cleared up.

Chapter 7

"**W**as that the other reason you were coming to visit yesterday?" Luke plonked the saucepan of spaghetti bolognaise in the centre of the pokey kitchen table.

Melita nodded, fishing some disposable plates out of her basket. He'd asked her to get some on her way over, as the place was scant on eating utensils. It was okay if there were only one or two guests, but push it to four and the facilities were exhausted.

She'd arrived with Flynn after phoning earlier to say they needed to speak to his grandfather. Baffled, he hadn't argued and suggested they come over for dinner.

A quick phone call to his grandfather and the issue of what to have for dinner was resolved.

Jim pulled out his chair and invited the others to follow. "Sit, everyone. Dinner's ready."

Luke pulled out his chair and looked up as Flynn nudged Melita with his elbow. She scowled instantly, only making Flynn look more determined than ever.

Melita dropped her gaze, a blush creeping over her cheeks. "Oh, all right."

She came around the table to Luke's side and put her hand on his arm to stop him from sitting down—not that he was close to doing so; he had an inkling of what was going on—then, without hesitating, she wrapped her arms around his neck and squeezed hard. Her warm breath as she counted to five brushed over his skin. He refused to let her go when her numbers were up. Instead, he squeezed tighter. He'd debated all day about what to do next. Should he tell her, or should he not? But when a whiff of frangipani assaulted his senses, he was a goner and quickly forgot his dilemma. He brushed his lips across her cheek before he released her.

She stepped back, looking embarrassed, and wouldn't meet his eyes when she returned to her chair.

Jim cleared his throat. His poor grandfather was probably stumped as to what had just happened and why they weren't hoeing into the food he'd prepared—no doubt he thought there was something wrong with this young generation.

Luke was starving, so he reached across for the spaghetti server before anyone else had a chance. Another blasted humid day and he could eat a horse. The others would have to fight him for seconds if they dared.

"Luke tells me you want to talk to me," Jim interjected before a single mouthful was taken.

It sounded like Jim wanted to know their reason for coming over and wasn't about to waste another minute.

Flynn nodded. "We know you grew up in the area and went to school with the granddaughter of the owners of the mafia house."

"Yeah, she was a nice enough kid, but you couldn't help feeling sorry for her. Everyone knew her story."

Luke twirled spaghetti around his fork and sat forward as he listened.

"We'd like to find her," Flynn said, "but it looks like everyone is keeping her whereabouts from us."

"Why do you want to find her?"

Flynn and Melita detailed their plan. With each mouthful, Luke couldn't keep back his apprehension. If his nightmares came again tonight, it'd be a telltale sign this was a bad idea. Why bring into the picture some poor woman who'd lived a crap life? Why reignite all her memories when she would rather squash them? It didn't make sense to him, but then what did he know about marketing?

What he *did* know was that bad luck could strike at any moment when he was around.

"Easy."

"What?" Luke looked up.

"I said easy," Jim repeated.

Forks dropped, mouths stopped chewing and quiet filled the kitchen.

Jim shrugged. "When Luke told me you pair wanted to talk, I wondered whether it was about Patricia. I've heard a few things around town. Caught up with a couple of old mates and they told me you were sniffing around for her whereabouts."

"They did?"

Luke could see this hurt Melita. She wasn't a bad soul and having the local community treat her like an outsider wasn't sitting well. Would she abandon the idea of finding polio girl? It would relieve him of a lot of explaining if she did. He could happily ignore his issues if she walked away from the entire project.

"Wondered why the hell you wanted to upset her," Jim said matter-of-factly.

"But that's not fair. I don't want to upset her," Melita objected.

"Calm down. I know that now. In fact, I think she deserves a lot of good attention after all the bad. I quite like your suggestion and I know where she is."

"You do?" Melita and Flynn said in unison.

"I do, but I'll only give you her whereabouts if you promise me one thing."

Melita nodded, sitting ramrod as she waited for the verdict.

"I know you're not short of a quid and the folks here tell me she's been doing it tough. She recovered from polio, but her body has begun to deteriorate. They call it post-polio syndrome. She needs better facilities to make her life easier and I was hoping you could pay for them. The money from the sale of the house you bought is not enough. At the moment she's in the local aged-care facility because she can't afford to make changes to her home. Maybe you could arrange to make it wheelchair friendly."

Melita leaped up, raced around the table and embraced him. His eyes popped out at the sudden attention and Luke couldn't help smiling at the obvious impact of Flynn's training.

"I promise you, Jim, I'll do whatever is needed. You're right. I don't lack money and with the sale of the gold there's going to be a lot more." She released her arms from around his shoulders and walked back to her chair, stood thoughtfully beside it for a moment and then tilted her head. "I have an idea."

Only Luke was eating; the others couldn't seem to eat and talk at the same time.

"Why don't you help me, Jim? She knows you and will feel a lot more comfortable if there's a familiar face close by. I could make her the patron of the charity I'm going to set up with the proceeds of the gold. She could be the public face." She sat down and reached for her fork. "I've noticed the locals don't take too kindly to outsiders."

Detecting a note of sarcasm, Luke chuckled. Who in the local community had been game enough to give her a hard time?

Jim lifted his fork and absently twirled spaghetti around and around. "I suppose I could. Maybe you could come with me on the first visit and I could explain everything before you fill in all the details."

Melita nodded. "Sounds like the way to go."

Eating resumed until the clang of Jim's fork on his plate had everyone looking at him.

"How long is this charity project going to take?" Jim asked, uncertainty palpable on his face.

"As long as you want it to," Melita answered.

"Are we talking days, weeks, months? What about my garden at home?"

Melita placed her fork down and wiped her mouth with her napkin. Luke could see, when she sat back in her chair, that she would take her time answering. The importance of Jim's participation in this project had just become clear to all of them. She was a smart cookie and determined to succeed with her first real venture into business. One day, Luke mused, he'd be no match for her. She'd be way above his station and where would that leave him?

"Jim, there are a couple of options."

Luke's grandfather nodded solemnly.

"I can employ a gardener and fly you back every few weeks to check on your home, or ..." Her solution sounded like a plea.

"Is it going to take that long?"

"At least a few months."

"Can I stay here with Luke?"

"You can stay anywhere you want. I'll pick up the tab wherever you go."

"What was the other option?"

She scratched her head and frowned. "I don't have one. I wasn't sure what I'd need to do to convince you to stay and help."

"I'm convinced. At home, I'm just a lonely old man who talks to himself a lot." He laughed, pushing his finished plate away and sitting back. "And you know what?"

Luke grimaced at the picture his grandfather painted of his life. He placed his fork down keen to listen to what he had to say.

"I like you a lot. I like your ideas and your generosity. This is going to make a big difference to Patricia's life. She'd be crazy not to accept some sort of deal, so I'll do my best to convince her." When he paused, he looked in Luke's direction. "Was that something I'm supposed to know about, you know, whatever you pair were doing before?"

Flynn laughed and Melita turned a bright crimson.

Luke couldn't take his eyes off her, but it took a few moments before she caught his gaze. By God, the chemistry was there—the blood pumping through his veins, the ache in his groin. Was she feeling it too? Could he forget his fears and just go for it? Her money, be damned?

"Because I'm okay with it," Jim told them, "except I have a couple of conditions before I agree."

Oh, God, what now?

Even Melita tensed.

"I'd like a few more plates and some decent cutlery. If I'm going to be cooking for more than two on occasion, we're going to have to do better than disposable stuff."

Melita looked relieved and chuckled. "I'll open an account for you at the local supermarket. I'm hooked on your spaghetti bolognaise, so I might drop in more often, if you don't mind. Actually, could you teach me how to cook it?"

Jim turned Luke's way and nodded. "I like this one. You could do a lot worse."

Ah, shit. Until the next brush of bad luck. How did he break it gently to his grandfather—and Melita?

Chapter 8

Melita wiped her hands on her jeans and straightened her blouse. Jim reached across and touched her arm. They sat waiting in the visitors' lounge of the aged-care facility where Patricia resided.

Melita turned to him.

"This means a lot to you, doesn't it?"

She nodded. "I don't know why, but I have a bad feeling that if I don't get Patricia's help, the whole project will fail. Which is stupid, of course, because with the right marketing any business can succeed."

"I know what you mean, what with the history of the place and all that. If you can get the locals on your side, it'll be a bonus."

Melita nodded and picked up a well-worn magazine. Idly flicking through the pages, she wasn't taking anything in. Her thoughts were in turmoil. Call her stupid, but she was even getting negative vibes from Luke. He'd only said it once or twice, but he'd expressed his concerns about the gold, her safety and whether it might hamper her success. He even hinted that she should look for another location for her boutique.

If money was something she had to be careful about, she might've thrown the towel in by now, but this project brought out a new side of her, a determined one, and she was hell bent on carrying it through to the end. She wanted her business to succeed. Had first dreamed of a combined tea house and boutique years ago. More importantly, she wanted to get all this sorted out and fast, so she could get back to designing. It was where her heart lay, but she'd been unable to find her creative muse lately and that really upset her.

Thank God for Flynn. Marketing ruled his universe; he insisted any adversity could be overcome with good marketing. Even bad publicity could eventually turn into good was his motto.

Not only was all this planning stressful, it was also taking her away from Luke. She hadn't been anywhere close enough to practise, as Flynn called it, and lots of practice was required. Nothing had changed when it came to how her body reacted to him. And it did, every single time he was within arm's reach.

Waiting patiently to visit Patricia, she leaned back and closed her eyes. She infused her head with his special scent of freshly cut timber and remembered the feel of his work-hardened hands on her cheek. But good Lord, she wanted more than that, and she would practise long and hard until she could comfortably remain in his arms for hours.

Except this new determined version of herself was nervous. What did she want? A successful business, the man she loved—or was she greedy enough to want both?

That was one half of her brain. The other half was stuck on a new design. She couldn't get the strap right on a bikini. *Ugh!*

"Mr Harvey?"

Melita's eyes flicked open and she sat up. Jim rose when the nurse approached.

"Patricia is awake and happy to visit with you and your friend. Would you like to share afternoon tea with her?"

Jim nodded and thanked the nurse, then began following her down the corridor.

Apprehension wound its way around Melita's stomach. The thought of eating and drinking wasn't a good idea. She walked beside Jim, his stride steady; he was reasonably fit for a man in his seventies. And if Luke didn't look every inch his grandfather in fifty years, she'd eat somebody's hat.

She grimaced. Who knew where she and Luke would be in fifty years? She wished she could guarantee they'd be together, but this new version of herself didn't quite know anything about relationships yet—press her buttons, though, and she was unwavering in her resolve to give it her best shot. She had Jim on her side. Next step, Luke.

They padded softly along the carpeted corridor. At the end they turned left and the nurse knocked on a door.

"Go in. She's expecting you."

Jim went in first, giving her time to appreciate the bright and airy room. Relatively new in construction, the place sported brightly coloured curtains and a large window with a view of the gardens and the forest further back. She wasn't sure what she'd been expecting, but she wasn't surprised to see Patricia out of bed and sitting in a wheelchair near a table. A vase of mixed daisies and gerberas caught her attention. Their colours matched the cheerful blouse Patricia wore. Was this a reflection of her personality? Melita hoped so.

"Jim, this is an unexpected surprise." Patricia raised her hand and Jim pressed it in a shake. "I'm wracking my brain trying to recall where I remember your name."

Melita stood back and let them get reacquainted. After all, this was their plan.

Jim chuckled. "I'm not surprised. It's been about forty years since I've been in these parts. I've been catching up with a few old mates."

"Take a seat, please, and your friend, too. I think they've offered to bring us afternoon tea."

The staff had brought in two stackable chairs for their visit. Jim rearranged them close to Patricia and motioned for Melita to take a seat.

"Patricia, this is Melita."

Patricia extended her arm and smiled. "Do I know you?"

Jim answered for her. "No, but I wanted to introduce you to her."

A knock on the door signalled the catering staff's arrival. Melita rose and did the honours and when they were all seated again, Patricia quirked an eyebrow and, in a no-nonsense way, stated, "I have an inkling I've heard your unusual name recently, Melita. Why do I get the feeling I know what this visit is about?" She turned to Jim and added, "I'm confused as to why you're involved Jim? You were one of the nice guys. I don't believe you're here to give me a hard time."

Melita's heart boomed inside her chest. This woman was one shrewd person. It was unlikely anyone could put anything over her.

"You're right, Patricia. I'm not here to harm you, but I'd like you to listen to what Melita has to say." Jim chuckled. "You were always ten times smarter than the rest of us and it doesn't look like anything has changed. I'm not surprised you guessed the reason for our visit."

Patricia smiled and Melita could've sworn she witnessed a slight blush to her cheeks. Patricia turned to Melita and said, "Okay, young lady, hit me with it. Before you do though, I want to say one thing. I want nothing from that house, ever. I know you found something you'd like me to know about, but trust me, nothing would ever convince me to take it. If you don't want it, burn it."

Melita took a deep breath and pictured trying to set fire to the metal case of gold bullion. If the idea wasn't so impossible, she might've laughed. Instead, she slowly released the air trapped in her lungs and placed her mug on the nearby table. Unclenching her fingers from around its handle was a superhuman task and she hadn't even started talking.

"Thanks, Patricia. Thanks for, um, not throwing me out, for starters."

Jim and Patricia both laughed, already relaxing together. Like they'd been close friends for the past forty years.

"Go on, tell all," Patricia prompted.

"When I bought the property at the South Johnstone turn-off, believe me, I had no idea of its history. Nobody had told me a thing."

"Hmm, I can't imagine any real estate agent offering the information freely. They were probably in shock that someone wanted it." She waved her arm to dismiss any response Melita might've made. "What were your plans for it?"

"What *are* my plans, you mean. Nothing's changed. I have every intention of turning it into a boutique and tea house where I can sell my own designer swimwear and accessories."

Patricia's eyebrows shot up. "Really? How come I haven't heard this?"

Jim piped up. "You're not talking to the right people." Again, they laughed together comfortably.

"Anyway, carry on. I still don't understand why you're bothering with me."

Melita squared her shoulders and took another deep breath. "Well, recently, while renovating the property, we came across a metal box hidden between two walls."

"Let me guess. Full of money?"

Melita's eyes opened wide. Further proof of Patricia's perceptiveness. "Close but not quite. Full of gold bullion."

"Good Lord. Probably the reason they murdered my grandfather." She took another sip of her drink and eyed them over her cup. "Just between you, me and Jim, you should keep your mouth shut about the discovery. The Black Hand continues to be a sensitive topic in the area because family members of the murdered men still live around here." She paused, putting her mug down. "And what I said still stands. I don't want any of it."

"The truth is, Patricia, I don't need it either. I want to set up a charity for the local community and use the proceeds from the gold, which would be worth a pretty packet, to fund it. We could build a new hospital, repair damage from the last cyclone, build more aged-care facilities, install a town swimming pool, new sporting fields or whatever else the local community needs." She paused, letting her words sink in. "I'm talking about a lot of money if my lawyer's guess at the gold's worth is anything to go by."

"If it wasn't so tainted, I'd say 'what a great idea'."

"You don't like the idea?" Jim asked casually. "You don't think Melita was meant to find it and use it this way?"

Patricia put her mug down and shrugged. "I get a bit numb when I think about that property. It brought such turmoil and hardship to my father and grandmother, there wasn't a day that went by that I didn't want to torch it. 'If only I could walk,' I used to think." She pointed to her wasted body and grimaced. "I spent four years in a damn wheelchair and when I could walk again, I vowed to forget about the history surrounding my doomed family and try to make a life for myself. It's only been in recent weeks that it's been thrown back in my face and the memories made to resurface."

Melita knew this was her cue to stride in and sell her idea. "Patricia, I was hoping you would agree to be the face of my charity. The sale of the gold is going to make squillions and I'm determined to spend the money right here. Not a single cent will leave the local area."

"But I'm old and useless. Look at me. I had no idea what was happening to my body until I learned about post-polio syndrome ten years ago."

"Hey, who are you calling old? I'm the same age as you, and I, for one, am not ready to sit down and die. How about we do this together?" Jim suggested.

Melita watched the play of emotions between the two of them and was flabbergasted at how in tune they looked.

"Now what would you want with someone like me, wheelchair bound and withering away?"

"How about we start with going out for lunch tomorrow?"

Patricia looked lost for words.

"If you agree to come to lunch, I'll tell you the conditions I insisted on if you decide to help Melita," Jim added.

Still stunned, Patricia swung her gaze from Melita to Jim and back. "Am I being cornered?"

"Yes or no to lunch?" Jim wasn't backing down either.

"Yes," Patricia answered.

"Good. Now listen carefully."

Patricia turned to Jim and for the first time Melita could see past her tough veneer. Her bottom lip was caught between her teeth and her hands were clasped tightly on her lap.

"Melita is going to renovate your home and make it wheelchair friendly, so you can move back. She's also going to provide you with the best medical care money can buy. This'll include occupational therapists, physiotherapists, at-home care, whatever is needed to make you as comfortable as possible for the rest of your life."

Patricia's chin quivered, her eyes filling with moisture. Melita found a box of tissues and handed it over as tears splashed down her cheeks.

"Why, Jim?"

Jim shrugged. "As I told Melita, you had a rough time when you were a kid and you deserve this."

"But what's your connection? Are you related?"

Melita smiled when Jim leaned away from her, closer to Patricia, as though he wanted to prevent her from hearing his conspiracy theory.

"I think there's something going on with my grandson."

"Oh."

Quiet filled the room as Patricia took a few moments to compose herself and take in everything they'd told her.

"How about looking at it as spending some quality time with a crusty old fellow? I can tell a few jokes, they're not always funny but sometimes they are."

This brought another rush of tears mingled with laughter from Patricia. Her blush was very evident this time as she shushed him away. Then she picked herself up, straightening her back as much as her debilitated body allowed, and blew her nose.

"Lunch tomorrow, Jim, and I'll make my decision then."

This was a dismissal in Melita's books, but she was okay with that. They'd heaped a lot on Patricia's shoulders—it looked as if there was more happening here than Melita asking her to become the face of her charity.

Jim rose and Melita followed his lead. "You choose where we go. I have no idea where to take a beautiful lady."

"Really, Jim?"

"Just saying." And they all laughed when Jim reached for her hand and kissed it. "Until tomorrow."

"Thanks, Patricia," Melita said. "I hope you agree. I promise, you won't regret it."

"Yes, yes, we'll see. Give me some time to think on it."

They waved goodbye and closed the door behind them. As they walked towards the front entrance, she could hear Jim humming.

"Putty in my hands, she was."

"Oh, Jim. You're an old flirt! Wait till I tell Luke."

Jim winked at her. "Learn a trick or two from me, girl, before you waste your life away."

Huh? Had he just suggested she make a move on his grandson?

Chapter 9

L uke flicked to a clean page in his diary and detailed what had to be followed up in the next few days. With the plumbing and electrical work just about complete, the installation of the commercial kitchen would begin the following week. He'd already tested and inspected the piping and electrical outlets; it was crucial that they were installed correctly before the kitchen arrived. Once it was installed and the splashbacks were in place, the switch plates could be fitted.

Things were progressing nicely elsewhere on the property, too; the extra window openings would soon sport the French-style windows Melita had chosen and the concrete foundation for the detached building at the rear of the property had been poured. In a couple of weeks the steel frame would go up. Then there were painters and tilers to organise. His job was one long arduous surgery, where each task had to be completed in a specific order before he stitched everything up and handed over the keys.

Luke closed his diary, satisfied everything was coming together nicely. In the past few weeks, they'd experienced a few delays because of the weather, but nothing too drastic. The hardest part of managing the project was getting hold of local tradesmen when they were needed.

He heard Melita's laughter before he saw her. Her days were as busy as his and her father and his lawyers had been in town for the past week. She was a familiar face around the worksite and always had an encouraging word for those working on the project. Her laughter often rang out with the noise from hammer drills and saws.

It was time for a break and no doubt she carried delicious food with her. She was single-handedly increasing the turnover of the local bakery three-fold because she rarely arrived on site without a basket full of savoury and sweet snacks for the crew.

Luke looked up as Melita entered the kitchen and his gaze went straight to the red silk scarf tied loosely around her neck. It was such a bold accessory; it looked nothing like her usual designs.

"So, do you like?" She must've noticed him looking, because she twirled on the spot, modelling the scarf.

He tugged on her hands. "I love it, but my guess is it's not one of your designs."

She took a step back, leaving him disappointed at her inability to fully relax. Was it because there were a dozen tradesmen hanging around? The time would soon come when it was just the two of them and he wouldn't let her retreat so fast.

"Maybe not, but it's officially mine."

"What is?"

"As of today, Mr Luke Harvey, the gold bullion is mine." She twirled her finger around the scarf and added, "I thought I'd take the silk from inside the metal box as my prize."

Ah, now he recognised it. "So is this a good omen?" The gold still made him nervous.

"Definitely good. The plan is coming together nicely."

Fair enough. He could overlook that the scarf was connected to the gold and the story of the Black Hand; after all, it wasn't the scarf that had triggered his panic attack and bad memories. He would treat it as another fashion accessory. It wasn't as though Melita was short of them.

"Also, Patricia and Jim finally have a job to do."

This made him chuckle. "That should give them less time to make eyes at each other."

Melita's laughter tinkled around the room.

It hadn't surprised Luke that from the first lunch they'd shared nearly a month ago, his grandfather and Patricia had been a pair. Was there ever any doubt about Patricia agreeing to help Melita? Zilch.

"Does this mean your father and his heavy-handed lawyers will return to Boston now and allow *us* to make eyes at each other in peace?"

Luke was desperate for some time alone with Melita and was working on a plan. Flynn had left town for a few days and Jim was likely to be at Patricia's. With the modifications on her house well underway, she'd moved back and Jim had volunteered to help her settle back in.

Melita looked away shyly and concentrated on delving into her cane basket for his afternoon goodies. Her silence didn't go unnoticed.

"Hey, Mel?"

He wrapped his arms around her from behind, pushed his face into her hair and drank deeply of her essence. What was their relationship? A quick hug here, an even quicker kiss there. A lot of hours on the job site and shared morning tea. They were adults, for goodness' sake, and he wanted so much more. He was doing his best to ignore her vast wealth and was prepared to snub his history of bad luck. It was time to shake things up.

She dropped the basket onto an overturned cardboard box. When she turned in his arms, she managed a lop-sided smile. "Are you free on Sunday?"

Dumb question—or maybe not. He'd found himself onsite on quite a few Sundays, but with their families out of the picture, he'd make sure he was free.

Mesmerised by her grey eyes, he was content to look into her depths forever, could hold this position for eternity. "Saturday afternoon. Be ready. I have a surprise."

One of the tradesmen bellowing his name cut off their connection and he swore. "Sorry, I better see to it."

With disappointment etched all over her face, she said, "I'm on my way to Kelrick Kastle. I'm staying the night with Father and his lawyers and will drive them to the airport tomorrow. I'll be back by Saturday afternoon."

He squeezed her hand. "Drive carefully. Let me know when you arrive." He left her in the kitchen and darted out to see to the problem.

He'd been more relaxed these past weeks. The nightmares had left him alone and he could almost forgive himself for forgetting his fears. Any thoughts he'd had about ending things with Melita had long vanished.

Twenty minutes later, after he'd sorted out a problem with the supply of tiles, he crossed back to the kitchen to eat the food Melita had left. When he went to write a note in his diary first, he gasped. From between its pages, the silk scarf was sticking out. Red-hot blood coursed faster through his veins.

He opened the diary to the page she'd chosen. On Saturday's entry she'd written, 'Can't wait to be with you.' Luke pressed the scarf to his face, breathing in Melita's scent, dragging it into his lungs. It left him light-headed, so he relented and placed the scarf back between the pages. He and Melita would create memories with it, and he'd banish any niggling bad luck premonitions to the back of his mind.

All his fantasies of what he would do when they were finally alone came rushing at him. *Hell.* He wanted this and Saturday couldn't come soon enough.

⁂

Jim pocketed his phone and turned to Patricia. "Don't you look swanky?"

Patricia fiddled with the gears on her new scooter and smiled. "How did I ever manage without one?"

Jim knew the scooter was transforming the way she looked at life. "Beats me. The same way you coped without me all these years—with a great deal of difficulty."

Her laughter engulfed him. They were spending the afternoon in the park so she could practise manoeuvring the scooter in a safe environment before taking it on the roads. The assistance from her physiotherapist was also a godsend. She now coped with tiredness from muscle weakness and nerve damage better as she built the strength in her arms.

"That was Melita on the phone."

"Ah. What's she up to?"

Jim sat on a park bench as Patricia drove along the path in front of him. She turned in a tight circle and came back towards him. He waited until she was closer before replying.

"She's on the way to Moona Creek for the night with her dad. He leaves for Boston tomorrow, so they're spending the night with her brother and his wife. She wanted us to know the gold bullion is legally hers."

Patricia slammed on the brakes and looked up. "That means we're on the job, doesn't it?"

"Think you can handle it, Pat?"

She released the brake and, making her way to where he sat, gave his hand a light squeeze. "We're doing the right thing, aren't we, Jim? This isn't going to backfire on us, is it?"

Dappled sunlight made her face look like patchwork. He reached across and gave her a quick peck on the cheek. She blushed so easily around him. "What's the worst anyone can do? Shoot us?"

Patricia rolled her eyes but smiled.

"Look at it as the fast lane to heaven," he said. "If we're both there, who cares?"

She tutted. "Oh, Jim, you're never serious."

"Why do I need to be? I happen to think I was put on this earth to see through this project with you. I could so easily be in Brisbane, doddery as hell, in my garden and pretending to enjoy it."

"But you said you enjoy gardening?"

"I enjoy being with you more."

"Oh, Jim." Moisture shimmered in her eyes. "You say all the right things. Look at us, in our seventies but you make me feel like a teenager."

"Guess I'm just good at it."

She smiled but said no more. They'd spoken about his wife and marriage; in comparison, her life had been a lot lonelier. She deserved some good years and Jim was determined to shower her with as much love and affection as he could. If only she realised how less lonely his life was with her. They'd become friends, companions and carers to each other; he was never going back to a single life. He also hadn't counted out reviving his sex life—if it was humanly possible at his age. He planned on working on it. Test out what the old body could manage. Stranger things had happened!

"Melita mentioned she'll be employing a charity manager, some high-flying exec from the States she knows well and can trust, but it'll be our job to find out what the community wants. I have a feeling we'll be attending council and chamber meetings and writing up stories for the papers. We'll have to show up when we're told, smile at the camera when we're asked and cut the ribbon when a project is completed. As she said last week, she wants us both to be the faces of this charity."

"Are you ready to be busy, Jim? Or would you rather be pottering around the garden?"

He leaned back and held her gaze. "I'm going to be honest, Pat. I've enjoyed every day of the past month. I haven't felt so alive since my good wife passed away. I think we're going to have a stack of fun. It's what our old brains need, don't you think?"

She scoffed and switched on her scooter, looking determined to get in some more practice. As she drove away, she threw at him, "Careful who you call old."

Jim laughed. If running the charity meant they were busy, then so be it. They would transform this town and leave a legacy no one could tarnish.

He eyed her scooter. Maybe he should get one too and join her in the ride of their lives.

Chapter 10

Melita skipped a step as she walked along the beach beside Luke. Sand squeezed between her toes and little crabs darted in and out of their hidey-holes.

"How did you find this place?" she asked.

Luke wove his warm fingers between hers and she absorbed all the heat radiating off him.

"I overheard one of the tradesmen talking about the holiday house his parents owned, so I asked if it was free this weekend."

"And what beach are we on?"

"I'm not exactly sure. Mission Beach isn't far, but this is north of the touristy bit."

She slowed her steps and stared at the water. It sparkled under the late afternoon sun and the waves coming into shore barely made a bump with the surf so gentle.

Luke tugged on her hand. "Don't even think about it. You're not going in the water without a stinger suit on."

She'd noticed the outdoor storage cupboard in the garage with the stinger suits and the instructions to rinse them out in clean water before hanging them again. Still, she scowled. "But it's *so* deceiving. It looks harmless and inviting. How am I supposed to test my new bikini? It took me forever to get the strap right."

It was an intentional invitation and Luke was perfectly on cue. He wrapped his arms around her from behind and nuzzled her neck "That, my girl, is where I come in."

She smiled. This was the weekend she needed. She was prepared to put everything on the line. If Luke could love her, then maybe she'd find a way to accept how loveless her childhood had been. Closing her eyes for a moment, she let herself enjoy the flutter of awareness his stubble created against her skin.

Remembering where they were, she looked over her shoulder and cocked an eyebrow in his direction. "You're not worried about people seeing?"

Luke chuckled. "I should be, except that's what makes this place special. It's only a small piece of freehold, but as you can see the beach in front of the house is flanked by two large outcrops of rocks. So, unless a beach-goer walking from the connecting beach is willing to climb over them, there's little chance we'll see anyone. You can only get to this place by road like we did."

Melita looked left, then right. "It's barely a three-hundred-foot stretch."

"You mean one hundred metres?" Luke's heated body pressed up against hers. "And it's all ours for the weekend."

She tried to keep it together and swallowed back a groan. "I'm trying to remember to use metric and ... and that sounds very private."

He began to unbutton her thin cotton long-sleeved shirt. "You'll get the hang of it, and yes, it's just you and me here."

He stepped back and slipped off her shirt, so she was left wearing only her newly designed bikini. His strong hands wrapped around her bare waist and his arousal tormented her from behind. Blood rushed through her veins and she wondered whether her legs would hold up. Then his lips touched her neck, ever so slowly, and her heart did somersaults. She choked back tears. Is this what she'd been waiting for? How many years had she suppressed everything she felt for this man? Their one and only other kiss had sustained her all that time. Would she now have something new to keep her going?

She reached up and tangled her hand in his hair, drawing him closer. Emotions continued to zigzag through her and an unexpected sob tore from her throat.

Luke stopped and spun her around. "Hey." He took her chin in his work-hardened hands and gently ran his thumb along it. "You okay?"

She cried, laughed and nodded, while her emotions ran amok. Embarrassed to have caused the concern on his face, she flung her arms around his neck and squeezed as tight as she could. He tightened his arms around her and she garnered strength from this man.

Her man.

God help her. Since learning of Flynn's existence, they had yet to attempt a decent kiss. Why had it taken them so long to get to this point? It'd been months and she wasn't wasting another second. She loosened her hold on him and leaned back. It was time to push past her insecurities and be the woman Luke needed. When she lifted her eyes to meet his, she fell into his gaze, swimming a thousand miles into his soul. The message she got back was loud and clear; this was well overdue.

Three and a half years ago, she'd barely been out of her teens and everything about her and Luke's relationship had been uncertain; it was no surprise it had ended. She'd never stopped wanting him though. Now, with no tradesmen nearby, and no Jim or Patricia, it was time to let her inhibitions go.

Just do it, girl. You can.

She had to make the first move. Luke was too much of a nice guy to push himself on her after her embarrassing little outburst only moments ago. She laced her fingers behind his head and gave the gentlest of tugs to bring him closer. He raised an eyebrow in question—one she wouldn't answer with words.

At the first touch of her mouth against his, a ripple reverberated through her body. It was matched by a frustrated growl from Luke, then he wound his arms around her waist and pulled her in as tight as he could.

The afternoon sea breeze tickled her bare back and competed with the heat spreading to every pore. She held on tighter, wanting the kiss to go on forever, enjoying the heaviness between her legs pulling her down. Then, when Luke lost his footing, they tumbled onto the sand. He chuckled for an instant, but she wanted more and sank into another kiss like she was drowning and he was the oxygen. She refused to let him go, her heart bursting whenever his tongue touched a sensitive spot. She moaned against his mouth, having long forgotten how a simple kiss could bring so much pleasure.

The tiny sand granules against her skin were better than a massage and her hands knew no boundaries, moving up and down his strong, muscular forearms and over his firm shoulders. When Luke rolled her onto her back, she was shocked again by his arousal, which throbbed through his swimmers and against the thin scrap of bikini she wore.

He captured her bottom neatly in his palms and pressed her hard against him, and she let him. She seeped into his bones and melded to him. As long as their mouths were joined, the rest of the world didn't matter, time slipping from one minute to the next.

When Luke savagely pulled away, his heartbeat thundered in her ears. She inhaled, filling her lungs starved of air, and continued to run her hands over the hard knots of muscle on his chest.

While Luke took a few moments to get his breathing under control, she feasted on his good looks. He'd matured so much in the time she'd known him; he'd lost his boyish looks and had changed into a man. A bolt of awareness shot through her. They'd both grown up; the time was right to carry on from where they'd left off three and a half years ago.

Luke took one of her roaming hands and kissed the inside of her wrist with a tenderness so endearing she sighed with pleasure. He smiled, then rested his weight on her with his face on her breasts. His chest continued to rise and fall in time with hers, blanketing her insecurities.

She snuggled against him, her curves fitting perfectly against his muscled body as he pressed her into the sand. She closed her eyes and, enjoying the pressure of his weight, ran her fingers through his hair, gently stroking.

When Luke shifted, Melita hugged him tighter and wouldn't let go. He chuckled softly and kissed a spot on her neck.

"Did you want to put on a stinger suit and have a swim? Then we can drive into Mission Beach for dinner. After that ... we'll see what happens."

Luke's heated suggestion had her breathing in ragged puffs.

When he prised her hands away, he eased himself up.

She opened her eyes and dragged in a good lungful of air. Shyly, she looked up. "I want to do this Luke. We've wasted enough years."

He smiled that crooked smile of his that melted everything. "I do too. Trust me, it's taking more strength to stop right now than if I were holding a heavy beam in place."

She smiled and relaxed a fraction. "Okay, swim first."

This was all new to her, the way everything throbbed—and they hadn't started anything yet—but she'd be more than okay. God almighty, what would she be like if they *did* take things to the next level? She felt a shameless urgency and sharp pleasure with every touch. Their gazes spoke a thousand words; words that had long been wedged in her throat.

A simple brush of his hand against her naked skin and it left her worried she would drown the first step she took into the ocean.

⁂

Looking out towards the beach, the ocean breeze whispered over Melita's skin. They'd swum, eaten and now she waited for Luke to shower.

The Beach Hut boasted an unusual design. The single bedroom jutted out from the rest of the building and its three glass walls could be tilted open, similar to some garage doors. Once they were lifted, screens were pulled down to keep the insects out. It gave Melita the impression they'd be sleeping on the beach, yet protected from the mosquitoes and sand flies—which, Luke warned, could cause more pain than they were worth. Dense tropical rainforest surrounded the hut, making them feel as if they were the only two people on earth.

Noises from the forest punctuated the quiet and mingled with the sounds of the gentle waves hitting the beach. How savage could it get on a wild and windy night? The water was only about a hundred feet away—or thirty metres, she calculated in her head—so this was the last place she wanted to be if a cyclone was forecast.

She heard Luke padding around and gave him a few minutes to get dressed. It was still early, but they both knew what the night would bring. Every glance, every touch—it wasn't rocket science.

He came up behind her and wrapped his arms around her. She sagged against him, heat pooling at the base of her belly, every nerve ending rippling. She wore a silky wrap, but he smoothly dispensed of it. A groan escaped her lips when his warm, taut, naked body pressed up against hers.

He took her hand and led her to the bed where a bedside lamp cast a soft light. A patch of bright red fabric on her pillow caught her attention.

"What's that?"

Luke squeezed her hand before letting it go.

In the lamp's warm glow, she recognised the silk scarf. He'd rested three sunset frangipani flowers along it.

Something burst inside of her.

Here was a man with so much strength that he could easily carry a bag of cement on each shoulder. Muscle and power bulged from his biceps and corded muscles ran the length and breadth of his six-foot frame, yet he could still think of something as sweet as this. And they'd warned her Australian men weren't romantics!

He reached around her and, picking up a flower, tucked it behind her ear before kissing her.

"You're my frangipani girl," he whispered. "Their scent always reminds me of you."

Good Lord, he was saying all the right things and she couldn't utter a single word. How could she? He'd rested a hand on her naked backside, and with all the sensations swirling around her body, she felt as if she were about to collapse. His mouth covered hers anyway, so what was the point in trying to talk?

He reached behind her again, took the soft, silky scarf, touched it against her shoulder and let it drag slowly over her breasts. She gasped at the feel of it on her skin.

Luke lifted her and laid her on the bed. She wanted to burrow her face in his neck, but he was out of reach and tormenting her with the scarf. His hands whispered along her stomach, tantalisingly, ever slower, downwards, until the silk scarf lay across her tightly woven hair, where everything throbbed, and his fingers shortly followed.

The play between them went on and on, seemingly for hours. Isolated in this private haven, when he finally entered her, everything felt right in the world and her body was more than ready for him.

Luke woke when the first touches of dawn entered the room. It wasn't unusual for him to wake early, but everything about this morning was different. He'd woken once during the night and had gone hard immediately. He hadn't been sure if he should try his luck again, but he'd put a condom on, and as soon as he'd reached for her, she'd responded. They'd both slept like the dead after that.

Lying on his side, he let his gaze slide along her perfect length. She lay on her stomach, hair spread across the sheet. Would she be up to it again? Should he wake her? He smiled in the half-light as he spotted the red silk scarf tucked beneath her calves. He tugged on it, gently pulling it out. Never again would he associate the silk scarf with anything related to the Black Hand. They'd created new memories with it last night.

Holding it aloft, he trailed its end slowly down her back, letting it rest on every knuckle of her spine. She moved a fraction when it reached the rounded shape of her backside, then groaned when he dangled it between her legs. Her right leg was bent up on an angle, and the thought of where his mouth had gone the night before had him agonisingly swollen again and needing release.

She rolled onto her side and Luke dropped the scarf and pulled her towards him. "Good morning, beautiful."

She moaned against his mouth as he took hers with force.

"Would you like to do something different this morning?" he asked when he came up for air.

Pliant against him, she wiggled against his groin. The tension became unbearable and a mighty groan escaped his lips. She nodded her agreeance, so he lifted her from the bed and grabbed a couple of towels and a condom.

"Let's see if my theory about no one visiting this beach stands true."

He chose a shady spot underneath an overhanging tree, but when he went to put her down, she refused to release him. With her legs wrapped around his waist and arms secured around his neck, she rubbed against his hardness every time he moved to spread the towels.

He stopped once to kiss her hard and she giggled at his obvious discomfort. Then he lay down with her still attached and rolled to his side. He wanted to wipe every suggestion of laughter from that beautiful face and make her moan as he taunted her for a very long time. After he'd slammed his way inside—immediately contrite, in case he'd hurt her— everything exploded and he could no longer hold back.

As they lay spent on the rumpled towels, he tucked her face beneath his chin. When she giggled, he slid back and looked down at her. At the same time her mouth latched onto his swollen nipple and she mumbled, "Oh, please, do that again."

His laughter mingled with hers. Their bodies shook until they gradually calmed and sleep took over as the sun continued its gradual rise.

Chapter 11

Melita sat at Luke's pokey kitchen table looking at the latest reports with Jim and Patricia. She stifled a yawn, hoping they wouldn't notice how tired she was. Jim was busy at the coffee machine while Patricia had her head down writing notes.

I should be in the clear.

"What'll it be, Mel?" Jim asked.

Melita looked up from reading the report. "Better make it a strong one. No milk, thanks."

She tried to concentrate on the words in front of her but failed. It was three weeks after their beach getaway and life had certainly turned a corner. 'A bloody good one,' Luke would say.

Jim appeared at her side and the aroma of freshly brewed coffee wafted around her. "Here, Mel, looks like you need it. Just remember you can't live off coffee and sex alone."

"Ugh?" She looked up

With his own coffee in hand, Jim sat across from her and shuffled papers to the side. "You think I haven't noticed how Luke's barely getting any sleep? How you pair have turned nocturnal and are having a bloody good time?" He chuckled at that.

Heat raced along Melita's neck. They'd decided to keep quiet about their relationship for a while, but how could they? It was impossible, when they were in close proximity, not to touch, not to think of what they'd done the previous night, not to reach for a kiss—and usually in full view of half a dozen tradesmen.

"Is it that obvious?"

"Ah, yep, even if I'm rarely here at night anymore."

She covered her face with both hands and groaned. Jim and Patricia chuckled.

Flynn was yet to be informed, but she would confidently tell him that his training sessions had worked. He was due to fly back into Cairns in a week's time and would notice her absence at home straight away. He would get all the gory details out of her—except none of it was gory—and she floated inches above the ground every day.

She looked up at Jim. "Are you okay with it? Your grandson and ... and me some ..."

"Some hoity-toity, rich Yankee?" Jim supplied.

Melita's jaw dropped. Something speared her chest.

"Laugh, Mel. It's a joke," Jim prompted.

"Really?"

"Really. It's my job to hassle girls who deprive my grandson of his beauty sleep. I hope he hasn't turned into some cranky monster on the job site."

She tried to picture Luke as anything but the sensitive, loving man he'd turned out to be. An image of a tired Luke, with his hair on end, as though electrocuted, brought a smile to her face. She couldn't believe how transparent they'd been. Laughter erupted from her throat and Jim and Patricia joined in. It wasn't long until tears rolled down her cheeks.

"We decided to keep it to ourselves for a while. Are you saying we didn't even make it a week?"

"Yep." Jim took another sip of his coffee.

"And you've been waiting for us to say something?"

"Well, someone had to say something."

Melita took a tissue from the box that sat on the shelf behind her and dabbed at her eyes. "Are you sure you're okay with it, Jim?"

"Damn straight I am."

"Do you really think I'm some hoity-toity Yankee?"

"A bloody nice one if I have to be honest."

"Ignore him, Mel. I'll deal with him later tonight when I'm close enough," Patricia threw in.

"Hey, enough of that. We better get on with the job."

"Yes, we better." Patricia laughed gaily.

Melita smiled. They did have to get down to the nuts and bolts of the meeting. It was time to flick on a switch and concentrate. She had to push Luke to the back of her mind for now.

A few more sips of coffee and she'd be just about right. She made herself focus on the report from the Chamber of Commerce's last meeting. After a few moments of reading, she said, "It says here they don't want a new hospital."

Jim and Patricia nodded.

"But they could do with some extra facilities. Like what?" Melita asked.

Patricia was the spokesperson for the charity and was doing a fine job of it. "They're talking about a dialysis machine, x-ray and scanning facilities, and an improved birthing unit. Of course, they would need to be fully staffed with appropriately qualified persons."

"That's okay. I'll provide ongoing donations to cover the costs for at least the first ten years."

"That's very generous of you, Mel," Jim contributed.

She shrugged. "The money from the sale of the gold is starting to come through. When it runs out, I'll top it up with my own funds."

Jim and Patricia had no idea how much money she had. Being wealthy could be frightening, but for some reason she felt safe over here. Only in Boston was she nervous about the size of her fortune.

"What else could the community use?" Melita drained her coffee mug and rose to rinse it at the sink.

Patricia flicked through a couple of pages of the report and flattened the notes on the table. "They have a universal sports field, but they've suggested revamping the existing club house. If there were sufficient funds, they would appreciate a—"

"They know the money's there," Jim interjected. "Word's out that a bucketload of gold was found in the old mafia house."

"Really?" Melita had hoped the information would stay out of the news a little longer, but she should have known better. In such a small community word had been bound to get out. She returned to her chair and folded her arms. "What are they suggesting?"

"A building that incorporates a twenty-five–metre pool, commercial kitchen facilities, toilets, showers, lockers, a gym and a canteen where they can cater for home games. You know, provide hot chips, hamburgers, pies and drinks," Patricia supplied.

"It's easy to come up with ideas when the money's flowing freely, isn't it?" Jim wisecracked.

He had a point, though, cynical as it was. She understood human nature better than most her age, having seen how desperate people were when money was involved.

"Wouldn't it be smarter to have an outdoor pool, seeing as we're in the tropics?" Melita asked. "Part of the building could form a partial cover."

"I think they'll appreciate anything we do. They're in awe of this charity and can't believe their luck. By the next meeting they'll have the final plans ready for the parks that were damaged after the last cyclone. The local Aboriginal Elders have had a say in the design. I had a quick glance of some of them and I think you'll be impressed, Mel."

Melita nodded, thinking that Patricia looked to be in her element. She'd worried at first whether Patricia's medical condition would prevent her from helping, but with her physical well-being taken care of, Patricia was thriving.

Patricia had been interviewed by the local newspaper earlier that morning and her story, her history and news of the gold find would all be revealed. The community charity Melita had established, for managing the funds from the sale of the gold, would also be publicised. By tomorrow there'd be no secrets and Patricia looked to be holding up well.

"Okay," Melita said, "what else do they want?"

⁘

Melita wrapped her arms around Luke's neck and let the smell of wood comfort her. She was bone-tired. She'd spent all afternoon nutting out charity stuff with Jim and Patricia and now she had to prepare her report for Marcus, the charity's manager, who'd relocated from Boston to Cairns for the job; there were some services the local community couldn't provide, so the small city of Cairns provided the perfect base. There were a lot of plans to draw up and applications to make to different state and local council services—a lot for Marcus to do, but she trusted him. The charity was in good hands.

"I'm going home now, Luke."

"What?" His arms tightened around her waist, a clear sign he had no intention of letting her get away.

She loosened her hold and raised her head. "Your grandfather said we can't live on coffee and sex alone."

A frown stamped Luke's forehead. "He said what?"

She smiled and reached in to kiss his neck. "He knows about us, but I didn't say a word. Anyway, he's right."

"Who's right?"

"We both need some sleep."

Jim and Patricia had volunteered to clean up after dinner. Jim washed the dishes and handed them to Patricia to dry. She could hear their chatter and laughter in the kitchen.

Luke had a tragic look on his face. Just showered, he smelled delicious and it wouldn't take much to change her mind. "Are you joking?"

Melita chuckled. "One night, Luke."

"But—"

She twisted out of his arms, though he held on to her hands. "I'm going to drive home, have a shower and fall into bed. Nothing exciting."

"Tell me about it. Nothing exciting there."

She tried to put on a serious face but couldn't hide her smile. "Stop it, Luke. You're turning me into some sex-crazed person who can't think of anything else."

"That's exactly what I'm after."

She prised her hands from his and playfully slapped him on the shoulder. "Sleep tonight. Sex tomorrow." She whispered the last part. No need to advertise their every move. "I'll say goodbye to Jim and Patricia."

She backed away, towards the kitchen, and the expression on Luke's face reminded her of a kid whose favourite toy had been taken away. He sighed, pushed away from the wall and followed her.

⚜

As she drove the short distance to her rented home, tiredness hit with force. She parked the car in the garage and gritted her teeth. How fast could she shower and fall into bed? Sleep was all that mattered tonight.

Once inside, she walked down the hallway into the living area and switched on the light. She gasped.

Splintered glass lay in front of the living room window and the filmy curtains moved with the breeze. Her gaze was pinned to the gaping hole, the size of a soccer ball, almost perfectly centred in the pane. Her scrutiny dropped to the floor and she saw a bundled rag among the shattered glass pieces—the missile used to break through the window.

Now what?

Her heartbeat increased tenfold and her tiredness didn't lend any support to the way her body trembled.

This feeling wasn't new to her. She'd been threatened before, even with her father's expensive security guards close.

Was this the work of a random bunch of kids mucking around? Or had the local community found out who she really was?

As she approached the bundled rag, stepping gingerly to avoid crunching any further glass, a surge of anger swirled around her chest. What she really hated was that someone had violated her private space. How dare they?

When she picked up the bundle, she almost dropped it because of the weight. She wasn't sure why she needed to see what was inside, but human nature was like that. Duct tape was wrapped around it and it disassembled when she pulled it apart. A chunk of steel fell from her hands. She leaped away before it landed on her exposed toes.

Bloody hell! That was all she needed—to have to call the police *and* the paramedics.

As she reached for her phone, a thick piece of paper dropped at her feet. She looked at it for a few moments and swallowed her fear. She'd read enough books to know that a message, the likes of which she had no wish to read, would be on it. Probably a request for ransom money. She nearly passed out when she picked it up. She flattened it against her thigh. On the left-hand side was the image of a black hand, similar to a kindergarten kid's painted handprint. To the right of it were the words, scrawled in big, black lettering, '*IT'S OUR GOLD. GIVE IT BACK!*'

Her legs buckled and she fell to the floor, glass shards pinching through her jeans. With shaking hands, she scrambled for her phone, still in her handbag. All Luke's worries whizzed through her mind. The gold, her safety, his concerns.

What was she missing? Was she in danger?

Calmly, she talked herself through the next few steps, refusing to dwell on any potential danger. She'd ring the police but not Luke. He didn't need the extra burden—and she didn't need to be reminded about his warnings.

Except it felt wrong not to tell him.

Chapter 12

L uke rolled off the side of his bed and dropped to the floor—it was all he could do to wake up completely and dispel the nightmares. The thud of his body landing on the timber boards echoed around the room. Luckily, he was alone in the house; that sort of noise would've sent his grandfather racing in to see what had happened.

With his heart racing a million miles a second, he concentrated on his breathing. Slowly in, slowly out. He did it again. And again. And again.

When he was sure his heart wouldn't explode, he sat up and nursed his head in his hands. If Melita was ever around when something like this happened, how was he supposed to explain it? Bloody hell, you'd think he would've grown out of having nightmares by now. For the first time ever he considered seeing a counsellor.

He raised his head and glanced at the alarm clock, then groaned when he saw it was only 2.46 am. What chance did he have of falling asleep again? Zero. And what morbid bad luck lurked around the corner?

Whenever he experienced a bout of nightmares, he always feared what would happen next. And this time he had two enemies trying to throttle him in his sleep—the black hand of his childhood nightmares and the Black Hand connected to the hidden gold and the mafia house. The double dose of danger left him no choice but to fear the worst—something was going to happen to either his grandfather or Melita, because who else would suffer the consequences of his bad luck? It always struck close to home and he was convinced it lurked in the vicinity of the mafia house.

He fell back onto the bed and scraped his hands through his hair. He should've convinced Melita to stay the night. It'd been weeks since he'd consciously thought about the black hand reaching out to harm him, because with Melita by his side, the likelihood of anything going wrong had seemed minimal.

But that was bullshit.

The resurgence of his bad dreams, after so many weeks of none, only compounded his theory. He'd let sex soften his resolve when he should've said something to Melita ages ago. Yep, he'd only had to spend one night alone for bad luck to be back on the agenda.

Shit!

He rose steadily, his legs trembling. What sort of man was he? Could he present himself to the woman he loved when the attacks were still happening? Would he come across as unstable when he explained it? Would it send Melita scurrying back to Boston and into the arms of another man? Someone who wasn't so screwed up?

He walked over to the open window, allowing the early morning breeze to brush over his naked torso—his usual trick when he woke from a nightmare. Looking out at the inky night, he was dazzled by the stars. Tonight, he was lucky —they were visible— except he wouldn't be getting the good night's sleep he needed *and* he'd worry for days, if he had to wait that long, wondering where the next batch of bad luck was coming from and who would be its victim.

⁂

"What do you think, Flynn?" Melita ran her index finger along the stainless-steel benchtop in the new kitchen, excited by the installation.

"I love it. Luke's done a great job."

"Yes, he's very particular about everything. Almost obsessively so."

Flynn chuckled. "I suppose it could be worse. He could be a builder who didn't care about the finish or how it looked."

After collecting Flynn from Cairns Airport, Melita had insisted they stop off at the tea house so he could see its progress. The upstairs boutique and changing rooms were almost finished, and the painters would arrive within the next couple of weeks before the café furniture was delivered.

"Have you decided on a name for this place yet?" Flynn asked as he inspected Luke's work.

The name of the tea house would determine the direction Flynn took in marketing the place, so she had to give him something soon. She'd been certain before the break-in but had changed her mind that night. After the local policeman had finished inspecting her living room, she'd gone to bed and had tried to sleep. Her only comfort, as she'd lain alone and wide awake, was the red silk scarf. She'd held it close to her heart as she'd remembered all the things Luke had done with it during their weekend away. The thought of having a little part of him in the room with her had calmed her—and the name of her business had come during the hours before sleep had claimed her just before dawn.

The next day, she'd phoned Flynn in Boston and told him she wanted 'The Silk Scarf' added to the options they'd already discussed. Flynn wasn't enthused at first, but the name wouldn't leave her. Despite how much they'd discussed the other options, she'd made up her mind. Well, sort of.

"I think I know which name I'll choose. Can you give me a couple more days?"

Flynn nodded and didn't argue.

With the pressure off to choose a name, her thoughts returned to Luke. She still hadn't told him about the note that had been thrown through her window. At first she'd been certain he would've found out on his own, this being a small town and all, but the policeman had arrived in a nondescript unmarked car, so the attack on her home had managed to fly under the community radar.

She'd talked herself out of staying with Luke during the past week for a number of reasons. Strangely, Luke hadn't argued. His acceptance was as unsettling as the break-in had been.

"You okay, Mel?"

She pasted on a fake smile. "Sure, I just want to run the names past Luke and see what he thinks."

"You're lying. What's happened? Is it Luke?"

She frowned. "No, and don't say anything to him. Please." If thugs had learned who she was and were looking for easy money, it was her problem, not Luke's.

"Then what *is* happening between you pair?" Flynn had witnessed the kiss she'd given Luke when they'd arrived. "It all looked pretty rosy when we got here."

"It is, truly. There's just something I have to deal with and I don't want Luke suffering because of it."

Flynn leaned against the shiny new kitchen counter and arched a brow. "Tonight, you can tell me what's going on."

She closed her eyes and groaned. There was no escaping Flynn.

"No ifs or buts, Sis."

Yep, he'd prise it out of her. He'd apply his usual tactics and within minutes she'd be spilling the beans. Maybe by sharing it, she'd get some relief from the tension constantly pulling on her in every direction.

"Not a word to Luke, okay." She heard someone enter the kitchen and spun around to see Luke making his way towards them.

Did he hear anything?

Flynn must've sensed her alarm because he stepped in and made immediate conversation with Luke, complimenting the work and praising his renovation skills.

"Hey, Luke, do you mind if I steal Mel tonight? There's some stuff we need to go through so I can get the marketing campaign on the road."

Luke glanced in her direction and she shrugged.

"Sure, as long as I can have her back tomorrow."

The boys laughed at the joke, but something stirred inside her. Luke was giving in too easily. That last night they'd spent together, he'd been ferocious about not wanting her to leave. But now he'd turned the tables completely and it was confusing the hell out of her. She knew what her own problem was, but she had no idea why he was suddenly backing off. When should she bring it up? How did you start such a conversation?

She approached Luke and wrapped her arms around his neck, no longer caring who was in the vicinity. All her shyness had gone, but she couldn't shake the feeling that Luke wasn't hugging her back in his usual way. Even his kiss was lacklustre.

Holding her emotions in check, she blamed herself. Maybe she was giving out vibes and Luke had latched on to them. Maybe she was the problem and needed to sort herself out. Fast.

Groaning inwardly, she took a step back and tilted her face to his. "Sorry about tonight. I'll make up for it tomorrow."

He nodded. "Better get back to work. I'll have a word with you tomorrow about the light fittings."

"Okay."

He disappeared and a little piece of her heart went along with him. She'd wait a couple more days and see what the police uncovered, then get Flynn's advice before she decided whether or not to tell Luke.

Flynn spoke out the side of his mouth. "Something's off, Mel. Let's drive by the bottle shop and pick up a bottle of wine. I think this might be a long night."

She gave in. It was going to be a long life if she didn't get a handle on her relationship with Luke soon.

Melita dropped Flynn off so he could have a shower after his long flight, then made her way to the shop. With a couple of steaks and some pre-dinner nibbles in hand, she veered in the direction of the town's only liquor shop. It was an add-on structure, attached to the rambling old hotel. The hotel's design matched that of other pubs, as bars were affectionately called, built in every regional town in Australia. Most were about a hundred years old and double storey, and every time Melita entered one, she thought about how they each smelled the same. She loved how casual they were and, on lazy nights, easily succumbed to a pub meal.

The drive-through service area looked busy, so she parked the car and walked in. Flynn had rattled off some names of wine he preferred and she made for a display of bottles, in neat rows, away from the counter. She scanned the labels, slowly moving down the aisle.

"Don't move."

She tensed when a hand clamped around her wrist. A man stood directly behind her.

"I have a knife and I'll use it if you say a word."

The strong smell of cigarettes filled her nostrils, making it difficult to breathe. His rank breath touched the skin behind her ear.

"You have two weeks to hand over either the gold or the money. Don't turn around straight away. We'll meet again."

As soon as he was gone, she let out the air trapped in her lungs and with shaky hands grabbed the closest bottle of wine. From habit, she looked up and spotted security cameras. Then, forcing her stiff legs to move, she made her way to the cashier, her heart doing laps around her chest. For a split second she feared dizziness would land her and the bottle on the floor—with a horrible mess to clean up. Instead, and with great difficulty, she placed the bottle on the counter and proved how challenging it could be to retrieve her purse.

"Are you okay?" The man serving her looked concerned.

She almost let out a burst of laughter, except it would've come out as a sob. The poor man. How bad she must look, to be buying a bottle of wine and shaking so much. No doubt he figured she was an alcoholic—or worse. She wouldn't be surprised if he slipped her a flyer for Alcoholics or Narcotics Anonymous.

She paid and, forgetting to thank him, left as fast as her stiff legs would allow. Taking furtive looks in all directions, she fumbled for the car keys and almost dropped the wine bottle.

She didn't see any likely suspect.

Chapter 13

"The steak!"

"What?" Flynn, with his arm around her, helped steady her tears.

Exhausted from crying, she sniffled. "The steak is still in the car. It needs to be put in the fridge." Though eating was the last thing on her mind.

"I'll get it. Don't move."

When he left a jolt of panic made her heart leap. She rationalised that he wouldn't be long.

Stretching along the comfy grey lounge chair, she rested her head against a cushion and forced in another deep breath. She eyed her handbag on the floor and debated her next move. After barging into the room, shaking and crying, she'd dropped it. Decision made, she reached for the bag and dug out her phone. It was time to ring her father. He'd know what to do.

Flynn returned while she was on the call and she let him know she was speaking to her father. When she ended the call a weight lifted off her shoulders and the phone slipped from her hand, landing on the carpet.

"What did he say?" Flynn sat on the floor with his back against the lounge.

Melita inhaled, long and deep. "He's putting his best two private investigators on a plane to Cairns tonight. They're ex-undercover cops he trusts. They'll find these thugs and corner them with enough evidence to put them behind bars. He can't believe the local police haven't found anything yet."

"What did he say about them wanting the gold?"

"That they'll be in jail before they get the chance to write their next ransom note to me."

Flynn chuckled. "His guys probably deal with this every day in Boston. This little outpost isn't going to know what's hit it."

She smiled. When her father said he was sending his best, she didn't doubt him. The incident at the bottle shop had amped up her fear, and her father's reassurance that these guys would sort out the problem was what she needed to hear. She was close to a complete meltdown. What if she'd come home to an empty house? She didn't want to think about her state of mind if Flynn hadn't been here.

"Dad will fly here once the job is done. He'll only get in the way in the meantime. Said his guys will want to set up the blackmailers and I'll need to play along with their plan."

Flynn frowned. "Will it put you in danger?"

"He assured me they're professionals."

Flynn shrugged. "I hope so." He sat with his knees up, tapping his phone. "Listen to this. There aren't too many results for the Black Hand in North Queensland, but there's one article written by a local a few years back. The Black Hand was a gang with a simple objective. They wanted money and obtained it from their fellow countrymen who'd begun to prosper in the north as cane farmers. Hardworking Italian migrants were threatened with death if they didn't pay extortion demands. Says it was prevalent in the 1930s. It mentions a few names and how they would send a notice to pay, with an imprint of a black hand."

Melita shuddered. She hadn't realised the imprint dated back to those days.

"The author warns readers that the deaths and incidents relating to the activities of the Black Hand remain, to this day, a very sensitive topic.

Families of those either involved or murdered still live in the region and continue to feel strongly about it."

Tell me about it.

Flynn continued reading out snippets while she closed her eyes and tried to ignore the chill creeping into her chest. Her father was adamant she didn't involve the police any further. Sometimes they were tangled up with the criminals, and until his private investigators had sussed out the situation, he wanted the local police to stay out of it. After all, they already knew of the break-in and ransom note, and 'if they haven't done anything yet, it's highly unlikely they'll move fast on anything else,' he'd said.

"When are you going to tell Luke?"

Flynn's question jolted her out of her thoughts. The whole time she'd wished Luke had been right there with her.

She sat up and winced. "I should've told him sooner. He's not going to be happy."

Flynn swung around on his backside to face her. "I can't believe you didn't tell anyone and stayed here alone the entire week."

She rubbed her eyes, her shoulders falling forward.

Flynn rose from the floor, sunk onto the couch and put his arm around her. "You're my sister, my one and only, and I only just found you. If you don't start taking better care of yourself, I'm going to get nasty."

She smiled, despite tears threatening again. She hadn't felt so included in a family since her sister Ella had stormed her way into her life. Now, since meeting Flynn and finding love with Luke, it was as though she mattered; she was needed, and her death, if premature, would cause heartache for those around her.

She swiped at her eyes and picked up her phone. "How much time do you want to spend going through the marketing?"

"Give me two hours, that'll be enough for now. I have to work the next couple of days in Cairns, but it'll give me a head start."

"Okay," she tapped on her phone, "I'll ask Luke to come over about eight and we'll have dinner first. I'll feel better when I've told him everything."

"Me too."

She rose and made for the kitchen. "You make the salad, I'll cook the steak."

"And I'll pour us each a glass of wine. Whatever you brought home, we'll stomach it."

She grimaced. Just the mention of the wine and she was back in the bottle shop. Her heart raced, but she clenched her hands and tried to fight her fear. By tomorrow night her father's men would be here, trailing her every move. If she could stick close to Luke, she might be able to manage her fear in the meantime. She wasn't letting those bastards put her off her game and under no circumstances were they touching one ingot of gold.

She put the book down. Not a single word had penetrated.

Frustrated, she glanced at her phone. There was no flashing light to tell her she had an unread message. Her fingers itched to call Luke.

She had to get everything off her chest. After a whole week of keeping quiet she was impatient to tell him—now that she'd made the decision to do so—except he hadn't replied to her message. He'd probably seen it and ignored it. Damn it. She'd sensed something wasn't right with him. If only she'd pried. Why did she lack the confidence to do so? Why couldn't she just come right out and ask questions instead of bottling everything up?

She rolled over and groaned into her pillow.

Flynn was sound asleep. Jet lag had finally caught up with him; he'd struggled to stay awake after they'd finished going through the marketing plan. He'd even refused a hot chocolate—and that was saying something.

She may as well sleep too. As long as she saw Luke before her father's men arrived, she could tell him everything and explain their presence. Before switching off the lamp she grabbed the red silk scarf lying beside it, bundled it against her chest and tried to relax. Before the break-in it had been easy to lose herself in dreams and fantasies; it was impossible since the bottle shop incident. Instead, she lay there going over possible scenarios for broaching the subject with Luke. He'd be upset at finding out a week later, but she would explain that having money meant you were an easy target, and she wasn't the first Van Der Meeliko to be targeted. He'd get that.

She snuggled further under the covers and turned on her side. She loved him and would show him. The three weeks they'd spent in each other's arms had been paradise. She wanted to go back there. They'd get through this.

The bedroom door swung open and crashed into the wall. She gasped and froze, as if electrocuted by fear. Torchlight pierced the dark. Screaming, she scrambled against the bedhead and within seconds a hand pressed firmly against her mouth.

"Shut up if you want to live," the man hissed.

A black balaclava covered his head and deathly dark eyes held her captive.

"This is a taste of what you'll get if you don't hand over the gold or the money when we ask for it."

He shoved something inside her mouth and she struggled to breathe. Her heart thrashed as she kicked her hardest. His hand connected with her cheek and her face was thrown sideways. She fell backwards, limp, struggling to get enough air in through her nose. As she lay paralysed, her fear level spiked.

The man bound her wrists and ankles to the bed with tape. She couldn't scream. Couldn't move. Couldn't call Luke to come to her rescue. How was Flynn sleeping through this?

Within minutes the man made his escape, but not before a crashing noise came from the hallway. How she heard it over the booming of her heart, she'd never know. What she did know was that to cry like she wanted to meant she wouldn't be able to breathe at all. So she lay very still, eyes wide open, sleep a long way off.

Chapter 14

Luke rubbed his eyes. This was the part of his job he least enjoyed. The volume of paperwork to catch up on never lessened—quote request emails to send, quotes received to compare, orders to compile and tradesmen to coordinate. It wouldn't be so bad if he didn't have a hundred other things on his mind.

The television went silent and he heard his grandfather's slow steps coming towards the kitchen.

"Want a cuppa, Luke?"

Luke nodded.

"The usual?"

"Yeah, thanks, Grandad."

Luke hid a smile behind his hand. It was a rare night in for Jim; he was in love and having the time of his life. Patricia must've needed some sleep for him to spend the night away from her.

Luke's smile slipped. He was in love too, but he wasn't having the time of his life. Melita was never far from his thoughts though. The need to tell her of his fear and its implications was at the forefront of his mind every day, but Flynn's arrival this afternoon had let him off the hook for another day.

When Jim placed a steaming mug of Milo in front of him, he picked it up and savoured the first sip.

"Want to talk about it?"

Luke fumbled and the mug landed noisily on the table, spilling some liquid. Jim rose and grabbed the dishcloth from the sink.

"Is that why you're here and not with Patricia tonight?"

"Maybe." Jim cleaned the spill, then rinsed out the dishcloth and hung it over the spout. He took his seat again and scraped it closer to the table. "What's happening between you and Mel? One day things seem picture perfect, the next day they're dark and hazy."

The tension drained from Luke's shoulders. He'd never told anyone about his nightmares and fears. Not his family or his mates. But his grandfather cared about him, and for the first time, he wanted someone else's take on what happened all those years ago and their thoughts on why the nightmares kept coming back, so he told his grandfather everything. His unfinished Milo was lukewarm by the time he was done; he grimaced when he took a sip.

Jim remained motionless for a long while.

Eventually, Luke asked, "So do you think I should see a counsellor?"

Jim shook his head. "I'm still getting my head around the fact you never told anybody about the nightmares. Yes! Bloody hell, of course you need to see someone. If they can help you, then yes."

Luke toyed with the handle of his mug. "What do you think about the bad luck that always strikes after I have a nightmare?"

Jim mulled over the question, his mouth twisting. He wouldn't strike it off as superstitious rot—he wasn't that insensitive.

"Does the bad luck strike straight away?" he asked.

"Not necessarily."

"And you're worried about the gold?"

Luke shrugged. "I'll know when the bad luck strikes, but yes, I'm worried about Mel and the gold. The house is bad luck enough, what with its history, and I had a panic attack the day we found the gold. Now the nightmares I had last night will bring their own lot of bad luck."

It sounded stupid, even to his own ears. How the heck did he expect his grandfather to take it all in? He slumped down in his chair. His fear was insane, but he'd lived with it for too long to simply dismiss it. "Should I tell Mel?"

Jim didn't hesitate. "Of course. She's probably sensed your worry, or your reluctance. She'll know something isn't right. Jeez, for a few weeks I couldn't tear the pair of you apart, day or night, then all of a sudden it stops. Tell me what you'd think if you were in Mel's shoes."

He knew exactly what he'd think. The hardest thing he'd ever done was stay away from Melita. The thought of rising for work without seeing her, day in, day out, and doing it for the next forty years didn't rate a mention. He would rather be dead—and that thought had never entered his head before.

He rose to rinse his mug. "I need to see her tonight and explain. I don't think I can wait another minute. Does that make sense, Grandad?"

A smile finally graced Jim's face. "Perfect sense. Get your phone and send her a message. If I know Mel, she won't be sleeping peacefully."

Leaving his mug on the sink to drain, Luke stood on the spot, suddenly at a loss as to where he'd put his phone.

Jim must've understood his confusion because he said, "It's not in the lounge room."

"It must be in my bedroom." Luke found the energy he didn't have a few minutes ago and walked briskly to his room. In the darkness, a flashing green light indicated he'd received a message. Thinking it was likely to be his mother or one of his sisters, he groaned when he realised it was from Melita and had been sent a few hours ago. It was nearly ten p.m. and she'd asked him to come over at eight. *Damn.*

He tried calling her, but it went to message bank. He tried again but still got no response. Call him paranoid, but he couldn't leave it at that. He had to tell her tonight, even if it meant waking her. For all he knew, she and Flynn might have the stereo up too loud to hear the phone.

He threw on a jacket and picked up his keys. Back in the kitchen, Jim was tidying up.

"I'll see you in the morning, Grandad. I'll pop over to Mel's now. I have to."

"Good idea."

Luke gave his grandfather a hug. "Thanks for listening. For years, I've been going crazy. It's nice to finally tell someone."

"We'll get to the bottom of it and sort it out. Trust me, you're not alone with this anymore. And I'm sure a therapist will help."

Luke squeezed once more and said, "Right. Now to sort things out with Mel."

"Good luck," Jim called as Luke made his way past the kitchen door.

⟨⟨⟩⟩

Luke swore when he drove onto Mel's street and saw all the lights switched off. He didn't doubt Flynn was sleeping off jet lag, but Melita's car was in the garage, so something didn't add up—she never muted her phone and always worked late into the night.

He sat in his car and tried to call her once more. As it went through to message bank he noticed that the front door was ajar. A shiver of fear crawled down his spine and for a split second he froze. Bad luck always accompanied his nightmares, but this was odd. Melita was meticulous about ensuring doors and windows were shut every night. You didn't grow up wealthy and from Boston without learning the basics of security, she'd told him once.

When his heart jolted, it was enough of a wake-up call and he wrenched the utility door open. He grabbed a pry bar from behind the seat, just in case.

Within seconds, he was past the front door, and he didn't hesitate to turn on the hallway light when his sneakers crunched on broken glass. He swore. The vase Melita kept on the hallway stand had been smashed and the dried flowers were scattered all over the floor.

He licked his suddenly dry lips, unable to call out her name. He swayed dizzily when he tried to move around the shards of glass. If Melita was hurt, he'd never rest easy again. Horrendous images ran through his mind and a fear so strong rooted him to the spot. He'd spend the rest of his life looking for the culprit, wouldn't stop until the person was put behind bars.

'Go and find her,' a voice kept telling him.

Why was he wasting time when it could mean the difference between life and death?

'Go now. Fight the fear. You can do it.'

It was as though sharing his lifetime of fears with his grandfather had released something. Now was the time to move on and put the past where it belonged. He shook his head and found the strength to face this latest round of bad luck.

Racing towards the back of the house, he began shouting her name and didn't stop until he reached her room.

When he switched on the light, he screamed. Her mouth was full of blood and she lay there wide awake, her arms pinned above her head and her fear so palpable he wanted to reach her quickly. She began to whimper and cry.

He realised it was a cloth in her mouth, not blood, and it took him less than a second to grab it out. He shoved it in his jacket pocket, then began tearing at the tape. He took a little longer with the tape around her ankles because she grabbed hold of his shirt and wouldn't let go.

"Oh my God, Mel, are you okay?"

She nodded feebly but looked unharmed.

He shushed her when she coughed and struggled to speak. "I'm here now, Mel. You're okay. I'm never letting you go again."

Finally, he deciphered her words.

"Flynn, Flynn. Check Flynn."

Christ almighty. He'd forgotten about Flynn in the face of trying to calm Melita.

"Ch-check him, please," she croaked.

He laid her back and bolted for the spare room. When he switched on the bedroom light, he found Flynn, bound up and looking terrified. He sagged with relief when he saw Luke.

Luke quickly removed the sock that had been shoved in his mouth.

Flynn coughed, then spat out, "Mel. Is she all right?"

Luke nodded as he tore at the tape binding Flynn to the bed. Once he'd freed him, they both bolted back to Melita. Brother and sister embraced and tears spilled down their cheeks.

Luke slumped to the floor, desperately trying to get his head around all this. "I'll call the police."

Melita and Flynn came apart instantly and said in unison, "No, don't!"

Luke rose on unsteady legs. "What the bloody hell do you mean? Are you crazy?" His bad luck had never had such serious consequences and his patience with it was long gone. He raked his hand through his hair, dumbfounded.

Melita rubbed at her wrists where the tape had been. "I'll explain."

Chapter 15

"A break-in and a ransom note and I know nothing about it?" Luke shoved his hands in his pockets, fighting the urge to slam his fist against the coffee table. "Would you have told me about what happened tonight if I hadn't come over and found you?"

"Luke, ease up, hey?" Flynn had made an icepack for the blossoming bruise on Melita's cheek and held it against her face.

Luke rose from the couch and paced. Nothing made sense. Maybe he was overtired, but the only thing he understood right now was that Melita hadn't trusted him enough to tell him about the break-in a week ago.

"Luke, I wanted to tell you, but it's *my* problem."

What? That stopped him in his tracks.

"I didn't want you worrying. This sort of stuff is normal for someone with my background. In Boston, we deal with the possibility of blackmail every day. I'm not the first Van Der Meeliko to go through it."

"Bullshit." *By God, she's holding her ground.* She might look apologetic, but she was far from sorry. He roughly ploughed his hand through his hair. "Crime is crime no matter where it happens and those criminals have no more right to the gold bullion than the guy next door. You've put yourself at risk because you're *different* to me, yet I'm the man you're supposed to trust, maybe even love."

Flynn's look of disapproval signalled it was time to end the slamming match. Luke took the hint but still shook with fury. He walked away, needing to calm down.

As he made his way towards the front door for fresh air, he felt the chasm that existed between her world and his open up. She was right. She did come from a different world.

When the shattered glass crunched beneath his shoes in the hallway, he veered off course to look for a broom and dustpan.

Why didn't they want the police involved? It went against his every belief. The police were supposed to be on their side. Why wouldn't they report it? Melita was adamant that they wait until the ex-undercover cops arrived. It would be another twenty-four hours before they did.

With the glass cleaned up, he walked outside and tightened his jacket around his chest. If he were a smoker this would be the time to light up and try for calm, because he knew now that it was not only Melita's life under threat. His nightmares were bringing terror into his world. No longer was it about Melita. The tables had turned and no one was safe. Anyone connected to him was in for a rough ride and last night's nightmares had delivered beautifully. He couldn't have choreographed it better.

A stirring breeze whistled through the leaves of the jacaranda in the yard and he heard a couple of its large seed pods fall onto the lawn. It wasn't a chilly breeze, but he bundled his jacket tighter. Iciness was finding its way to the tropical north and no amount of warm clothing would make it go away.

Once he'd calmed down, he realised he still hadn't spoken a word to Melita about his fears. To bring them into the picture now would only add to the confusion. It was better to say nothing.

Melita had managed to get some sleep that night. After she'd had a warm shower, both Luke and Flynn had insisted she try to rest. She'd almost laughed hysterically when she'd come into the lounge to say goodnight to them both. Luke, stretched out on the couch, had a long-handled shovel and a crowbar lying on the floor next to him.

"Nobody's going to get past me. If they do, they'll leave in an ambulance," was his blunt response when she'd eyed the tools.

Oh, how she'd wanted to fling her arms around his neck and rest alongside him. But he'd erected an ice-cold barrier around himself that not even a bloody Eskimo could penetrate, so she'd gone to her room alone instead. A frantic search for the silk scarf that came to no avail was the last straw. Without it, she felt adrift. Her anchor was no longer in place and any moment now she'd be thrown against jagged rocks. She broke down and cried herself to sleep—a dreamless sleep thanks to her exhausted body and mind.

When she woke this morning, she'd found both the lounge room and Flynn's room empty. The house was so peaceful it was hard to believe that in the past twenty-four hours she'd been threatened with a knife, tied up hostage-style and had driven away the only man she'd ever loved—all because she hadn't trusted him. She'd never forget the hurt written all over his face. Luke demanded trust if they were to be together. He'd been raised in a traditional household—his parents had lived and breathed together. Her own experience was different. Her parents had led separate lives in their huge mansion. If that was the kind of relationship she wanted, then Luke was the wrong man for her.

As if I know what I want.

By all accounts it was probably too late. His final words before she'd gone to bed had been, 'I'm not sure about us.'

She sighed as she brushed her hair. In a few minutes she and Flynn would leave to meet up with the ex-undercover cops. The men were booked to stay at a resort in Mission Beach, posing as a couple on a fishing trip.

She'd fielded phone calls and texts from her father all day and the investigators had been in contact for the past few hours. She didn't doubt her father's sway would influence what happened over the next couple of weeks and knew with certainty that he wouldn't skimp on anything when her safety was at stake. He'd come a long way in the parenting department and for once she was grateful and happy to embrace his wealth. Damn it, she had a life she wanted to live! She was desperate to squash these horrible toads getting in her way.

Reminded of the ghastly cane toads always in and around the yard, Melita managed a lopsided smile in the mirror as she tied up her hair. The horrid cane toad that had long since become an unwanted pest in the Far North; the need to eliminate the species was just as important as getting rid of the Black Hand thugs. It made sense to compare them.

But still, there was little reason to smile. She hadn't heard from Luke all day and had spent most of the day at the workshop concentrating on a new halter-neck swimwear design that *wouldn't* come together. The image of the galah wasn't sitting right, and by the afternoon she'd discarded half a dozen designs. That's when she'd given up and had left the workshop in the care of her supervisor. She'd considered buying snacks from the bakery to bring to the mafia house, like she did most days, but lost her nerve and had come home instead.

"Ready to go, Mel?" Flynn called from the front door.

She picked up her purse. They'd been instructed to drive to the resort, keep an eye out for any vehicles that might be tailing them and take down number plates if possible. She was to keep her mobile phone handy and record anything unusual. If they believed a vehicle was following them, they were to meet at a specific restaurant. If there was no suspicious activity, they were advised to go straight to the resort.

It was all so cloak-and-dagger. Was this how her life would be from now on? Would her wealth always put her in danger? Would she get to a point where she didn't want to live anymore? Like her mother had chosen not to?

If her mother was still alive, how might she have protected her? What advice would she have given about how to deal with Luke?

As for her father, he'd been working on overcoming a history of aggression and bullying since Ella had re-entered their lives, which gave her hope that humanity wasn't all bad.

Except for these criminal bastards trying to get their hands on my gold.

She made her way to the front door, more determined than ever to spend the proceeds from the gold in the local community. She didn't care one iota about any Black Hand thug who thought he had a right to it ninety years later. They'd all go to hell before she handed over anything.

Except she wasn't prepared to die. Heck no. She had a job to do and a project to complete, and damn it, a man she loved. She just had to prove it.

Bring on those ex-undercover cops! She would play any role beautifully and watch those thugs go down in a big way—and then she'd splash the news everywhere that the gang calling themselves the Black Hand were a bunch of criminals. She would explain how the proceeds from the gold were being spent, so anyone else who thought they had a right to it would realise it was gone. And despite all the negativity, she would continue to donate to medical research with every sale she made. Any family still connected to the Black Hand would be filled with shame and embarrassment—and then she'd know the job was done.

She lifted her jacket off the hook by the front door, squared her shoulders and locked the door behind her.

When she got in the car, Flynn asked, "Got your phone handy, Sis?"

"Sure do, Bro. Let's go catch these bastards."

Flynn laughed as he reversed the car onto the street, which helped her loosen up and lose some of the tension.

"I hope your father's right when he says these guys are good."

"They want to watch my house, Luke's place, the workshop and the mafia house. Six specialist detectives are coming from Brisbane in the morning to assist them, which means they'll be authorised to carry handguns."

"Wow, Daddy-o has been busy."

Melita nodded and checked the side mirror for any traffic tailing them.

"Wait," Flynn said, "I thought we weren't going to involve the local police."

"We aren't. The local police won't know a thing until they need to be told. This is a unit from the Australian Federal Police set up for this one incident."

"And what's the incident?" Flynn asked. "The discovery of the gold or everything that's happened since?"

She shrugged. "Both I suppose." Just then she noticed car lights in the side mirror. "Two cars behind us. Bugger, if they're tailing us what do we do?"

"Some fancy driving, by the looks."

As much as she wanted to feel safe, she couldn't completely keep the fear at bay. Although they'd only attempted to scare her into releasing the gold into their greedy hands so far, who was to say they wouldn't eventually try to hurt her or take her life? All day she'd fought with the belief that the only way they would get the gold or money from her was if she were alive. Made sense, but who knew what their motives were. Sure, they could target her family in Boston, but for now this was a local issue, and she didn't know how intelligent they were. If she'd learned anything coming from one of Boston's richest families, it was that criminals were dumb a lot of the time.

When Flynn veered sharply off the road to execute a U-turn, Melita was thrown against the door. She caught her breath and asked, "Where're we going?"

"Sorry about that. We'll head back in the direction we were coming from for a couple of miles. See who we lose."

"Kilometres. You have to talk metric over here."

"Nah. When it's you and me we can talk how we like. Okay with that, Sis?"

She smiled, loving her brother more.

"Looks like we lost one vehicle, but the other just turned around," Flynn said.

Her legs stiffened as fear ramped up again. She wasn't coping with this at all. Her fingers curled around the edge of the car seat and she squeezed hard until she remembered she was supposed to be gathering information. "I'll never be able to read their number plate from this distance."

"Hang tight," Flynn said, "I'll pull into the service station up the road and give them plenty of warning. If they're tailing us, they'll follow us in. Get ready."

Melita's jaw tensed and she frowned. She hated this. Reaching for her phone, she tapped out a message to let the detectives know their latest movements.

"Here we go." Flynn indicated left and slowed down. "Ah yep, they're following us. Get ready, Mel, I'll pretend we're going to fill up."

But Melita didn't get the chance to send the message or register anything about the other car, because as Flynn slowed down, it sideswiped them and she was thrown sideways. Flynn swore as he swung the vehicle away, narrowly missing a fuel bowser before slamming on the brakes.

With her heart hammering tenfold, she looked up in time to see the black Mazda fishtail ahead of them, wheels squealing as it exited the service station driveway. Flynn flashed the high beams for a split second on the rear of the Mazda, enough for her to catch the details of the number plate. MAD MOB 01.

As she rubbed the shoulder that had taken the brunt of the hit, it was easy to remind herself that some criminals were just plain dumb.

Chapter 16

B leary-eyed after the crappiest night's sleep, Luke prepared to face another day on the worksite—with things between himself and Melita at an all-time low. Had he really said those words to her before she'd gone to bed? What sort of unfeeling bastard was he? Even a three-year-old would've seen she was upset and had needed comforting. Hell, *he'd* needed comforting, and it wouldn't have taken much to convince her to join him on the couch.

After she'd gone to bed, Flynn had thrown him a scornful look, causing his conscience to twinge, then had said, 'Don't be too hard on her,' before heading to his room, which had only emphasised how badly Luke had screwed up again.

He ploughed a hand through his hair, issuing a gruff greeting to the three local carpenters he'd hired for the week. They'd sheeted the interior of the tea house a few weeks back and now they were here to sheet the interior walls of the workshop building that had been erected at the rear of the property. Piles of gyprock, delivered the previous week, lay on the concrete slab inside the steel-framed building. The workshop exterior had been sheeted with a beige roofing iron, its design allowing for it to sit discreetly in the background while the tea house got all the attention from the main road.

At least Luke could smile about the progress they'd made. He was proud of his work and the integration of innovative features to lessen the environmental impact the building would have over the years. Louvered windows and exterior venting would increase the airflow through the building, which, along with extra insulation, would minimise the need for air-conditioned cooling during the hotter months of the year.

"A stringline over this way, boys." It was a painstaking job to measure to the millimetre where the sheets had to go, but the time it took was worth it. There was nothing worse than getting it wrong.

"I can't find the stringline, boss. Any idea where it is?" A young, burly tradesman named Pete rummaged through the toolbox of assorted hand tools.

"Must've left it over at the tea house," Luke replied. "Yeah, I think I put it on the kitchen bench yesterday arvo. Want to duck over and grab it?"

Pete nodded. "Sure thing."

"Here, you'll need these." Luke threw across a small bunch of keys. With the tea house now at lock-up stage, he carried the keys in his pocket.

Pete was out the door in a flash, and Luke and the other tradesmen strapped on their nail bags and readied their screw guns. Someone had a radio blaring in the background and Luke whistled to a song he recognised. He couldn't remember what age he'd been when it topped the charts, but the words came back to him easily.

He looked up when Pete rushed back inside.

"Boss, quick! You better come and see this."

"What?"

"Come now. Holy crap, what a mess! Didn't need these either." Pete threw the bunch of keys and Luke caught them. "The lock on the front door was busted."

Pete didn't wait for a reply and turned back in the direction of the tea house.

Luke broke into a sweat as he shrugged off his nail bag and jogged outside with the others. His heart thumped wildly; he was probably going to confront his worst building fears.

He wasn't disappointed. Every newly sheeted wall was spray-painted with stencilled black hands—downstairs, upstairs, the kitchen, toilets. *Bastards!* They hadn't missed a single sheet.

His muscles quivered as he slowly made his way around again, inspecting the damage for a second time. Heat flushed through his body as rage built and he felt the beginnings of a headache.

He ground his teeth as he took a moment to reflect. The vandalism, at least, hadn't brought on a panic attack, but bloody hell, he was close to exploding. His vision blurred as he viewed the handprints in one of the upstairs changing rooms.

He used a carefully controlled tone to talk to Pete. "Mate, could you run into town and pick up a ten-litre drum of undercoat, a roller and a paint tray. I want you to get two coats on every print by the end of the day. Get them to charge it to my account."

"Sure, boss, I'll get onto it straight away."

Just as Pete was about to leave, Luke remembered the damaged lock. "Hey, Pete, we'll also need another entrance lock. See if you can get a replacement. I think the empty box with the code is still sitting near the front door."

Pete nodded and left quickly.

There was nothing more Luke could do other than instruct Melita to get after-hours security in place. He could've waited for the painters to obliterate the ghastly vandalism—they were due to start painting in less than two weeks—but he couldn't do it to Melita. Seeing the handprints would turn her world upside down. The faster he could hide them, the better. He'd upset her enough.

Stoney-faced, he made his way down the stairs. If the other tradesmen thought it was strange that he didn't call the police, he didn't care. It wasn't a discussion he wanted to have, so he called out, "Okay, boys, back to work."

His steel-capped boots dragged as he trudged back to the workshop. After what happened last night, he wasn't surprised by the vandalism.

What about his local tradesmen? Did they know what was going on? Didn't everyone know everybody's business in a small town? Was he employing someone who was feeding information to the thugs? Someone had known it was the perfect time to graffiti the tea house.

Shit! He wanted to call the police. Melita's warning that they wait for the arrival of the ex-undercover cops rankled.

He dreaded the long day ahead. Hopefully he'd be too busy to dwell on the mess and the day would pass quickly. He also wasn't looking forward to telling his grandfather about last night and all the drama Melita had kept from him.

He thought *he'd* been the one holding back in their relationship. Christ, she had a notebook full of reasons she could've used to back off. Enough valid reasons to halt everything between them.

His face fell when he reached the shadow of the workshop eave. All he wanted to do was growl and grimace, tear at his hair, wallow in self-pity and lie around depressed all day. Damn it, things had been perfect for a few sweet weeks and life had started to shine again. Now he could see little reason to smile. It didn't help that he'd said nothing to Melita about his nightmares and the bad luck they brought. What would his grandfather think of that?

He hefted on his nail bag and groaned. They still didn't have the stringline, so he sent another one of the boys back to the tea house. It was going to be a long day. They had a shitload of work to get through and he was one man short.

⁘

"I don't have to ask you how last night went, do I?" Jim placed a huge steak in front of him, with a side serving of roasted vegetables, and positioned the salad in the middle of the table.

Luke looked at the juicy steak and found it hard to believe he didn't feel like eating. He had a pain in his gut—nerves, winding their way into a tighter, smaller knot. "Thanks, Grandad, this looks delicious."

"Except you're not going to do it justice, are you?"

Luke's fork slipped and clattered against the plate. He'd half-expected Melita to turn up at the mafia house that afternoon and had dreaded having to tell her about the graffiti. But he hadn't heard one peep from her, which had at least saved him from having to explain the mess. It would only distress her further if she knew about it. She had enough on her plate with the ex-undercover cops arriving.

"So, what happened?"

Luke looked up into his grandfather's concerned face. "Shouldn't you be with Patricia? She'll forget who you are." He wanted to make light of his grandfather's concern, but it really touched him.

He tried to chuckle when Jim's brows rose—he was clearly telling him to stop with the bullshit—but it came out sounding like a choke.

Giving up the charade, he let his shoulders drop, inhaled a long, deep breath and released it slowly. "It's a mess, Grandad. Everything. Nothing was resolved last night, it only got worse."

"Let me guess, you didn't sleep well either?"

"Do I look that bad?"

"Worse than bad. So, you gonna spill?"

Luke pushed aside the delicious-smelling steak and rubbed his eyes. If he wasn't careful, he'd fall asleep at the kitchen table. Somehow, he had to find the energy to tell his grandfather everything that had happened since he'd walked out of the house twenty-four hours ago.

Chapter 17

Flynn walked into the kitchen after inspecting the damage to her car the next morning. "The hit didn't do too much damage, but now it looks as if someone destitute owns it."

He was right but Melita couldn't have cared less. Her wariness heightened every sense in her body. "I'll trade it in today and buy a new one," she said, dismissing Flynn's concerns.

No one had followed them after they were hit, so they'd driven to the villa where the ex-undercover cops were staying. All the while, Melita was thinking ahead. What was going to happen next? When would the Black Hand strike again? Would they hurt her? She could see they were getting desperate. Things could turn dangerous. She was relieved help had arrived.

"Want me to come with you?"

Huh? She'd spaced out for a moment, losing the thread of the conversation as they made their way inside.

"Oh, the car? No, I'll be fine. Don't you need to be in Cairns today?"

Flynn placed the breakfast cereal on the kitchen bench and pulled some plates from a cupboard. "Yes, but I'm nervous about leaving you alone."

"Don't be." Something tightened in her chest, but she needed to brave this out. "You heard them last night, I'll be tailed twenty-four seven." She checked the time on her phone. "And the detectives from Brisbane should be here and in position by now."

Everywhere she went, she'd get a sense of someone watching her, she'd been told. There was nothing to worry about, as every detective in position was armed and had been authorised to shoot if she was in danger. But knowing that did nothing to ease the tight ball of nerves in her stomach.

She put her phone down on the kitchen bench just as it began ringing. The name of one of the ex-undercover cops flashed on the screen, so she lifted it to her ear. The need for words were unnecessary, and as she listened carefully, her mouth curved into a smile for the first time in days. When she ended the call, she chuckled.

Flynn arched a brow, waiting for the news.

"They've got positive leads on the owner of the MAD MOB number plate. 'Like taking candy from a baby' were his words."

"That's great news."

They sat down to eat and Flynn finished his breakfast in record time. He picked up his briefcase and swooped in for a hug before dropping a kiss on her forehead.

"I'll be off. Don't forget, tomorrow's the day you give me a name for the tea house. I want to know exactly what we're calling it. I can't give you another minute longer."

Ugh!

Then, remembering something she'd thought of while having dinner with the cops last night, she waved Flynn off before dashing to her room. Dropping to her knees, she scouted under the bed for any sign of the silk scarf.

Damn! Where could it have gone?

She'd been certain she'd find it under the bed—the only place she hadn't looked yet. She'd already pulled off the sheets and doona, had even looked inside the pillow cases. But it was nowhere to be found and she couldn't hold back the anxiety wavering around the outskirts of her mind. Why was the damn scarf becoming so bloody important?

For God's sake, give it up. Get your new car and get the hell back to work. Everything else is pointless if you don't have any swimwear designs to sell.

Despite her weariness, she'd achieved a good day's work and had closed the workshop an hour early, sending everyone home. They deserved it after working hard to fill an urgent order from a Hamilton Island boutique.

She wanted to make it to the shops in time to buy a small gift for Luke. They hadn't spoken since the night he'd found her tied up. She didn't blame him; she should've told him everything from the beginning. Why had she held back? Sometimes she was so messed up she couldn't remember her reasoning. But then again, what past experiences could she draw on to navigate her way around this relationship? *None!*

The township of Tully boasted a small gift store, where she'd seen photo frames with meaningful messages on display in the front window. If she lacked the ability to express her feelings verbally, this option might work. She'd taken some great snaps of the two of them during their weekend at the beach—a framed picture might remind him of the fabulous time they'd shared. Maybe he'd even consider giving her another chance.

God, I miss him.

She locked her new white Mazda 6 Sports Edition and swung her handbag over her shoulder. They'd delivered it to her after lunch and her lungs were full of new car smell. She inhaled the damp, fresh air outside, replacing the smell of new leather in her lungs.

She looked up, unsurprised to see dark, heavy clouds about to drop their bundle. It always rained in Tully. It wasn't called Australia's wettest town for nothing—despite the neighbouring town, Babinda, disputing it and claiming the title as their own. She shook her head and smiled. Two towns fighting over which was the wettest? Only in North Queensland.

She fiddled with the zipper of her handbag before putting her keys inside and closing it again. On the footpath, she glimpsed the frames on display and slowed her steps to read some of the messages before going inside. 'Sometimes the heart sees what is invisible to the eye', 'Today I caught myself smiling for no reason, then I realised I was thinking about you', 'All it takes to make my day is a glimpse of you'. The messages were exactly what she was after.

She made to enter the store when a shadow moved behind her and a man said, "Don't move. I've got a knife and I'll use it if you scream or run away."

She gasped, reaching up to touch her neck. It felt as if her heart had stopped. Her breath was trapped in her chest and she didn't think she could take another one. Cold shivers ran down her legs and within seconds they began to shake uncontrollably.

His gravelly voice struck fear through her and his breath stunk of garlic and cigarettes. She swallowed, doing everything she could not to gag when he pressed himself up against her.

"I'll take this," he whispered in her ear as he pulled her bag off her shoulder. "Now I want you to walk nice and quiet to the car parked beside your swanky new one. And make it quick. Don't think we don't know about the cars tailing you. The drivers are busy parking and won't notice you're missing if we hurry up." He shoved her towards the car. "*Move*, bitch, or you'll pay for it."

She turned on stiff legs. To any passer-by, they'd look like lovers, given the gentle way he caressed her shoulder. Wanting to recoil from his touch, she prayed the under-cover cops were close by and watching. She held onto that hope before despair at not seeing anyone she recognised had a chance to invade.

Where are they? How could they still be parking?

Given that every available resource Thomas had secured was trailing her every move, this man had approached her way too easily. She would hear the wrath of her father from across the Pacific if anything happened to her.

The windows of the dark blue car were tinted almost black. Melita was roughly shoved inside and to the middle, and a hood was placed over her head before she could make sense of anything. Barely a minute had passed since she'd locked her own car. How had these thugs snatched her from underneath the noses of her father's private investigators and the experienced team from Brisbane?

She resisted the urge to burst into tears. Instead, she bit into her trembling bottom lip. There was only so much more of this she could take.

*

Luke picked up the scent of the sunset frangipanis sweeping in through the front door of the tea house. He didn't know what ideas Melita had for a business name, but he might drop the hint that 'sunset' and 'frangipani' worked well. They embodied every good memory they shared.

He raked a hand through his dusty hair and checked the work Pete had done to cover the stencilled black hands. He nodded, satisfied. There was no obvious evidence of the vandalism, and with the distance growing between him and Melita, there was a good chance she wouldn't come inside the building before the painters arrived anyway. As long as it remained a one-off incident, there was no reason to tell her about it. He had every intention of telling the undercover cops but wanted to give them a few days to get themselves sorted first.

The tradesmen had all left for the day and he began tidying up. He felt close to Melita when he was alone in the tea house. They'd shared so many good moments here and he missed her. Then he remembered his last words to her and knew he should stick to his guns. He was trouble in her life and was doing her a favour by staying away.

Except the lump in his chest said differently. It physically hurt, worse than a tough day on the job, every time he envisaged life without her.

Looking out the front French windows, he noticed the car that had been parked a little way up the road all day. It was reassuring to know he was being watched. It wouldn't hurt to say a quick hello on the way home.

He turned away and made for the rear entrance, which led to the partially sheeted workshop. As he locked the door, a shadow moved across his path before someone grabbed him and pulled a hood over his head.

"Don't move, or you're dead."

Luke stiffened, his back ramrod straight, his breathing shallow. *No fucking way. This is not going to happen to me twice in my lifetime.*

"We have a knife." One of them jabbed it against his chest and he felt the prick through his hi-vis shirt. "One wrong move and the girlfriend loses an ear and then her fingers, one at a time."

His heart thrashed and his memories threatened to choke him. *No fucking fear. No. No. No.* He tried to jerk his arm away, but their hold only tightened.

"Hurt her and I promise I'll kill you personally," Luke hissed through the hood.

One of the men gave a depraved chuckle and every hair on Luke's body stood on end. His muscles stretched taut; he was ready to react if given half the chance. This time he'd fight back. No longer a frightened ten-year-old boy, he'd fight them until he breathed his last. God help them if they hurt Melita.

They shoved and dragged him towards the workshop, then past it to the trees he knew shrouded a section of the property. *Shit!* Hadn't he seen an undercover cop parked there earlier in the day? Where the bloody hell was he? On a fucking coffee break? Without someone on watch, this was the perfect time and place to conduct a kidnapping. The detective at the front of the tea house would have no idea what was happening behind the workshop if his backup crew had packed up and gone home.

Damn! Why hadn't he taken Melita's situation seriously? He should have insisted on going to the police after he'd found her tied up, or he should have at least met the undercover cops when they'd first arrived.

If these bastards hurt her, he would never forgive himself. How could a simple nightmare bring so much bad luck? How could he have caused so much grief to someone so perfect, so lovable, so, so—*damn it!*—someone he was so in love with. Wanting to scream until his lungs burst, he kept quiet and hoped his grandfather would alert Melita when he didn't turn up for dinner.

For now, he'd play it smart. It'd take some time for the detective to realise he was missing. Hopefully someone would notice he never left the tea house. His utility parked out the front should be an obvious sign.

He heard a car engine idling. Before long he was pushed inside and bit back a curse when his shin connected with the edge of the door. Feeling the presence of a man on either side of him, he assumed they were in the back of the vehicle. He tried to keep his wits about him and concentrated on where they were driving, but he soon lost his bearings. He had no idea where they were; all he knew was that the roads had been rough for about twenty minutes, and when they stopped, the tell-tale song of crickets told him that dusk had fallen.

The men forced him out of the car and bound his hands with rope and tape. The only other sound in the quiet night was the squeak of a steel hinge. He was jostled towards the sound and within seconds they removed the hood. When his eyes adjusted to the darkness, he had just enough time to see a farm shed before he was pushed inside.

"Be sure to take a good look at your girlfriend before the boss pays a visit later tonight. It might be the last time you see her pretty face."

What? The smell of sugar cane and dirt rose to mingle with his confusion.

He turned around but the door was shut and bolted from the outside. Inside, a lone lantern was perched on a shelf.

"Luke!"

He spun around, but with his hands bound he lost his balance and stumbled, then fell on something sharp. He swore and pushed away the farm implement before recognition penetrated his fear. *Melita? She's here?*

Getting awkwardly to his feet, he twisted around and spotted her—she lay curled in the darkened corner—and his heart lurched at the sight of terror looking back at him.

"Mel."

He wanted to curse but only managed to choke. The look of resignation on her face said it all. She couldn't take it anymore.

He had to let her go before she was killed. Whatever it took to save her, he'd do it.

Chapter 18

A lone and frightened, she'd cried hard. Nobody had seen her abduction. And being unfamiliar with the area, she had no idea where they'd brought her. Their threats about what would happen when the boss arrived scared her witless. How was she expected to be brave under those circumstances?

These bastards were serious about wanting the gold and she was beginning to have second thoughts about keeping it. Was it worth dying over?

In theory, yes. But compared to living life to a ripe old age, maybe not.

When a car had pulled up outside, she'd grown tense. The door hinge had squeaked and she'd held her breath, expecting the worst. She'd pushed herself further into the corner with her legs, trying to minimise the friction from the rope and tape on her sore wrists.

Too afraid to look at whoever had come to interrogate her, her eyes had snapped open when Luke swore and she'd been unable to hold back from calling his name.

Now, her heart plummeted. This was the price you paid for being wealthy. You put good salt-of-the-earth people like Luke in grave danger. How had they kidnapped him without the undercover cops seeing anything? Her father would be livid when he heard about this.

Luke stumbled towards her and tears began to fall down her face once more.

"Mel, Christ, are you okay?" He fell to his knees beside her.

She noticed they'd bound his hands too.

What could she say? Even if she knew, she was far from capable. Her body convulsed with a fresh wave of tears.

"Sit up, Mel, please. Come on, wipe your face on my shirt."

She sat up clumsily and, resting her face against Luke's shoulder, made a solid attempt to stop crying.

"That's better." Luke planted a kiss on her forehead. "They'll find us. We have to be positive."

"Before or after they chop off an ear or a finger or two?" She hadn't meant to sound so harsh.

"Bastards. They told me about that threat." Luke bent his knees and rested his bound hands on them. "Listen here, Mel, we have to play their game for as long as we can, but if there's going to be any cutting or hacking off, *I'll* volunteer, okay? This is my fault and I'll sort it out."

"What?" *His fault?* The only thing he'd done was befriend her, become her lover and the one person in the universe who meant everything to her. Voices floated in from outside the shed door and she lowered her voice to a whisper. "What do you mean?"

Luke swivelled to face her. The paltry yellow light coming from the old camping lantern was enough for her to see turmoil in his eyes. Goddamn it, she loved this man and wanted to remain by his side forever, but what did he mean? How was this his fault? Did he have any concept of what life was like for someone as wealthy as her?

She pushed against his shoulder with her chin. "Luke, talk to me, please."

"Oh, Mel, I've been trying to for weeks. Some days I think I can, but other days I want to forget it."

Wanting to shout until her voice was hoarse, she restrained herself to a harsh whisper. "What are you going on about?"

He rested his forehead against hers and she took all she could from him—his aura, his scent of freshly cut timber, his strength. God help her, she needed it. When something trickled down her temple, she jerked back. She'd never seen a grown man cry before.

She lifted her bound hands and touched his face. "Luke, I love you."

"I more than love you, Mel. Enough to let you go."

"No," she wailed, tears trickling once more down her cheeks. It would barely be tolerable if she were the one letting him go—and she had darn good grounds to do so. She was not okay with him giving up. What reasons could he have? "Tell me, please."

His shoulders dropped, and when he sighed, the nerves in the pit of her stomach strengthened. How bad was this going to be?

"When I was ten, an intruder broke into our home through my bedroom window. He bound my wrists and legs and gagged me. He said if I made a single sound, he would kill me. I was left that way all night. I thought I'd die. It was so hard to breathe. I almost did ..."

Melita never let her gaze leave his face as he relived the childhood tragedy. It had been a random act and they'd been given no explanation for why his family's home had been targeted. Repeated nightmares coupled with bad luck had left a cursed streak on his life—and he'd kept all that to himself until he'd shared it with his grandfather a couple of days ago.

When he finished, he hung his head low.

"Luke, look at me." She wanted him to see how her heart sat perched on her shoulder for all to see. But if he didn't want her in his life, where did that leave her?

He shook his head, as though not wanting to be swayed. If she didn't do something quickly, he'd leave her just to save her. He needed to be reassured that there were ways to deal with his recurring nightmares, and that she wanted to be by his side to help him do that. He'd already said he should've asked for help years ago.

"Luke, please."

Slowly, inch by inch, he lifted his face. The sadness seeping out of his expression tore at her insides.

"Luke, this"—she twisted from left to right, highlighting their current situation—"isn't your fault or because of bad luck."

Like an old man giving up on life, he bowed his head, as though refusing to share the blame with anyone.

"It's true. This sort of thing happens to people like me all the time. I can count on both hands, plus more, how many times it's happened to a Van Der Meeliko."

He continued to shake his head. "I'm sorry, Mel." His voice broke, catching her unawares. "Too many bad things have happened to me and the people I care about for it not to mean something. I have to let you go …"

"No!" she shouted, not giving a damn who heard.

Determination seeped past the barriers of sadness written all over his face, relegating them to a back seat. "Yes, Mel. But my bad luck is only one reason we can't be together. As time goes on, our differences will become glaringly obvious. Christ! We come from different planets. You'll always have more money than you know what to do with, and I'll always be penny pinching to make ends meet."

She couldn't believe what he was spouting from his mouth. How had he gone from bad luck to this? It rendered her speechless and scrambled her brain, then shock set in. "So this … this is about money, is it?"

All her years of hoping she'd find someone who wanted her for who she was, and not for her wealth, had been a waste of time. It always came back to money. *Always.* She wanted to yell loud enough to tear the roof off the shed. Stamp her feet until blisters formed. Punch a wall and watch the blood drip from her knuckles—except she couldn't. The thugs waited outside and her hands were bound. She was no longer free and her life would never be her own. It would always be ruled by her godforsaken money.

She shook but she was done crying. She'd curb it to get through to this idiot of a man that he was wrong. For once in her damn life she was going to get something right!

"I'm doing what's right, Mel. You can do a lot better than me, and you will."

"No, Luke, you're wrong and I won't stop until I've—"

The door bolt moved and the hinge squeaked in the night.

Luke pressed his face to her ear and whispered while he still had the chance. "Don't agree to anything and let me do the talking."

A thug swung a leg towards Luke's shin, kicking him hard. Luke kicked back with his own steel-capped boot and caught the thug a good one on the ankle. If it was the last piece of satisfaction he got, he would enjoy every second of it.

"Ouch, you bastard!"

Luke copped another blow to the lower back and pain riddled every nerve ending. He bit down hard to keep from screaming out.

"Hey, Johnny." A brawny and malicious-looking brute sauntered over. "I said there was fun to be had, but can you wait a minute?"

Luke eyed the mean glint in the man's eyes and figured he was the boss the others had mentioned. His sort never let anyone stand in their way.

Johnny, who looked young enough to still be in school, limped over to a crudely made bench and sat down, rubbing his ankle. "Hurt him, boss. Hurt him real good."

Luke flinched at the boss's depraved laugh. Melita whimpered.

"We're going to have a nice, pleasant conversation, then I'm going to hand over a laptop and you're going to transfer all the money you got for the gold to us. Simple, really, isn't it, sweetheart?"

It took all of Luke's willpower not to move when the boss ran a finger down Melita's face and cupped her breast. She shuddered at the touch.

"We'll give you ten minutes to agree." He touched her hair with his dirty fingers and lifted some strands. "If you don't"—he tucked her hair back neatly and fondled her ear—"chop, chop. One at a time."

"Touch her, you bastard, and you'll regret it for the rest of your life."

The boss had taken it too far the second he'd touched Melita, and for all his good intentions to play it smart, Luke was prepared to die an ugly death if it meant saving her. He'd do anything to distract the guy.

The boss turned and landed a heavy blow across Luke's face. Luke fell back, his legs twisting uncomfortably.

"No, don't!" Melita screamed and pushed against the boss.

"Transfer the money from the gold."

"Okay, okay, I'll do it."

My God, what was she saying? Luke wanted to throttle her. He rolled awkwardly to straighten his legs and slid closer to her. Pain exploded from his nose and he bit back a curse. *Probably broken.*

"Ten minutes, you bastard. Get your filthy hands off her and leave us to discuss it alone."

Instead, with lecherous hands, the man took a leisurely tour down her shoulder and along her arm. Melita kicked at him and again his sadistic laugh rent the air.

"I might just enjoy you, instead, while you make up your mind. I don't think your boyfriend will mind watching. Do you?"

Ignoring his pain, Luke lunged at him again, hitting him on the leg.

The boss turned to one of his henchmen. "Tie his legs up, now!"

For his act of bravery, Luke copped another hit to his upper thigh and the realisation that there'd be little chance of him saving Melita.

Chapter 19

S he swallowed hard. *Keep it together, girl.*

She'd been trained for this. Knew she had to give them what they wanted. Had to offer it to them and make them think she was giving in to their demands. The opportunity was being handed to her on a platter. Textbook stuff, but she didn't think it would be presented so neatly.

"Untie my hands and give me the laptop."

The boss jerked his head in her direction and she flinched. He was a mean-spirited one. What'd gone wrong in his life to bring him to this point? He didn't know it, but things were about to get much, much worse for him.

"One thing at a time, little girl."

"Wait, Mel!" Luke's anger showed in his posture. "Take the ten minutes."

She shook her head then turned from him. He was in pain and it was *her* fault. They needed to get out of here, fast. "It's over, Luke, I don't want the money anymore. It's caused us enough grief. They can have it."

Luke hissed, his pain and frustration hitting her square in the back.

She did her best to shut him out. *Keep the charade going. Make them believe you've capitulated. Let them think they have the upper hand.* The things she'd been taught about how to deal with thugs like these came back to her as easily as her Sunday school lessons.

She raised her bound hands. "Untie them." *And don't patronise me, you bastard.*

He smirked and placed a kiss on her shoulder. "Do you think we're stupid? We picked up on the extra surveillance in Tully. It's a small town, bitch, but we're one step ahead of you. We'll have the money and be outta here before they realise you're missing."

Luke growled behind her; she didn't need to look to know his helplessness would be like a knife going through him.

"Gag him, Johnny."

"No, don't!" she begged, twisting to face Luke. *God, no.*

He'd only just finished telling her about his childhood trauma and his inability to breathe, how the fear of dying that way was always there.

"He won't say another word, I promise." She pleaded silently to Luke.

"Gag him, Johnny, and give him another reminder to shut his fucking mouth."

Melita wanted to spear his chest with a knife. Instead, she bit her bottom lip until she tasted blood. She couldn't bear to watch Luke being kicked and punched, so she turned away—it was the hardest thing she'd ever done—and blocked out the sound of him choking. She had a job to do, but she made a promise to fix this brute good and proper. She wasn't Thomas Van Der Meeliko's daughter for nothing.

With a jolt she realised it was the first time she'd ever wanted to be like her father—and it was to channel his ruthlessness. A sinister smile made her lips curl.

She pressed her bound hands into the boss's chest and demanded he untie her. He waited until Luke had been bound and gagged, kicked and punched, but he did as she bid.

The relief was sweet and she rubbed her wrists vigorously until the pain ebbed.

"What's your plan for after I transfer the money?" She was all business now.

"We'll leave you and your lover boy nice and cosy together. The police will get a tip-off in a few days. Do you want to be tied up together or separately?"

She kept every vestige of emotion off her face. "Where's the laptop?"

Someone walked out of the shadows carrying a device. The glare from the screen was blinding in the yellow half-light.

"Don't do anything stupid. I'm watching everything you do."

Be my guest. "It'll take up to fifteen minutes for me to set the money aside and transfer it to you."

He swaggered towards Luke and hurled another booted foot in his back. Melita nearly threw the laptop at the back of his head when Luke muffled a painful groan.

"We can wait fifteen minutes, can't we, boys?"

There were a few grunts and replies from all corners of the shed. How many thugs were there?

Concentrate, girl. Remember the codes and passwords.

Remember she did—they'd been drummed into her from an early age.

She opened the webpage for The Bank of Boston Central—seemingly authentic but fictional. As soon as she logged in, using a code that was specific to her, alarm bells would ring loud and clear in her father's office and the offices of at least three other managers, signalling that she was in trouble—her way of shouting for help from half-way across the world.

She entered her code and the page loaded. Next, she had to give them some idea of the problem she faced—different coding specified different scenarios. She typed in the number series that indicated she'd been abducted, which would send her father and his men a GPS reading for the laptop she was using. Within minutes, they'd be able to pinpoint her exact whereabouts.

Doing her best to keep a smile from spreading across her face, she entered the code to signal that she was about to pay ransom money to her abductors. This would send alerts to her bank. Their security department would then watch the money move through cyberspace to the bank account she nominated. It would stay there for half an hour—enough time to show the scumbag the money had reached his account—before it was confiscated.

"One more transaction and then I'll need your bank account details."

"A little Boston bitch we got ourselves here, boys. I bet Daddy's got lots of money we could take."

Try your hardest, low life.

She gritted her teeth, wanting more than anything to turn around and look into Luke's eyes. To check he was okay and not unconscious.

She entered one last series of numbers—a call for medical help. Luke needed an ambulance—and fast.

She pressed the tab key, extending the time it would take for the money to be transferred. She hoped twenty minutes wasn't pushing her luck. Every step was visible to the boss, but he had no idea that every press of the button gave her another five minutes. She almost tapped it again but stopped herself. She didn't need his suspicion aroused.

The little bars at the bottom of the screen crept along slowly, indicating the transfer was on the way to being completed. She couldn't hear a sound coming from Luke. Her heart beat and pulsed inside her as she waited, and each breath she took was a struggle.

Fingers crossed her father would have enough time to contact the undercover cops and alert the local police. Hopefully, the ambulance was on its way so the medics were ready to treat Luke as soon as the cops stormed in and took this rotten crowd away.

These monsters had no idea of the hornet's nest they'd settled on. Her father would wield his power and money, ensuring every last one of them served time—for a long time. She'd heard her father say once—to her half-sister, Ella, after she'd received death threats—that 'no one messes with my girl.'

The laptop beeped loudly to indicate the setup was complete and she almost screeched in the deathly quiet of the shed. Not even a muffled sound escaped Luke. Worry pushed against her chest and she struggled to calm her racing heart.

"Write down your bank account details," she said, enunciating her words carefully to keep from screaming them instead.

The boss pulled a notepad from a briefcase and smirked. The weasel was probably congratulating himself on how easy this had been.

Like taking candy from a baby. The undercover cop had said something similar when he'd told her about the lead they had on the car with the MAD MOB number plate. She didn't doubt it was owned by this criminal idiot.

She was getting the greatest satisfaction from duping him. So long as Luke wasn't seriously hurt. If he was, so help her God, she'd come down on this swine like a tonne of bricks and use every goddamn penny she had to silence him, put him in prison and fight every parole opportunity he was given. Trusting that Luke would come out of this okay, she found the strength to appear calm.

Her fingers shook as she typed in his bank details, and her teeth refused to release her bottom lip. If she wasn't careful, she'd taste blood again.

Where was the rescue party? There was only so much she could do to use up time. But she had to believe she'd mobilised everyone into action. Had to remain positive that they were steadfastly creeping towards this shed, stealth-like in the dark.

Come on, come on.

"It'll take about fifteen minutes for the money to land in your account. You can watch its progress, just let me check on Luke." She also needed to get out of the way, in case the shed was stormed by armed personnel.

The threat of this monster raping her seemed to have passed. His eyes glistened with greed as the small squares on the bottom of the laptop moved slowly from left to right. He waved her off, giving her permission.

Not wanting to give him a chance to change his mind, she stumbled over to Luke. Without hesitating, she dropped beside him and wrenched the gag from his mouth. His eyes opened slightly and his breathing sounded raspy. Blood was splattered across his face and upper torso, but she couldn't make out where it'd come from. The light didn't reach this far into the corner. She was desperate to tell Luke that help was on the way, but she kept quiet, knowing it wasn't safe to do so.

Seven or eight men were gathered around the bright beam of the laptop, following the transfer's progress for themselves. Turning away from the tight knot of nasty humanity and concentrating on Luke instead, she felt for his pulse and was reassured. Her biggest concern was the hits he'd taken to the head. But she wouldn't go there yet; she couldn't or she'd crumble. His breathing sounded better, and she took his head in her lap, hoping to offer comfort. It was all she could do while she waited.

Someone whistled and the conversation from around the laptop filtered back to the corner. "That's a lot of loot, boss."

"You gonna share with us?" another asked.

"You'll get your share, you bloody parasites. We're family, remember." His menacing voice was gravelly, as though his vocal cords had been severed at some time.

There was laughter and ribbing and discussions about how they would spend the exorbitant amount of money she'd falsely transferred.

She turned her attention back to Luke and whispered, "Stay with me, Luke. Help's on its way."

He flicked his eyes open for a few seconds, but they looked distant and she worried he might be concussed.

A deafening boom assaulted her senses, and, startled, she jumped. Luke's head slipped from her hold when the doors to the shed shot open and heavily-clad officers raced in shouting, "Get down, get down! Now, now, now, on the ground!"

The cops waved their rifles at the criminals, all packed neatly together in a tight knot around the laptop. She almost laughed at the comical sight as relief poured through her limbs. Luke stiffened beside her and she shushed him, trying to reassure him that everything was okay. The cops were kicking away guns and knives and shining bright torches into the thug's faces. It was only as they were clicking on handcuffs that she heard the faint sound of sirens approaching. Her relief was complete. Help for Luke had arrived.

Then a flash of white tore across her peripheral vision and Flynn entered the shed behind a couple of local police.

"Mel, Luke, where are you?"

What's he doing here? She didn't get the chance to ask. Didn't get the chance to reassure him that they were okay or ease the anxiety on his face, because in the moment that followed, Johnny reached inside a pocket, pulled out a handgun and pointed it at Flynn.

She screamed—at least she thought she did—before the noise from the shot reverberated around the shed. More noise followed as one of the policemen sent a second bullet into Johnny's body. He jerked and flopped for a miniscule of a second before lying deathly quiet.

Then Melita found her voice.

"*Flynn!*" She screamed, coming to life as she rushed to her brother's side. Blood poured over his face as she sank to her knees and howled his name.

Chapter 20

Melita tapped her phone, checking for the time. Flynn had been in and out of consciousness for a couple of hours, and she'd promised his parents, John and Mary, that she'd be there each time he woke up. Not that she had anywhere else to be. Until Flynn was all fixed up, she wasn't leaving Boston.

She closed her design sketchpad and glanced at the flowers, sent from family and friends, scattered around the room, which Mary had also decorated with photos. Melita was grateful. While she respected the care and compassion most nurses showed their patients, she had an inherent dislike of hospitals. With no prior bad experience to blame, she couldn't explain why she loathed the sterile rooms. Perhaps it was the smell of disinfectant and the lack of warmth and laughter.

She sat back in the padded chair and closed her eyes, her mind flicking back to the mayhem of the hours after the shooting. The ambulance had been on its way when the police stormed the shed, but it was Flynn they'd taken, not Luke.

Within hours of arriving at Cairns Hospital, Flynn had stabilised, enough for them to put him on a flight to Brisbane for the first and crucial operation to put his face back together. Melita hadn't left his side and didn't spare any expense in caring for him. After his surgery in Brisbane, she had him loaded on a plane, with a fully equipped medical team, to Boston.

With the blame for his injury landing squarely on her shoulders, the least she could do was have him near his family with the best medical services America could offer—and she'd done just that. He was now waking up from his fifth and final operation to put his chin back together. It was two months since the incident, but as the surgeons explained, mending it was no different to completing a jigsaw puzzle—each piece placed carefully with enough time for the body to repair itself. It could've been so much worse, but remarkably, the rest of his face had been left unscathed.

"Mel."

Her eyes snapped open and she leaned forward. "Hey, Flynn." She reached for a cup of water and held the straw to his lips.

After a few sips, he managed a whisper of a smile. "I'm feeling more awake this time." His voice was less croaky and his words didn't slur as much as they had when he first woke a couple of hours earlier.

She pushed his hair away from his eyes, careful not to disturb the bandages around the lower half of his face. "Are you in pain?"

He chuckled, despite all the bandages. "I'm sure I'm drugged enough not to feel any. Just a bit numb when I talk."

Guilt, always guilt, speared across her chest. Of all the bad luck to come hurtling her way, why had she been the one to find the lost gold that had been the cause all those murders during the 1930s? Luke thought bad luck trailed him—well, her tally of bad luck was marching right alongside his. She'd never let it get to her before, but she could see now how constant bad luck could affect you. It could drag you down and leave you in a dark place. No wonder it was such a big deal for Luke. They'd both experienced their fair share of it lately and quite frankly she'd had enough!

"Have I missed any news while I've been out of it?"

Melita smiled. She didn't doubt it must hurt like blazes for him to talk, but she didn't try to stop him. On his good days between surgeries, while he recuperated at home, he insisted on working as usual, despite the pain. She neither pushed him to work nor held him back.

"Where do you want me to start?" she asked.

He'd only gone under the knife that morning so hadn't missed anything, but he asked the same question after coming out of each round of anaesthetic. It was his way of confirming he was good to go just as soon as he could feel his chin again.

She'd delegated everything except her design work, which was her only source of solace during the many tense-filled days of the past weeks. It was the only task that allowed her to switch off and push everything else to the back of her mind.

And there was plenty to push.

Flynn touched her hand. "Thanks for staying. Will Mom and Dad be here soon?"

"I insisted they get some sleep, but they'll come back after dinner."

"They'll never hold out that long. Now do you get what it was like for me growing up?"

Melita laughed. Flynn always succeeded in bringing a smile to her face when she least felt like it. "They're the best, so stop your moaning."

"Not complaining." Laughter sparkled from his exhausted eyes. "Except for all the hugs and kisses in public when I was a teenager."

John and Mary had taken her under their wing immediately. She'd told them everything in the days following her and Flynn's return to Boston, and Mary had tucked her under her protective arm and became the mother she needed. They'd insisted she stay with them and their love surrounded her like the soft comforter they'd put on her bed. Regardless of the road she took, she knew there would always be a warm and loving home with them.

"How are Patricia and Jim going?"

"They're doing what they love best and coping just fine with Marcus's assistance."

"They're pretty good together, aren't they?"

She nodded. They were getting through the community projects quickly, with the funds dwindling at a steady pace. If it weren't for Patricia and Jim, she'd have no idea what was happening in Tully. In Jim's words, shit had hit the fan after her departure. There was huge community backlash against the criminals, especially since the money from the gold was being put back into the township. The culprits were sons of the local families once connected to the Black Hand, so there was no sympathy for them. Certainly nothing from her father, either. With his best lawyers on the job, the case against them was progressing nicely.

Only the death of the young boy, Johnny, had continued to gnaw at her conscience. He'd been too young to die. With time, he might've evaded the clutches of the boss and made a decent life for himself. Anonymously, she'd sent a cheque to his family to help with the cost of his funeral and to ease the pain of learning what their son had been mixed up in.

"And Luke?"

She groaned, though she hadn't meant to, and slumped back in her chair. The sound reverberated around the sterile room and made Flynn smile, despite his swollen face.

"Ouch."

She sat up, tense with alarm. "Are you okay?"

"I'll have to wait a few days before trying to smile."

She dismissed his remark, more concerned about his comfort. "Can I get you anything? Would you like some water?"

"No, Sis, I don't need anything from you except an answer. What's happening between you and Luke? Every time I ask, you manage to evade the question or say nothing at all. You've been here two months. Don't you think it's time you went back?"

She caught her bottom lip between her teeth, tears dangerously close. Why was the mere mention of Luke's name enough to undo all her hard work? Hadn't she spent the last two months burying everything?

"Oh, Mel, I didn't mean it like that. If you love the man, shouldn't you go ba—"

"Yes," she said, stopping him in his tracks, "I love that dumbass." She fisted her hands into tight balls as anger swamped her. "Do you want to know what we talked about while we sat bound up in that shed?"

She hadn't shared the details of the conversation with anyone. Not Flynn or John or Mary. Instead, she'd let Luke's words eat away at her, and they now sat in a tightly woven knot lodged securely inside her chest.

Flynn didn't say another word. With all the patience in the world, he let his brotherly love reach across to her, instilling her with confidence to share the heartbreaking secret. She didn't know why she had refrained from telling him, but he always managed to dissect her heart and knew when to prod enough for her to release her pain. So she told him that the thing that mattered most to Luke was that she came from money and he didn't. At the end of the day, her wealth was the white elephant that would always stand between them.

Flynn reached for her hand and squeezed once, but she wasn't surprised he lacked strength in his drowsy state. "Foolish man," he said. "Wait until I get my hands on him."

She choked back a sob jumbled up with a sad laugh. Flynn was her brother and protector all rolled into one. She'd never known anything like it before—Patrick had only become her protector after moving to Australia and getting cleaned up—and she wasn't sure his love was hers to take.

After the incident in the shed, Luke had bounced back after a few days with only bruises and a broken nose. For that she was grateful. She'd shared only one phone call with him in the past two months during which he'd assured her he would take care of the work at the tea house. The only other contact they'd had was by message, so she could pass on construction and refurbishment information as required. He never mentioned their last conversation or asked if she was coming back.

Despite all that, the longer Melita was in Boston, the more the urge to follow through with her dream was cemented in place. It *would* happen. Fear of reverting to her old life, with nothing to fill her days, was a constant threat to her peace of mind. But she had to take care of Flynn first, then she'd get back to it. If she could get the designs finished and sent to her capable supervisor in Tully, the conveyor belt would churn along for now.

"Hey, Flynn?"

"Yeah?" He managed another squeeze.

"You never did tell me, and I've been meaning to ask you for ages, about how you ended up at the shed." Every time she thought to ask him, he'd been under the knife or asleep.

He shrugged. "I don't remember exactly how it happened. I was frantic when I arrived home to an empty house and you wouldn't answer your phone. None of the detectives watching over you knew where you were and I remember panicking when a message came through that your new car was parked in the main street with no sign of you anywhere. Then suddenly, they were receiving urgent phone calls and I hitched a ride to the main street with one of them."

Melita nodded. That would've been the moment her father had activated all channels of assistance.

"The local police were hovering around your car and I jumped in with one of them without thinking."

"Oh, Flynn, I just wish—"

"Shh. It's only a chin, and with all the borrowed bone bolted together, I'll look as good new."

She smiled at his positivity, but although the surgeons were doing a great job, his chin would never look the same again. His scars would always remind her that life was vulnerable. Why the local policemen had allowed him anywhere near the crime scene would be something her father would get his lawyers to question. But even if they had tried to stop him, she doubted Flynn would've listened. Fear had a way of blinding common sense.

He slowly loosened his hold on her hand. "I might close my eyes again, Sis. It's uncomfortable to talk with my numb mouth. You don't mind?"

She smiled and reached up to straighten the sheets. "I love you, Flynn. I'll be right here."

His mouth tilted a fraction before his eyes closed.

She sat back and massaged her forehead. The police had recovered her handbag, phone and car keys outside the shed. She'd arranged for her new car to be garaged at Patricia's and had given Jim strict instructions to use it occasionally. Her handbag, transported via police channels, had been returned to her in Brisbane as she'd waited for Flynn to stabilise. It was all insignificant stuff really. What mattered was that the criminals didn't get away with their plan—the money from the tainted gold was being put towards the community and Flynn was healing slowly.

But nothing between her and Luke had been resolved. Two months was a long time to be apart and she really loved him. Except, stubborn fool that he was, Luke couldn't see past his own bad luck to make their relationship work.

Chapter 21

Luke checked all the windows, secured the French doors and did a final walk-through of the finished tea house. He'd barely taken a day off since the shooting, and now that the project was done and dusted, relief coursed through his veins.

"What do you think, Grandad?"

"I've been watching it transform week by week, but now that it's finished, I can see it's very, very impressive. Your father would be proud."

As usual, muscles tightened across Luke's chest at the mention of his dad. On days like this he really missed him. He was proud of the work he'd done here. It'd been challenging in a lot of ways, but he'd persevered and conquered each problem, one by one. It would've been the icing on the cake to share it with his dad—and the dollop of cream on top of the icing if Melita were here to share his pleasure. Handing over the key to a finished project was the reward he constantly looked forward to, but for now, that moment would have to wait. He still had no idea if or when she was coming back.

"This old beauty has come a long way. If only old ghosts could talk. Wouldn't they have something to say?"

Jim's words interrupted Luke's wayward thoughts but didn't stop pride from filling his chest. He enjoyed this type of renovation and looked forward to many more. Even if nothing happened with Melita, he'd always be grateful for this opportunity to broaden his building experience.

"Melita will love it. Once Flynn's out of the woods, she'll be on the next flight over here."

Luke turned to his grandfather, the afternoon sun slanting in through the French doors. "You think so?"

"What makes you say that?"

Luke sighed. The conversation he and Melita had shared came back to haunt him. "I said some pretty dumb things when we were holed up in that shed."

"Puh. That girl loves you. Get yourself over there and be sure to remind her how much *you* love *her*."

There was no other option and no use fighting it. He'd booked his flight a couple of weeks ago; it was time to face Melita and apologise. He'd put his other work on hold and was taking the break he deserved, a tiny voice telling him not to leave Boston unless he convinced her to come home. He was over using his nightmares as an excuse, and as for how he'd handled the money issue … well, he might be paying the price of that for a long time yet.

Once outside, Luke locked the front door and peered at the frangipani trees. Now leafless, their grey, bare branches were a stark reminder of how lonely he was without Melita. They looked lifeless in the hazy afternoon, and it'd be a long wait before they once again filled with colour and fragrance. His heart was no different, stripped bare of leaves and flowers. It seemed his life was one long wait.

He turned at the touch of Jim's hand on his shoulder.

"We better get back. Patricia will have dinner ready and it wouldn't hurt to get a decent night's sleep before your flight."

Luke nodded and made his way to the utility. Sleep always helped, if he could manage it.

"Did you look into any of the counsellors on the list I gave you?" Jim asked.

Luke shook his head. "I promise I will when I get back. I honestly haven't had time to do anything but finish this job."

Jim tutted.

"I know, I know. I've had two months to fix this shit and should've made time for it. If Melita throws me out because I keep using my nightmares as an excuse, I won't blame her."

"She'll understand. You had to finish her tea house."

"Yeah, but I have to step up and be the man she needs. Not some loser who can't sleep through the night without waking up in a sweat."

Jim patted him on the shoulder. "Don't be so hard on yourself. The past couple of months have been tough on both of you. You'll work through it."

Luke hoped so, but it was hard to fathom how. His nightmares had magnified and changed. Far from receding, they now had new fodder. When they came, it was with a blast, featuring a bit of the past mixed with a whole lot of the new. Sometimes he laughed it off, amazed at how his head worked. Most times he lived in dread of the next round of bad luck.

All things considered, he'd managed okay over the past couple of months—but okay wasn't enough anymore. He wanted more, and Melita was number one on his list. The first thing he had to do was accept that she was filthy rich and love her as she was—he couldn't believe he'd ever uttered those hurtful words in the shed—then he'd seek help from a counsellor to rid him of his nightmares.

He *would* move forward, but he wanted Melita to walk by his side, so they could heal together.

Only Flynn knew Luke was arriving in Boston. On Flynn's good days, between his surgeries, they'd messaged and discussed many things—including Melita and the discussion in the shed. Luke had a need to offload and Flynn had been a supportive ear.

Flynn had organised Luke's accommodation—a self-contained room in a house owned by friends. It was only a couple of streets away from where Flynn and Melita stayed with his family. But Luke wanted a shower, a feed and a good night's sleep before he presented himself on their doorstep.

When he exited the airport, he joined the taxi queue, planning to stay the night at a motel he'd booked before leaving Cairns. It was a chilly autumn evening in Boston, and when he reached the head of the queue, he zipped his jacket and helped the driver load his luggage.

Settling into the back seat, he stifled a yawn and relaxed, wanting nothing more than to close his eyes. *God, how I hate long-distance flights.* They zapped his energy, and sleeping sporadically never cured his jet lag once he arrived at his destination.

After a few minutes his eyes began to droop, but he caught a speck of bright red in his periphery. Suddenly alert, he noticed something red poking out of his jacket pocket and pulled it out.

What the? The silk scarf!

His jaw dropped. How had it ended up in his pocket? Was he having a nightmare? He tapped his head to make sure he was awake first before thinking back to the night he'd found Melita gagged and tied to her bed.

His spine stiffened when he remembered thinking her mouth had been filled with blood. *Bloody hell.* That one moment had terrified him the most. He vividly recalled pulling out the gag but couldn't remember shoving it in his pocket. He hadn't worn the jacket since.

Holy shoot, he'd had the scarf all along. Not that he'd given it a passing thought. Christ, there'd been a million other things to think of since that night—the scarf the least important of all. Anyway, he'd thought Melita had it.

The rest of the taxi ride was spent recalling how he'd tantalised her with the silk scarf on that long-ago weekend. It didn't take him long to harden up, and he shuffled uncomfortably in the seat, relieved when the taxi finally parked outside his motel.

It never ceased to amaze Luke how a good night's sleep cured almost anything. He'd slept for ten hours straight, enjoyed a hot shower and ate a massive breakfast. Just what he needed.

Having paid for a late checkout, he had time to stroll the streets of central Boston before he collected his luggage and met up with Flynn, who'd insisted he was well enough to drive, despite only having his last surgery a week ago.

Luke hadn't argued. He wanted the chance to talk to Flynn alone and owed him a face-to-face explanation of what'd gone wrong between him and Melita and how he planned to fix it.

He walked out onto the street and smack bang into a ... photo shoot? Or maybe it was a film set.

"Oops." He sidestepped, only just avoiding a cameraman. Unfortunately, he didn't see anyone else, and a person hit him from behind.

"Blast, didn't someone warn the motel that guests were to use the other entrance?" a petite woman grumbled.

Luke rubbed his side and back, where something sharp had hit, as the man who ran into him, apologised.

"Are you okay, man?"

Luke didn't hesitate to respond. "Sure, mate, I'm fine. I'll get out of your way."

"Hang on, hang on."

The same woman had spoken and Luke made tracks to get out of her way, but she grabbed his shoulder to halt his progress.

"What do we have here? Did I just hear a sexy Australian accent come out of that gorgeous mouth?"

Luke looked from left to right as the woman took a long and hard look at him—from the tip of his hair and all the way down his jean-covered legs. She eyed his joggers momentarily before snapping her gaze to his again. With his height advantage, Luke thought she might've been intimidated, but he didn't get that impression. This was one woman used to getting her way.

"Guys, gather around. *This* is what I was looking for."

Luke made to leave—surely they were talking to the wrong person—but within seconds he was surrounded by about a dozen people scrutinizing him.

"Um, you must be mistaken. I've just arrived in Boston, so I'll leave you to get back to work and—"

"Wait, don't go yet. You're just the person we need. My goodness, look at the colour of his skin. So naturally tanned. We'll never find anything as good after the miserable fall we've just had." The petite woman said.

Luke tugged at his arm. "Excuse me, I have to go. It was nice meeting you, but you've got the wrong person."

"Stop! Everyone, step back." The petite female was at it again.

Before Luke could make his escape, she thrust her hand towards him, expecting a handshake. "Sorry about all the excitement. I'm Bianca."

Reluctantly, Luke shook her hand. "Hi, I'm Luke and I don't belong here."

"Look, my apologies for all this." She waved her arm to encompass the others and the equipment. "It's just that the city of Boston holds a big photographic competition each year. The winner's shots get posted on all the city buses for a year. This year's theme is 'anything foreign' and you'd be the perfect model. What do you say?"

Was this another variation of his weird nightmares?

"Sorry," he said, "but I have no idea what you're talking about. Why don't I walk away and leave you to it?"

Panic flared across Bianca's face and she pointed to a café down the street. "Can I buy you a coffee and explain. If you accept, we'll pay you an agreed fee. If we win, you'd be paid royalties for the rest of the year."

This was absurd. A model? Did he look like model material? Heck, he'd barely combed his hair that morning.

"I'm only here for three weeks."

Bianca didn't miss a beat. "We only need you for a week. Five hours each morning and we'll get our required shots. Oh, my God, it's going to work." She turned to the others. "My earlier idea. He'll be perfect for it. I hated the cityscape plan from the start, but now that he's appeared out of nowhere, I can make it work. Jeffrey, I can make it work."

Jeffrey held a notebook and posed with one hand on his hip. "Bianca, you're bloody crazy. It's always last minute with you. If you didn't manage to impress me every bloody time, I'd quit and leave."

Bianca squared her shoulders and puffed her small chest out. "So, you trust me on this, Jeff?"

Jeffrey pointed Luke's way. "You haven't convinced said foreigner yet."

Alarm swished across her face when she turned back. "My offer of coffee still stands. Can I convince you to listen to my plan?"

Luke wasn't immune to her pleading look. With a few hours up his sleeve, should he? What harm could it do?

Chapter 22

L uke stirred sugar into his cappuccino while Bianca explained how the competition worked.

"We produce a series of five images and together they have to tell a story."

Luke nodded. *I'm getting it so far.*

"I was thinking of a 'local Boston girl meets foreign Australian man' kind of thing. A romance of sorts."

Luke sat up. The stupidest thought just careered through his mind. Fobbing it off as dumb, he ploughed a hand through his hair before taking another sip of his hot drink and continued listening to Bianca.

"I want to do 'Boston girl meets Australian boy holidaying.' Maybe a subway shot, followed by a surprise meeting in one of our beautiful city parks. You'll both be dressed to match our cooler climate, then girl follows boy to Australia. We'll do a beach scene, oiled bodies, that sort of thing. Maybe use an iconic Australian landmark as a backdrop. You can give us some ideas."

Another idea zoomed through his mind. *Fuck, stop it! This isn't your show. Grab the money and run.* He coughed to clear his throat and said, "Yeah, plenty of places you could use."

She smiled enthusiastically and continued her explanation as Luke slowly sipped his drink. Jeffrey sat to his left, tapping his pen against his clipboard. He was clearly wary of the whole idea, his posture speaking volumes, probably doubtful Luke would accept the assignment. Hell, what did Luke care? It'd fund the cost of his trip and give him extra pocket money. No complaints there. Except Luke's mind had taken a track of its own and his ideas were multiplying by the dozen. It was so unlike him.

Bianca stopped talking and drew her shoulders back. "So, what do you say, Luke?"

The million-dollar question. Luke drained his cup and sat it down beside the plate of cake. "I have a few ideas of my own to run past you."

Bianca's mouth opened. She must've been so convinced the upfront fee would entice him to do it. It had, except Luke couldn't hold back the ideas that were steamrolling around his head, vying for attention.

"And they are?" Bianca asked warily.

Luke sat back and casually crossed his arms. *Here goes nothing. Is this when she scoffs at me and tells me to get lost?* "Well ... um ... each shot has to feature a red scarf, like a recurring theme. I want it to be something everyone looks for. I want people to be standing on the street, and as a bus whizzes past, they'll ask 'where's the scarf?'"

Bianca's eyebrows rose, surprise written all over her face. "Ah, anything else?"

Luke scratched his head, no doubt making an unholy mess of his hair. "Um ... yeah. Any swimwear worn in the shots has to be those designed by a certain native Boston designer. She's spent the past few years in Australia but happens to be in Boston now visiting family." He leaned forward and rested his elbows on the table. "You have to promise you won't tell her who gave you this info. If you can't do that, I won't accept. If you can keep it quiet, you won't be disappointed by her work."

"Oooh," Bianca rubbed her hands and turned towards Jeffrey. She looked like the kid who'd won the jar of lollies. "I can't believe it! It's falling right into our hands. There's divine intervention happening here. Can you feel it, Jeffrey?"

Jeffrey, who was too busy writing notes, ignored Bianca.

Bianca smiled wide. "Anything else, Luke?"

"One last thing." He told them what he wanted for the last image to round off the series.

And this time even Jeffrey gasped.

⁂

Melita ended one call just as she received another. She didn't recognise the number and, inwardly groaning, hesitated before swiping to answer. After being on the phone for hours that afternoon, she went in search of her charger.

"Hello, Melita speaking."

"Hello, this is Bianca Douglas from Boston Silver Images. I've been given your contact details because I'm looking for someone who designs swimwear, with an Australian theme, in particular."

All thoughts of charging her phone disappeared.

"Hello? Do I have the right person?"

"Yes, yes, you certainly do. How did you find me?" Melita walked backwards until her legs collided with her bed. She collapsed onto it and flung one arm out wide, the other holding the phone tight against her ear.

"I can explain it all later. I just want to clarify why I need your swimwear."

"Sure." Who cared how this woman had gotten her contact details?

"Are you aware of the photographic competition the City holds each year?"

Melita nodded. "Sure, of course I do. I grew up here." Who didn't know of it and all the hype that surrounded it? At the very least, it decorated the city's buses in a fun and imaginative way every year.

Enthralled, she listened as Bianca explained the different scenes she wanted to create and how her swimwear would be featured.

"Do you have anything suitable?"

Did she have anything suitable? She fist-pumped the air uncontrollably. Was this woman crazy? *Oh my God!* She was going to wet her pants if she didn't calm down. The current collection she was working on would be perfect.

Restraining her excitement, she spoke as calmly as she could. "The designs in my current collection are colourful and vibrant, in one and two pieces, each with an iconic Australian animal splashed across their front. So far, I have a platypus, galah, cockatoo, kangaroo, emu and echidna in some stores. I'm still working on other animals."

"Um ... I haven't heard of some of those animals, but that's the magic of this competition. If we win, most of America will soon learn what they are."

And they'll know who I am. She wriggled, too excited to lie still. This was beyond her wildest fantasies. Without hesitating another second, she asked, "Can I send you some images?"

"Of course. I'll need to see them by tomorrow morning, and if I like them, you'll need to get the actual swimwear to me about five days later. Is that possible?"

Five days! She'd move heaven and earth. In fact, she would get one of the girls in Tully to personally deliver them to Boston. She'd be on the next flight out of Cairns.

"Yes, it's possible." Melita spoke with confidence. "You'll have prints before the morning. Send me your email address and I'll get onto it straight away."

When they ended the call, Melita jumped up from the bed and danced a jig. The room she was using in Flynn's family home was small in comparison to her bedroom in her father's house, but it was stamped with love and all things soft and cushy.

She registered a knock on the door and knew it was Flynn. He'd phoned earlier to say he was on his way home and had a friend with him.

Unable to stand still, probably resembling an excited kid, she opened the door ready to spill the news.

Her smile vanished faster than an ice cube left in the sun. Flynn was on the landing, but Luke was standing beside him, and without understanding why, she burst into tears. Luke walked in and hesitantly took her in his arms. It was exactly where she wanted to be, if their last face-to-face conversation had never happened.

She sobbed against his chest and tried to push the memory of it away. But it kept twisting and tangling up in her head, making her unsure of everything between them. Her money wasn't going anywhere; it would always be an issue. *So why is he here?* If he didn't believe they could survive as a couple, why didn't he stay away?

All the while, Luke soothed, rubbing his hands over her back and whispering things she couldn't hear over her crying.

When she calmed down, she loosened her hold on him and stepped back. Flynn materialised with a handful of tissues, which she gratefully accepted.

"What are you doing here?" Her voice was muffled by the tissues as she blew her nose.

Luke gave her a lop-sided smile. It wasn't his usual blinding one—but then, they'd never had that conversation before either.

Enviously, she looked at him—all tanned and healthy. There was no way any Bostonian would look like that at the end of a dreary fall.

He reached into his jacket pocket and she heard something rattle. "I came to give you the keys to the finished tea house." He swallowed and, looking unsure of himself, shrugged. "That's all."

"That's all?" she squeaked.

Luke's gaze didn't leave hers.

"And to see me, of course, the most important person in the world," Flynn added, watching their spectacle as he casually leaned against the doorjamb with his arms folded.

Flynn could joke all he liked, but she didn't need words and reassurances from Luke. He loved her, she knew that much—it reflected in the way he'd pinned his gaze on her—but it would be impossible to overcome their very big issue unless they started communicating better or she gave her wealth away.

She pressed her lips together, still annoyed with what he'd said all those weeks ago. About to blurt that he shouldn't have bothered coming all this way, she decided it was time to put on the 'big girl' act. She could deal with this. There was zero chance her money was going to disappear, so if he couldn't love her as she was, she'd look for love elsewhere.

Yeah, easier said than done. Her heart had nose-dived when he'd claimed his only reason for coming to Boston was to give her the tea house keys. But he didn't fool her; he was here for more than that.

She squared her shoulders and glanced between Luke and Flynn. It was time to divert her thoughts. "Well, I'm going to pour myself a wine. If you join me, I might tell you something exciting."

Flynn and Luke shared a look, each raising their eyebrows, before Flynn swung an arm towards the door and said, "Well, let's get going."

Chapter 23

"I don't understand why Bianca won't let me attend the photo shoots. Damn it, it's my swimwear!"

Luke tightened his jacket around his chest as they walked down the street, the chill penetrating its flimsy layers. He'd instructed Bianca that Melita come nowhere near the photographic shoots, but in an attempt to pacify, he said, "Didn't she say you'll be a special guest at the gala event when they announce the winner?"

"Yes, but—"

"Well, that's good enough, isn't it? Come on, show me your Boston. You've got two days left. We've already wasted two. You know I'm committed after that."

Stand-offish since his arrival, Melita wasn't impressed with the secrecy surrounding his plans. "And I suppose you *still* can't tell me what's going on next week?"

Luke stopped and faced her, then took one of her hands and held it gently. Their time together in Boston was quickly disappearing and they needed to talk things through. To reconnect and be reminded of how strong their feelings for each other had been at the start. He wanted nothing more than to disappear somewhere private and have her all to himself.

"I've missed you, Mel."

Even with a pout she was cute—until she growled.

"Why didn't you say so when you gave me the keys? You come all the way to Boston and don't say a word?"

"I'm saying it now."

She turned away. "You're still keeping a secret from me."

He shook his head. What didn't she understand? He was trying to surprise her.

He let her hand fall out of his grip, not sure anymore if the surprise would last. If *they* would last.

Things had gone from bad to worse. He'd come to Boston to tell her the money didn't matter, but last night they'd had dinner at her father's stately Louisburg Square home, and it had been glaringly obvious that money made all the difference. His upbringing was more than a continent and ocean away from the way Melita had been raised.

Luke had never felt so out of place—he hadn't spilled his food or wolfed it down—but it was something he couldn't quite pin down. Only years of living in a world where some skills were carefully cultivated on a daily basis could a person hope to fit in. Luke was never going to fit in, nor did he want to. His biggest concern was if the startling differences between their worlds would eventually drive them apart.

Except he loved Melita. There *was* something between them and it was strong. Strong enough to keep him from looking at another woman for a shitload of years. He wasn't about to toss their relationship overboard, but they needed to sort this out. To talk it through and come to terms with their differences. He grimaced. It wouldn't happen in one day.

"Do you want to show me this city of yours, just in case I want to live here?"

"Wait." She spun around. "What do you mean, live here? I'm not staying much longer."

He delved into her beautiful eyes. "I was beginning to wonder."

She eyed him suspiciously. "The tea house *is* still there and in one piece, isn't it?"

He broke into a laugh. "Yes, of course it is." He sobered up and added, "But you haven't said *one* word about when you're coming back. I wasn't expecting you to rush back to me, but what about your dreams?" He paused, his fingers digging into his palm. "I'm just checking my options. If I have to live in a city hellhole, I will."

She turned away again. "Well, maybe you can discuss that with your next girlfriend."

Words jammed in his throat. She hadn't forgotten their last conversation.

"Mel."

She didn't turn back and avoided making eye contact.

"Mel, I'm an idiot." He moved in her line of vision and cupped her jaw. She dropped her gaze. "The money isn't going away."

A lone tear trickled down her cheek and he brushed it clear with his thumb. "When we get a minute alone, can we discuss it?"

They'd been too busy celebrating with Flynn and his parents to get any private time and Melita had been tied up finishing off a couple of the designs for Bianca. Despite her exciting news, she'd remained aloof with him the entire time he'd been in Boston. He wasn't surprised an invitation to stay the night had never eventuated; he hadn't given her a single reason to believe he'd changed his mind, so who could blame her?

Lifting her gaze, she shrugged half-heartedly, then reached for his hand and entwined her fingers with his. "So," she said and took a deep breath, "what would you like to see today? Do you honestly think Boston has what it takes to keep you here?"

Luke arched a brow. "You tell me."

"Well, it doesn't have amazing waterfalls, incredible beaches, dizzying rainforests or dangerous animals that can kill you."

He smiled at her interpretation of Australia and shrugged.

"It has museums, libraries, monuments, burial grounds with a stack of history, America's first lighthouse, churches, and a very tall high-rise …

owned by my father." A grimace touched the edges of her mouth. "I'm coming home, mate. Soon."

Her attempt at an Aussie accent brought another quick smile to his face but didn't break the tension between them. Her words brought him some relief, at least. The two of them had some steep barriers to get over, but if she was in the same country as him and away from the glitz of Boston high society, he was certain they could work through them. There was no way he would live in Boston—hell would freeze over first—but he wasn't telling her that. Not yet, anyway.

He tugged on her arm and turned back towards her father's high-rise. The sun disappeared behind the tall buildings and the breeze whipped around them as it eddied between the high-rises. Since she was coming back, he'd play extra hard at keeping his plans for next week a secret.

He hoped the surprise worked. He'd look pretty dumb if they were no longer in a relationship when the contest winner was announced. But that was a few months away. First, he had to work out if he could shelve the money issue. And his nightmares be damned; he would see a counsellor on his return home and put them to rest.

When they got the chance to discuss things privately, he wanted her in his arms. On a bed and in between soft cotton sheets was a good place to start. His body stirred just at the thought and they still had a full day of sightseeing ahead of them. *Shit.* He'd never keep his hands off her for that long. Thank God Boston didn't have beaches fringed with tropical rainforest—he needed to steer clear of those memories. Maybe they could ditch the whole idea of sightseeing.

"This secrecy is twisting my insides. I hate secrets. In fact, I've had enough big reveals to last a lifetime."

Damn, she was back to that. He stopped and wrapped his arms around her waist. "I know. I get it."

For the first time since his arrival, he kissed her, long and hard, only stopping for air when he heard wolf whistles.

When he stepped back, she gazed down. His bulge looked huge from *his* height.

His skin heated when her brows arched. She was probably wondering how he could be thinking about sex when she was thinking about secrets and what he'd said in the shed that night.

A frown marred her adorable face until she started to laugh.

Now it was his turn to raise his brows.

"Well, it is funny, isn't it, even if you *are* kissing a rich girl."

Luke groaned. How come a bulging groin didn't take her mind off things? What did that say about him? She wouldn't let him forget what he'd said about her being too rich for him. As for the secret, it was getting harder and harder to keep his mouth shut, but everything hinged on the surprise.

She had no idea the request for her swimwear was connected to his week of modelling. As he didn't want her to know he was modelling, the only clue, or little white lie, he and Flynn had let slip the day before was that his commitment required he fulfill a request for Jim. Out of respect, they'd let Jim tell all when they returned home.

"It has nothing to do with me?" she'd asked yesterday.

"No." Luke promised himself it'd be the last little white lie he'd tell her. The need to explain further had vanished when Bianca phoned to reassure Melita the designs were perfect.

Now it was time to distract her again. "After we visit your dad, what's the plan?"

Her beautiful face showed a hint of a scowl. "Luke Harvey, we haven't resolved anything."

Okay, so his current strategy wasn't working. He stroked her forehead with his thumb, igniting everything in his body, hardly giving his bulge an excuse to calm down. "Please, just this once, could you humour me? You'll learn all about it in good time."

She sighed and rested her forehead against his. "I have no idea what the hell you want with me, but if you remember, two big secrets completely transformed my life. I like how things are now. I don't want any more big reveals."

The thought of what he wanted to do with her when they were finally alone was taxing. He loved her, damn it, and wanted to kiss her again but refrained and took a deep breath instead. As he released it, he planted a gentle feather-light kiss on her lips. "Will you try to be patient?"

She groaned against his mouth. "Okay, but stop kissing me. We're standing in the middle of a Boston street. Unless you want our picture plastered all over the papers tomorrow morning, please don't. We need to discuss *us* first, before things get out of hand. Today is strictly for sightseeing."

Luke frowned. "Really? Is that what you want?"

She stormed off towards her father's high-rise and answered over her shoulder. "Yes."

Chapter 24

With Luke beside her, Melita waved goodbye as Flynn got into his car and drove away.

"Your brother is the best," Luke said.

Melita grimaced as they watched the tail lights on Flynn's car disappear. The time had come for their big talk. She was unsure how the night would end, but step one was to get away from family and tourists.

It hadn't felt right to invite Luke to stay the night. Flynn's parents were old-fashioned in their thinking but good people. She'd never do anything to upset them but had welcomed Luke's plan to convince Flynn they needed time alone. She was also determined to protect her own heart. Until they sorted out this mess between them, sleeping together was a no-go zone in her books.

When Flynn's car disappeared around the corner, the street quietened down in the early dusk. Luke opened the door to his rented apartment and held it open. "So, we're here to come up with some new ideas for your Australiana swimwear?"

She nodded. It was the excuse Flynn had used to get them some time alone. "Got any?"

Once inside, she couldn't suppress the nervous butterflies spinning around her stomach. What was her problem? They'd been alone together before. It wasn't like she'd forgotten those precious weeks after the beach weekend. Was she worried the night would end disastrously?

Luke closed the door and watched her intently, his fingers curled in towards his palm. "I have."

They stood only a couple of feet apart but his mesmerizing look pinned her to the spot.

Could he be as nervous as her? They'd finished the day with a late lunch and a relaxing tour of some of Boston's parklands. Now, this was the discussion they had to have. Two months was a long time to be apart and it couldn't be put off any longer.

"And?" she asked, registering his response.

"I'll get us each a glass of water first. I'll be back in a tick." Luke disappeared towards the kitchen she could see.

Why hadn't they used the past two months to communicate better? They might've been on opposite sides of the world—she nursing Flynn, and Luke finishing the tea house—but what a loss it was when she thought of all the quirky messages she might have sent him, all the bad jokes he might've sent back, the goodnight emojis they could've shared before bed.

Since the shed incident, she'd managed to get through each day by convincing herself that things weren't over between them. If Luke had changed his mind about her, she would have to fight to keep from spiralling out of control. She'd been smitten with him since the day they first met, and when they'd come together that one weekend at the beach, she'd believed she was being rewarded for her patience. That maybe, just maybe, she was capable of being loved. Damn it, she wanted the stubborn-ass man, but she wouldn't live with the shadow of her money hanging over their heads. If they couldn't sort it out now, was there any point in going further? It'd always come between them.

Luke handed her a glass of water and she gulped most of it down. "Thanks, I needed that." She put the glass down on the round table.

Luke put his empty glass down too. "Okay, here goes. How about jellyfish, sharks, crocodiles, pythons and the good ol' stinging tree."

Despite the turmoil whirling inside her, she burst out laughing. "Hey, you know what? I like them. I like them a lot." She spun around. "My handbag. Where did I leave it? I need a pen and notepad to write them down."

Once she had them, she sank back onto the couch and got Luke to recite them. When she put her pen and pad back into her bag, she plonked it on the floor. Luke was sitting across from her.

They took in their fill of each other. God, she missed his permanently messy, sandy-blond hair. Reminded of how she'd longed to see his healthy and tanned face each day she'd been in Boston, the ache inside her chest expanded. After two months here, her skin had paled, her freckles almost non-existent. When she'd been in Australia, colour on her skin had emphasised the freckles she'd once hated as a teenager but had since grown to love.

She thought about the past couple of days and the joy they'd shared in doing all things touristy. She'd amassed another great collection of snaps, and time had slipped by quickly as she'd waited for her swimwear to arrive.

"You know you're such a dork when you're a tourist." It was the understatement of the century. A bubble of laughter escaped her throat.

"Do you think I'll make it into any of the Boston papers? I tried really hard."

Her beautiful Luke was laughing right along with her and it felt good. She'd pushed everything aside to ensure they enjoyed the past couple of days.

"I think we're safe. No one in their right mind would believe it was me with you. I think we got away with it."

"Damn, I'll have to try harder next time."

They continued taking their fill of each other. This was comfortable; this felt right. Why couldn't it work?

A noisy sigh escaped her mouth. Two things marred her days. The first was the secrecy behind what Luke would be doing next week. Her gut instinct *always* got it right; she knew her life was about to change again. She just had no damn idea how.

The second was the discussion they needed to have. Why spoil the veneer of the last couple of days? What was Luke's real agenda for coming to Boston? Was it to say, 'thanks but no thanks. I don't belong in your world'? She'd witnessed how uncomfortable he'd been at her father's home last night. Even drinking wine was a painful experience for him. He preferred beer and a more relaxed atmosphere. That was her Luke—the man she wanted. And what about his nightmares?

"Can we talk, Mel?"

She jolted at his words. The inevitable had finally arrived.

"Unless you'd rather do it slow first."

Huh?

"I'm nervous, Mel." He fidgeted with the corner of the couch. "I don't deserve you. Sometimes I'm an idiot, with little experience to brag about."

Exasperated but nervous herself, she pulled at her earlobe. "Luke Harvey, do you think you could start with what you said in the shed that night?"

"I think I'll be more relaxed if we do it fast first."

She rubbed her forehead; anything to remove the deep worry lines. "I'm going to find something to crack open your skull. Then I'm going to pour a bucketload of common sense inside and see where it takes us."

Luke started to laugh. It was a special sound that brightened the room instantly. Nothing could dampen the smile it put on her face.

"Go on," he said, "you know I need it."

She sobered up quickly, as she had no idea how to navigate this treacherous road.

He sank onto the couch beside her and didn't hesitate to take her in his arms. When he gently rubbed his hand across her nipple, it caused all sorts of reactions. If they'd waited this long to have the discussion, what was another half-hour, hour, entire night? It could be their last time if things soured between them—she'd have to feed off her memories until she picked up her life again. Who knew how long that could take?

"No," she said, "I think we should stick to slow."

His brows rose, creating new wrinkles. "You think?"

She kissed him. If she regretted the decision, she'd live with it. She'd missed him so much.

Darting in with her tongue, she revelled at his sudden gasp. He latched onto her shoulders, his fingers digging into her skin. She deepened the kiss deliciously, but with a swiftness she wasn't expecting, he pushed her away.

Confusion set in.

"I promise by the end of the night I'll tell you why I said those things. It's been eating at me ever since."

Relief swamped her. It could wait. She cupped his face and brought him closer. "So are we still on slow?"

"Woman, you'll be the death of me."

"Well, um"—they connected briefly with their mouths again—"cracking open your skull could bring that on."

He groaned as he trailed his hands down her hips. Then he started by kissing her on her neck, then finding all the other places she loved him to find. "I'm geared to take this very fast. The next round we can take slower."

Too busy touching and kissing him, she didn't catch on at first. When his words sunk in, she burst out laughing—the contagious type of laugh that had Luke joining her. "Fast, please. Very, very fast. Oh, Luke, please, *please* don't make me wait."

Luke collected her in his arms and in a few steps reached the enormous king-sized ensemble. In the brightly lit room, he gazed at her so hungrily that moisture instantly pooled between her thighs. There were frantic seconds wasted as clothes were flung off in all directions; a few buttons probably went missing. Melita moaned when they finally connected skin on skin and felt liberated when Luke's groans matched hers.

They were equals as hands touched and probed, breath mingled and set alight each other's skin, legs entwined and pushed, and their mouths touched places sacred to them.

They only had one end in mind, and as soon as Luke was sheathed, he thrust deep and hard, causing her to cry out. They shattered together, creating magic they were willing to repeat over and over.

In a tangle of arms and legs, she languished comfortably, their breathing loud in the quiet room. When Luke snuggled against her neck and let his mouth rest there, she surrendered to the calm and closed her eyes.

Maybe their discussion would go well.

Chapter 25

L uke forced the images plaguing his night from his mind. Had he thrashed about in bed? Had he shouted? Sometimes he caught himself and managed to wake up in time. Regrettably, he was an old hand at this.

He lifted his head and spied the digital clock. Two a.m. *Damn!* He'd promised to tell Melita what was eating him before the night was up. He'd spoken like a lunatic in the shed that night and had unloaded a lot of crazy shit. No wonder the girl was confused.

Still, relief clawed through him. He'd been lucky not to have his normal nightmare experience; maybe because the girl he didn't want to scare was lying beside him.

He'd switched off the light hours ago, and from the shine of the clock's bright digits and a good sliver of moon shining in, he could see her chest rise and fall. She slept soundly and he was reluctant to wake her, especially for the train wreck that could go two ways. Would she give him time to fix his shit, or would she walk away? But a promise was a promise, and in the morning, he had to be at Bianca's studio by nine o'clock—another commitment.

He rolled onto his side and tucked tendrils of hair behind her ear. She made soft sleep noises, bringing a smile to his face. He could wake up to this every day for the rest of his life.

"Hey, Mel," he whispered in the dark.

She moaned and shifted slightly.

"Mel, I need to talk to you."

Her eyes flicked open and shut a couple of times. "Luke?"

"Yeah, it's me," he whispered. "Sorry to do this, but can we talk?"

She shuffled closer and raked a hand through her hair. "Do you want to put the light on?"

Luke's heart pumped painfully. He was being a coward but couldn't help it. "Can we keep it off for now?"

She bit her bottom lip and he sensed wariness radiating off her. She glanced over her shoulder at the clock before slumping back and rubbing her knuckles over her eyes. "Please explain to me what you were trying to say in the shed?"

He dropped his face and nuzzled her neck. Melita's hand came up and tangled in his hair. When he pulled back, he licked his dry lips and stared into her eyes. It was too dark to pick out the brown strands that intermingled with her unusual grey. Instead, they were dark pools looking back at him with uncertainty.

"My nightmares are worse than ever since that night."

"Have you gotten any help?"

"Not yet. But I plan to when I get back. I know I should've done something already, but there was never a spare day until the tea house was finished."

"So, um, that's good, right?"

Luke groaned. "I hope so. I want this shit sorted and out of my life."

He blinked when she touched his nose, her fingers trailing over its new jagged edge, as though committing it to memory. Was her mind back in the shed and all the horrors that had occurred there? Her slight touch was waking up every nerve ending in his body.

"Your nose. It changed after it broke. Were you okay?"

"It was fine after a few weeks." He took hold of her hand and brought it to his mouth, his body stirring as he kissed each of her fingers. "What I don't understand is how the police found the shed."

"Oh, that. It was me."

He frowned. "What do you mean? I realise the money transfer was stopped in its tracks before it reached their bank account, but—"

"Sometimes you get lucky," she cut in. "By giving me a laptop they played right into my hands. The bank website I showed them was a fake one intentionally designed to deal with a ransom attack. The codes I entered alerted my father and the bank authorities. Within minutes, they knew my exact location, what sort of crime was being committed and what help was required. If my father obsesses over anything, it's security. Since money isn't an issue, only the best is used. We try to keep it low-key, but it's very common among families like ours. Doesn't always work, but it did for us."

Yet another example of the gaping differences between them. Luke crumpled into the mattress and closed his eyes, knowing he'd never be able to compete with that.

"Luke?"

He reluctantly opened his eyes when she tugged on his arm. Her gaze pinned him to the bed. This was crunch time. He didn't want to lose her, yet he didn't want to lie. He took hold of her hand and squeezed it. "Mel, I was so sure when I boarded the plane for Boston that I'd be a fool to bring it up. You have billions. So what? If you loved me, it shouldn't make any difference."

He lowered his gaze and tried to breathe normally. He sensed things were about to go wrong, and he was too lame to fix it.

"And?"

He didn't have the guts to look up. "I'd be lying—to you, to me—if I said it didn't matter. It *does* bother me. I feel insignificant beside you. Never in a million years will I come close to having what you have. I *do* have issues with the money and my gut is telling me that one day you'll tire of penniless Luke. I'm not from your world. Shit, you saw how it was at your father's place the other night. You fit in perfectly, but I don't. Call me a loser, but I can't even sleep through most nights without thrashing around. I've been that way for years. What if a counsellor can't help me?"

She stiffened beside him. "Your nightmares weren't a problem tonight."

"One lucky night where I was able to shake myself out of it before I woke you. That's all it was."

"But I love you, Luke. There's never been anybody else. This is me." She stopped, as though holding herself short of pleading.

He took her hand, but she pulled it away. "I love you, Mel but ..."

Silence punctuated the space between them and the air sucked out of his lungs.

"But not enough."

He heard the despair in her voice and it sliced through him. Tears trickled like diamonds down her cheeks.

"Oh, Mel, can you give me time to sort myself out? I know I can get over the money thing. When we're in Australia, it'll feel different. Here, I'm like a square peg in a round hole. I stand out, I don't fit, I'm not as polished as you. We're good together but I need to make sure my messed-up head is sorted first. I have to."

"Haven't we wasted enough years?"

"I'll see a therapist when I return home. I need to. I can't keep putting it off."

In a softer voice, she murmured, "What if you can't get over the money thing?"

The slow procession of tears down her cheeks was breaking him up inside. He rose from the bed and sat on the edge. Resting his elbows on his thighs, he raked his hands through his hair. "Maybe I just need a decent night's sleep and I'll see things differently. I don't get too many in a row."

Seconds passed in silence ... until he heard a sob. He twisted around. She'd bunched up the sheet into a ball and was holding it against her face.

"Mel, Mel, come here." He joined her on the bed and wrapped his arms around her. As he cradled her against his chest, he debated the wisdom of what he'd just done and if there was any road back from this. He didn't want to leave it like this.

"Hey, Mel," he whispered against her hair, "do you remember our first kiss?"

She pulled back, her finger tracing a line down his cheek, her tears still a trail of tiny diamonds down her face. "How could I forget? No one has ever made me feel like that before."

Luke touched his mouth to her temple. "It was like that for me too and it's never changed. You still do the same things to me."

They'd been in the car, Luke teaching Melita how to drive. They'd stopped at a lookout west of Brisbane to enjoy the view of a vast wooded eucalypt forest with a river snaking its way through the centre. Luke couldn't remember much more about the view. He'd been distracted by Melita for weeks and hadn't needed any encouragement when he'd accidentally brushed his hand against hers that day. Alone, with very little passing traffic, their kiss had gone on and on, while the forest worked its magic on them in that tiny isolated spot. Luke had driven back; Melita had been too jittery.

"I wanted you to kiss me again. You never did. Why?" Melita asked.

"I still don't know."

He held her close and thought about the future. He wasn't in this for a good time; he wanted the long haul and he wanted it with this woman. Yeah, he was young and inexperienced, but he wanted the whole package—marriage one day and the kids that would follow. He had his parents to thank for that dream. Until his father's accidental death, they'd shown him how it was done.

"I'm going to get better, Mel, I promise. I just need time. Will you give me that?"

"Can we do slow?"

Huh?

She reached across him to tug a couple of tissues from the box on his side of the bed. Luke didn't take his eyes off her as she wiped her tears away.

Melita scrunched the tissues and let them drop to the floor. She turned her sad eyes directly on him. It might've been seconds, or minutes but there was enough light for him to see the slow defiant lift of her chin and something new pass over her face. His lungs froze with air trapped in their depths. He'd never seen her like this before. Nerves scattered around his body. He was dreading what she was about to say and wondered whether he should prepare for doomsday. Thank God the room wasn't brightly lit, or he'd be able read every expression on her face. That would be worse.

"I love you, Luke. I've loved you for a very long time. I'll help you get through your nightmares. We'll do it together, see a counsellor. Maybe they can help me too. But my money isn't going anywhere, and if you can't learn to accept me as I am, I won't wait around forever. But so help me God, I'll take what I can, when I can. So give me slow, damn it, and don't make me wait forever."

His chest constricted at the ultimatum. He deserved nothing less. Telling the truth had been the right thing to do, but why wasn't he feeling better?

He managed to release the constricting band and could breathe again. With infinite care, he took her on the slowest and longest journey they'd ever chartered, where she shed tears on his skin in defiance of her strong stance, and where his heart discovered the new meaning of grim.

When it was all over, she rose from the bed and dressed slowly. He didn't have to ask, already knew what was happening, but he needed it confirmed. "You're leaving?" The whispered words left deep tracks in his throat.

He'd never forget her nod. Knew she'd contact Flynn and he would come at any hour to help his sister. Pity Luke wasn't man enough to fix things. He was damaged goods from another world and had to fix himself first before he stood a chance. Then, only then, might he see her wealth in a different light.

Chapter 26

M elita opened her eyes.

Slowly.

She blinked them closed and open, fighting exhaustion. The clock registered nine-thirty a.m. She stretched her arms and curled her toes, then froze. Memories of last night screamed at her. Luke's confession, their love-making. So screwed up.

She rolled onto her stomach and groaned into the pillow.

Now what? The dreaded words had left his mouth. He couldn't handle that she had money—but he was going to try. He couldn't see that she wasn't her money; it was just something she had. How many years would it take? She would always love him, but she hadn't lied when she said she wouldn't wait forever.

What about her own insecurities? Was she still the freak no one could love? After all this time, and despite Luke professing that he loved her, was she still that damaged little girl incapable of being loved?

Only her business could motivate her now. After her marathon love session with Luke, she'd made the decision to return to Tully and the tea house. She had a job to do and people depended on her, but if she hadn't walked out on Luke when she did, she might've lost the courage to do so at all.

Now it was up to Luke. The quicker he got himself out of Boston and back to his normal routine, the faster he could start working on his issues.

As for his fears about his curse, she had no idea where to go with that. It was alien with her upbringing to believe in such things. *She* was cursed, belonging to Boston's oldest and wealthiest family.

She thought she'd long shaken off the fear of something happening to her. Once she'd left the confines of her old life in Boston and the fog had lifted, she'd made certain to live each day to the fullest. The Black Hand and its scare tactics were a wake-up call. They'd been a reminder that even outside of Boston she was at risk. But she would *never* give in.

In a way she could understand Luke's reasoning and hoped with all her heart that sorting out his nightmares would cure his concerns about the curse as well. *Damn it.* She pummelled her pillow with her fist. She loved him—his scruffiness, rough edges and everything soft in between. He had a tender heart, like no other she'd ever encountered, especially not in the Boston crowd she'd once hung out with.

In sunny Queensland, she'd always felt like Luke's equal, not some rich girl. Apparently, he hadn't felt the same. How had she got it so wrong? She'd honestly believed that in Tully things like trust funds didn't matter.

Was she that naïve? Because, obviously, to those who didn't have a lot of money, it did matter. She dashed away tears that threatened to turn into a torrent. She'd walk every step with Luke and help him through the counselling. She had to believe he would get to the other side and see life, and her, in a different way.

Her swimwear was due to arrive in Boston in a couple of hours. She would have to courier them to Bianca because she was boarding a plane back to Cairns, where she'd wait for her invitation to return for the announcement of the competition winners. Seeing her swimwear on social media would certainly add a buzz to her life. But, in the meantime, Bianca didn't need her. She would've loved to contribute to the photo shoot but had accepted the verdict.

As for Flynn, he'd insisted weeks ago it was time she returned to Tully, but she'd wanted to wait until he'd had his surgeries. Now, there was no reason to stay. He understood her need to return and get her show on the road.

For some absurd reason, she also wanted to find the lost scarf. She dreamed of it often, always hiding in some ridiculous place. If only her dreams could give her a clue as to where it was. But no, just absurd scenarios that made her feel like a nutcase.

Her scarf held too many memories. She wanted to clutch it close each night when she slept. For one horrible moment she wondered if the thug who'd broken into her home had stolen it. God Almighty! Where was it!

But why did she want it back? So the memories could haunt her? Would it gradually kill her day by day? She should've never believed in romance as a teenager. Should've never hoped for the magic to happen to her. It made her believe that one day she could have the lot. A man who loved her *and* accepted her as she was.

She now understood that her view of the world was tainted. Maybe growing up without feeling cherished and loved, even for a moment, had ruined her. She couldn't shake the feeling that she was, in some way, broken and unfinished. She'd never experienced the sort of unconditional love others took for granted. The love she had dreamed of as a girl may be real, but did girls like her find it?

Okay, girl, get out of bed and get going. She had to believe she could stop moping. Had to hold tight to her dreams and go get them. Lying around here wasn't going to achieve anything.

⸙

People get paid to do this?

The thought would catch Luke unawares and he'd shake his head without thinking, usually as the cameraman was about to press the shutter. It was day three of the shoot and the initial uncomfortable feeling of having make-up plastered to his face had worn off. *If they want to pay me to wear make-up and sit around looking into the lovely face of a model, well …*

He smiled. Never in a million years had he ever envisaged doing this sort of thing. Boring as hell and repetitive as crazy—but doable if you had nothing else scheduled in.

He was reminded of Melita and how she'd high-tailed it back to Tully. Smart girl. He was the idiot. His smile fell faster than it took for rotting fruit to drop from trees.

"Luke, you're supposed to look like you're in love," Bianca reminded him. "Scowls are not allowed."

Oh, shit. He dragged his mind to their last night together and how wonderful it'd been between them—until he'd broken her heart and she'd left. It'd been the push he needed to sort himself out.

He'd ploughed on, trying to pretend that Sian, his modelling partner, was Melita. He struggled. It didn't help she was a blonde and clearly into him, or was pretending to be. She was gorgeous, but repeatedly ignoring her invitations to hang out was getting awkward.

"Hold up the hammer as though you're about to swing it, Luke," Bianca called out. When she'd discovered he was a tradesman, she'd squealed in delight. "Sian, hold your straw hat as though the wind is about to blow it off."

Bianca turned towards the crew and asked for the big industrial fan to be switched on. In this scene, Sian would be scouting the building site in search of Luke.

The fan blasted chilly air his way, causing goosebumps to prickle his skin. *Do they care?* He supposed you had to be one of those mega-rich models to have your demands met. Luke wasn't hanging around long enough for that. He was actually missing the action of being onsite. Sore muscles, sweat and all—and Melita. The differences between them were beginning to fade as each day passed.

"Next scene, please," Bianca called, jerking him out of his trance.

Were they happy with his expression? Bianca must be if she was calling for the next scene. You never knew in this game what they were thinking, unless they were irritated. He'd been on the receiving end of Bianca's annoyance a few times, but he believed he was okay at this modelling stuff—and improving every day.

The assistants hustled around him, changing the scene. It had taken until today for him to understand what they were doing. Jeffrey had explained that one scene would be made up of two or three images depicting the romance as it progressed.

In this project, Sian would be shown flying halfway around the world, then she'd be looking for Luke at a busy work site, and the following scene would be their reunion. For that shot, she would wear the silk scarf around her neck. For a second, he wanted to tear it off her. It didn't belong around her neck. It belonged with him and Melita, and a million memories to boot. But the silk scarf was what would make them stand out in this competition and Bianca had latched onto the idea very quickly.

He went over to the food van and asked for a drink of water. He spilled a few drops on his work shirt and swore. He'd never worn an ironed hi-vis shirt; he was certain the costume people wouldn't want water stains to show in the shots. He'd also never owned a brand-new tool bag like the one he wore belted around his waist. His old faithful had been a hand-me-down from his earliest days as an apprentice and it was still serving him well. For one wistful moment, he wanted to be back in his comfortable surrounds, with his trusty tool bag strapped around his waist.

At least these tradie scenes would be over by the end of the day. They were scheduled to begin the beach scenes tomorrow. He couldn't wait to see Melita's swimwear being modelled and was thrilled at the prospect of what this exposure would do for her if they won the competition. Even the social media campaign, before and after the official announcement, would help. She deserved all the success she could get—plus more.

The shit she went through with the Black Hand had set her back, but he smelled success around the corner for her. And by the end of this project, he wanted no doubt left in his mind about how he felt about her. Some days he wanted to be with her, but on others he believed he couldn't. He back-flipped on odd days and made stupid promises on even days. Hell, he needed that therapist faster than ever. And soon!

Maybe this secrecy was a dumb idea, because he wanted nothing more than to ring her each night and tell her everything. But that would ruin the surprise. Besides, Flynn was insisting he keep his mouth shut. He spent most evenings with Flynn and usually went back to his apartment feeling convinced he was doing the right thing.

When he arrived back at the set, he stepped up to the fan to dry his shirt. It was time to get back to work. The red scarf's inclusion had morphed into something huge. Long discussions were held each day as to where and how it would appear. Luke couldn't believe it had been his idea.

"No Luke, you shouldn't be smiling. You're supposed to be surprised and shocked that this girl has travelled halfway around the world to find you," Bianca explained, exasperated.

Oops. Shock and surprise.

Of course, he knew this. They'd been through the scenes that morning, but portraying different emotions at the drop of a hat was difficult. For Luke, it was more taxing and trying than rebating a hinge for a door. When he was having trouble, he'd look for the silk scarf and picture the things he'd done with it at the beach that weekend, and when his memories took him elsewhere, he managed to get his facial expression just right. When that happened, Bianca got a special look. A look that told him she was pleased.

Luke sat in the darkened studio as the first proof photographs appeared on the three- by two-metre screen. Bianca and Jeffrey conferred, heads together, at the small table in front of him. Sian had left for another assignment, leaving only a handful of staff, who were sitting on chairs placed haphazardly in the small space. Luke spotted a couple of unfamiliar faces.

"What do you think, Luke?"

Luke glanced at the staffer in charge of setting up the scenes and nodded. "I'm impressed. You guys are very good at what you do."

The shots all looked so professional. Was that really him? Where had ordinary everyday Luke—the bloke who rarely brushed his hair and preferred to walk barefoot—disappeared to?

The unfolding love story was clear, and the means of disguising the silk scarf was very clever. Once the public knew they had to find it, gazes would be glued to a shot until it was found. Even he had taken second glances at some of the shots—and he'd known where it had been placed!

He lingered over the swimwear shots and felt the hole in his chest. He missed Melita so much but didn't want to call her until the assignment was complete. Could he promise her he was coming home and that he was prepared to see a counsellor?

He had to repair the damage done in his past so he could move on with his future. Then he'd sort out how to deal with the money issue. With the project now over, he was free to leave Boston. He and Flynn were flying back to Cairns together in a few days.

The tension in his stomach grew as the images slowly slid across the screen. Bianca and Jeffrey deliberated on each one. They had to decide on the placement of the shots for each scene, but it wouldn't be long until the final scene was unveiled.

Everything he'd ever dreamed of hinged on the end product. He worried over the wording. Should he change it before it was too late? Was it too much, too soon, with so much unresolved between him and Melita? The wording wouldn't mean anything to the rest of the world—but to him it meant everything.

He glanced up and there it was—the final scene with the words he'd insisted be splashed across the top. The scarf was loosely scrunched in his hand and flashes of red were visible between his fingers.

The image asked a thousand questions, but there was only one that mattered.

Now he just had to wait until Melita saw it.

Chapter 27

"**Y**ou're not coming home?"

Melita berated herself. She hadn't meant to sound desperate, but Luke was supposed to be boarding a plane tomorrow with Flynn and now he wasn't. The last two weeks without him had hurt. She regretted her decision to leave so soon after their rift—she'd promised to go to counselling with him, so shouldn't she have waited? Now he wasn't coming home at all.

"Will you let me explain, please, Mel?"

She crumpled into the softness of the couch and folded her legs beneath her. "Yes," she managed, knowing she sounded as dejected as she felt.

"Aw, Mel. I never expected this to happen. I've been asked to do—ah … a spot of modelling."

"What?" Melita jerked upright at the announcement.

"You know, standing in front of a camera, make-up, clothing, that sort of thing. It's for some big advertising company."

"Really?" What else could she say? It was the last thing she expected Luke to do.

"They're telling me I'll be perfect for what they're promoting."

"You are?" Her Luke, who didn't know the first thing about clothing and fashion?

As he kept talking, she stuttered along, replying with one and two-word answers.

"They want to employ me for six weeks. They've got some huge projects that—"

"Huh ... six weeks?"

"Yeah. They want to head out to some remote places for a stack of advertising commercials for cars, tray backs, boats and power tools. They reckon I'm what they're looking for."

"They do?"

"I'll be roughing it a bit on the road, but I'll get to see some spectacular parts of the US."

"You will?"

She heard the rustle of paper over the line and Luke swearing when he dropped the phone.

"You there, Mel?"

"Yes," she muttered, feeling as if she were in some kind of trance.

"The contract mentions they'll be shooting at the Grand Canyon, Death Valley, Monument Valley and Yosemite. Heard of them?"

"Yes." She lay down on the couch and curled up, and the phone almost slipped from her fingers. Despite how she'd left him and instructed he sort himself out, she wanted Luke closer to home. The court case was looming and the solicitors needed to meet with them, and her staff were working towards opening the tea house. How could she officially open it without Luke?

"Is this okay with you, Mel?"

What was she supposed to say? *No! Get back here. I'm sorry I left in a hurry.*

He hadn't sent one reproachful comment her way about how she'd left Boston. It probably meant he was feeling guilty, so now it was up to her to turn the tables and support him in this great opportunity.

She racked her brain for what to say next and made an effort to put some spark in her voice. This was a chance of a lifetime and she didn't want him missing it. She knew he would be surrounded by gorgeous models, but she pushed that thought to the dark corner of her heart she'd labelled 'the jealousy place'. It wasn't her style, but sometimes that crazy monster reared its ugly head.

So, how should she answer? Tell him it was okay when it wasn't? She swallowed hard. Everything wanted to come out—tears, frustration, even grief, like she'd already lost him.

"Um, Luke, I ... I just want to say the tea house is amazing. Thank you so much. It's everything I wanted. You didn't miss a thing."

For a few seconds, he didn't reply. When he did, even she could detect his emotion over the distance.

"Your dream was easy to follow."

Oh, Luke.

"I didn't mean for this to happen."

She frowned. "What do you mean?"

"I didn't go looking for it. I was offered this assignment."

"Really?" It was probably the only day in his life he hadn't been wearing a sweat-drenched hi-vis shirt. "Jim will miss you. What about your work?"

I'll miss you.

"I've rearranged my projects and passed some on to a mate. And ... and I already miss everyone. I miss you, too, Mel."

She curled up tighter and hugged the phone to her ear. "And I miss you."

He'd hate not being at home. He was close to his mother and sisters, and being in Tully had tugged at his family ties. Jim's arrival had helped, but being away from his close-knit family had been tough on him while he'd been renovating the tea house.

"It's only for six weeks, Mel, and I'll see some amazing places. Will you ...?"

She held her breath, knowing the question before he asked it and not sure how to answer.

"Will you give me a chance to sort myself out?"

She'd told him she wouldn't wait forever. Six weeks, considering the two they'd already been apart, felt like forever. She wanted to rage and shout until her voice was hoarse. How could she open the tea house without him here? How would she *last* without him close by? The only reason she'd left Boston in a hurry was because she thought Luke was coming back soon. Had she been too smug in her decision? Had she subconsciously believed she could twist Luke around her little finger and sort him out?

She let the phone slip down her cheek and took a few calming breaths. Sometimes nothing went to plan, but when Luke was involved, rarely did things ever go how she'd envisaged.

She wiped away a couple of rogue tears and put the phone back to her ear. "I'll miss you, Luke, and ... and I'm sorry I left in a hurry."

She didn't answer his question. For some stupid, superstitious reason, she refused, not wanting to jinx his return. Six weeks was long enough. What if they wanted him for longer?

Silence hung between them and her heart hurt with intense pain. Had she really caused this?

"Mel, I'm going to see an expert at every stop I make. Everyone does therapy over here, so I should be able to find one easily enough when I have a few days spare. I'm going to fix this, Mel. I'm going to get started on it over here and then continue it when I get home. I'm doing it for you."

She believed him. She really did. She just didn't trust the industry he was working in. It was so alien to his normal everyday life; would he come back changed? Would her old Luke return? She scrambled to push those frightening thoughts away. It was time for some positive vibes.

She sat up and ran a hand through her tangled hair. "I'm banking on it, Luke. I wish you were here, but like you say, it's only six weeks. I've got lots to keep me busy."

"And I'll phone you at every opportunity. I can't share anything I do, as it's confidential, but I can talk about everything else."

"Okay." She coughed and held in her sob. This was harder than leaving him in Boston, when she'd reasoned they would see each other in two weeks. He'd organise a therapist, sort out his nightmares—job done.

"I've asked Flynn to stay close. There's a lot on your plate, I realise that. The charity will be taking up your time, plus preparing for the court case and getting ready to open the tea house."

She knew all this and would've loved to have him close by, so she could lose herself in his arms occasionally.

"Bye, Luke."

"Wait, wait, don't hang up yet, Mel!"

"What?"

"Are ... are we still in this together?"

She hesitated but only for a fraction of a second.

"Mel, please?"

"Yes, Luke. Yes, we are."

She heard his sigh from across the vast ocean separating them. "I love you, Mel. Take care."

"You too."

She pressed end and let the phone slip from her fingers. Why did she feel like she was being punished for running away?

Chapter 28

Melita stared at the email and her jaw dropped. There was no way she'd be picking it up any time soon.

Images of your swimwear were forwarded to me from a colleague and good friend, Bianca Douglas. Our magazine, Sports Illustrated Swimwear Issue, *would love the opportunity to work with you as we prepare for the next season of summer. Your swimwear collection, portraying native animals of Australia, is what our readers are looking for—something new, exciting and dangerous. Your designs are both stylish and sexy and I have no doubt they'll be a huge success.*

We have a team prepared to travel to Australia and ...

Melita lost it. Two weeks had passed since Luke's phone call and, with so much to cope with, she'd barely had a minute to herself. Now this!

Oh my God, my swimwear in Sports Illustrated!

She jumped up and pranced around her makeshift office in her rented home in Tully. Fist-pumping the air, she laughed and cried, and spun around and around. She needed Flynn. He was coming back from Brisbane tonight, but she needed someone to talk to now. This was the most amazing way to get her swimwear out there and yet the hardest. Who had given Bianca her name initially? She had no idea, but she'd find out eventually.

I'll ring Luke. He'd rung a couple of times when it'd suited his schedule, but this would be her first call to him. Should she? It was late at night and he might be asleep. She decided she couldn't wait a second longer. It was worth waking him up for this news.

The dial tone was only just audible over the pumping of her heart. She adjusted the Bluetooth piece to her ear, wanting her arms free to hug around her chest.

"Hello, Luke's phone."

Huh? The accented female voice threw her. "Is ... ah, Luke there?"

"Sorry," she drawled in an accented voice, "he's busy at the moment."

Why did some woman have access to his phone? What was he busy doing? Melita did a quick calculation and worked out it was around midnight over there.

"Want me to tell him you rang?"

She hesitated. "Ah ... no thanks."

She ended the call, her excitement after receiving the email draining from her. Luke was surrounded by gorgeous models, visiting amazing locations, had plenty of spare time and was one out-of-this-world hot male. She pulled the Bluetooth piece from her ear and sank to the floor.

How busy could he be at midnight? Had that woman just hopped out of his bed? Someone exotic and beautiful with a European accent? She cringed, hating herself for those thoughts. She'd loosened up on her beauty and grooming regime since arriving home from Boston and on some days she felt drab.

Her spirits dropped and squeezed through the joins in the floorboards. Who cared about the exclusive swimwear magazine offer? Or about getting her first tea house up and running? What about her swimwear business?

Alarmed with how fast her self-esteem could be crushed, she swallowed the hurt back, biting her tongue in the process. There was no way she would let her defeatist instincts win. She was never going back to being the person she used to be. No way would she return to a routine that led nowhere. Despite everything feeling right when Luke was close by, she hated that she'd come to depend on him.

But she was stronger than this, wasn't she? Capable of propelling her life in the direction *she* wanted, without him beside her? If he was playing around with someone on his adventure, she'd damn him to hell. God, this was hard. Everything inside hurt. With so much on her plate, she hadn't seen this possibility coming.

She would be a mess when Flynn arrived. Poor Flynn. She would unburden all her worries, apologise for heaping her problems onto him and then get on with her life. Didn't he have enough on his schedule? Wasn't adjusting to a new life with a disfigured chin hard enough?

Groaning, the pitiful sound reverberated around the room. The man she wanted was out of reach. His reason? She had too much money. Her conclusion? She was broken, damaged, unlovable. Another word kept circling around and around, just waiting for a vulture to pluck it off the ground—*freak*.

Luke eased onto the small fold-up bed in the cramped trailer. He was surrounded by all the comforts he needed in the desert—they even had reliable internet and phone reception—but, thankfully, tomorrow was the last day before they moved on.

They'd filmed at night for the first time tonight. The moon had needed to be in the right spot, so they'd waited until midnight. He grimaced, his back aching after the uncomfortable position he'd maintained while they'd taken shot after shot.

He snorted. *A few weeks away from hard yakka and I'm already getting soft.*

He'd been made to stand on a surfboard mounted to the tray of a four-wheel drive utility. The entire segment was intended to show the audience that the vehicle was a smooth ride, even in the roughest terrain—as smooth as a surfer riding the waves of an ocean. Why the surfer was out surfing during the night, he had no clue. He hoped it worked for them, but the idea hadn't caught on with him yet. At least he liked the soundtrack they were using with the advertisement.

He closed his eyes and willed his mind to shut down so he could sleep. It was a couple of days' drive to the next location and he wasn't important enough to be offered the option to fly by chopper.

He couldn't believe the money he was being paid to do this stuff. He'd stand anywhere, do anything, if it kept them happy. It wasn't like he would do this forever. He'd end up with a shitload of money to rival the balance of Melita's bank account ... well, maybe not quite that much.

The first thing he wanted to do was build his first home. The sizable buffer left over would enable him to take on bigger projects—including the tea houses Melita planned to build up and down the Queensland coast.

It was taking him a few minutes longer than usual to unwind. The shift had been tiring and his stomach grumbled, which was weird, because he rarely ate late at night. His nightmares had been tamer these past few weeks and for that he was hugely relieved. If he talked or thrashed in his sleep no one said anything. The walls of the trailer were thick enough, but even now he could still hear talking and conversations as others walked past on their way to the showers or communal kitchen.

The chilly desert air nipped at his face before he remembered to dig around in his duffle bag for his beanie and gloves. Snuggling down inside the generous sleeping bag, he closed his eyes and hoped sleep would find him soon.

"Hey, Luke, are you decent?"

Huh?

The familiar accented voice of Carmela, the lady in charge of feeding them, knocked on the door of his trailer before he had a chance to reply. He liked the buxom middle-aged European woman, who took no nonsense from anyone. Her olive skin glowed and she seemed always on the verge of laughing. She managed to feed every whinging and whining model, cameraman and organiser, while keeping them united in the project they were undertaking. No easy feat for anyone, but her jokes and ribbing rivalled the world's best comedians and he didn't think she'd ever offended anyone.

The job wasn't always easy for Carmela, but Luke took note of her strength and how others listened to her common-sense advice. This was an industry where beauty, ego and vanity overtook everything—unless someone like Carmela kept everyone under control.

Luke wasn't sure if he had nodded off, but he groaned when he rose from the bed. Carmela's knocking persisted, so he switched on the light and opened the door.

"They makin' you work too hard?" Carmela grinned apologetically. She had a keen interest in Australia and threatened to head Down Under one day if she could get her loafing husband off their couch. Luke was more than happy to share stories with her.

"Your phone rang earlier."

"My phone?"

"Yeah. It was pretty quiet around here and I was walking past your window. Your phone was ringing, so I thought I better answer it for you. The woman wouldn't leave a message and hung up before I had a chance to say why you weren't around."

Luke was instantly alert. "Shit." He raked his hand through his tousled hair. Turning around to look for his phone, he spotted it on the small crate where he kept it.

Luke tapped in his password, found the log of recent calls and recognised Melita's number. He slumped against the aluminium doorframe.

"I did something wrong?" Concern crossed Carmela's face. The whites of her eyes were luminescent in the strong moonlight.

"Give me a minute. I'll call her and explain."

"Tell her she can trust this big mamma. I got nothing for her to worry about."

Luke smiled despite his tiredness. "If she answers, I will. I know she has her phone handy all the time." He hoped she wouldn't be pissed off that some woman answered his phone in the middle of the night.

Luke swore when it went to message bank. He tapped out a message: **Mel, ring me back, please. Let me explain.**

"Not answering?"

"Yeah, something like that." He slid down the doorframe and sat stooped with his bare feet spread over the tiny trailer step.

"Want to talk about it?"

Jeez, was it that obvious? Or was he just tired. Something jarred. Someone had just asked him if he wanted to talk. Hell, there had been many times when he'd wanted to talk about things but hadn't.

He ran his hands through his hair and rocked back and forth. His mind kept blanking he was so tired. He looked up, not sure if Carmela would still be there. She was. He dropped his arms by his sides and rolled his shoulders—it helped to clear the fog from his head.

"I should've gone for help years ago and sorted out this shit. Melita's the girl I want, but I'm so screwed up in here"—he rapped his knuckles on the side of his head—"and if I don't sort myself out, I'm going to lose her.

"I also said some crazy stuff to her. She has a lot of money and I told her I couldn't handle it. The idea of not being her equal took over. What an idiot!"

He was so tired he could barely keep his eyes open, but he doubted he'd sleep a wink.

He jerked when Carmela touched him on the arm. Maybe he had dozed off.

"Okay, let's talk. Not now, because you're tired, but after you've had some sleep. Everyone in my family comes to me with their problems and I fix them. I'll sort you out real fast."

Was this possible? Could talking to the camp cook make a difference? He'd underestimated how easy it would be to find a counsellor when he'd promised Melita he would. Most days they'd been too far from the services of a town or city. How could he start sorting himself out if he couldn't access a professional? Gloomily, he hunched his shoulders. Not convinced he would ever get the help he needed, he slipped into a moodiness he hadn't experienced for a long time. "Good luck with that," he said, rubbing his eyes.

"You give me five minutes. I make one of my famous brews for relaxing and you have the best sleep ever."

He didn't have the energy to raise his head. Was it time to pack his bags and head home? The distance between himself and Melita was killing him, but the amount of money they were paying him meant he was resolved to see it through. Christ, he'd never realised how insecure he was about money, but this opportunity was the start he needed. He'd slaved since his apprenticeship years, but the amount was insignificant compared to what he would take home after this six-week stint. Not to mention the royalties he'd earn if Bianca's project won. He wasn't here to compete with Melita's wealth—heck, there was no chance of that—but a two-month modelling gig every year could be the physical break he needed away from the building game and provide the financial cream to his savings.

"Here you go, luv."

He looked up. *That was a fast five minutes.*

"You drink it all up, switch that damn phone off and I wake you up in the morning."

He wasn't in the mood for arguing. Besides, he missed his mum like blazes and Carmela was coming in at a close second. His mum was famous for her soothing herbal drinks; it looked like Carmela was too. He'd never told his mum about his nightmares—would it be better telling a stranger? His mother would be hurt that he hadn't told her the truth. He'd honestly believed he was man enough to handle the nightmares. But that wasn't the case; he realised that now.

He grunted when the hot liquid burned his lips. "Jesus, Carmela, you want to tell me it's hot?"

"Young man, don't take the Lord's name in vain and no swearing near me."

He chuckled before taking another sip, the temperature more tolerable now that he was aware of it. When she stuck out her hand, it took him a moment to realise what she wanted. He passed over his phone.

"That girl needs lesson in trusting her man. How she gonna get through life always thinking the worst?"

Luke shrugged. Carmela had a point. He couldn't remember ever wanting another girl since meeting Melita, so why wouldn't she pick up the phone? He sighed into the half-empty cup. Was it human nature to be suspicious when you were half a world away? He'd never seen this side of her.

When the chilly breeze penetrated his clothes, he drained the last of the herbal concoction and handed the cup back. "Thanks, Carmela. I'll take you up on your offer. You're going to hear some crazy stuff coming out of my mouth."

"Ah, nothing will scare me. I've heard it all. I saw a lot of bad stuff where I grew up. My neighbourhood was very poor. Nothing is gonna hurt me. You spill it all out and Mumma Carmela will sort you out."

"Thanks."

"Don't you worry about what everybody says around here. Your head is screwed on proper. Mumma Carmela fix you up and then I see the Luke I know is hiding in there." She jabbed a finger at her own head. "We all a bit crazy. Sometimes, a lot."

Her words were reassuring and he smiled before a yawn caught him unawares. His stomach, he noticed, had stopped grumbling. "I don't let that sort of thing worry me much."

"I know, I see it in you."

He rose and stumbled back into the trailer. Bidding her goodnight, he shut the door and had barely made it inside the sleeping bag when he fell back onto his camp bed. The next thing he knew, someone was banging on his door and he heard Carmela's cheery good morning.

Chapter 29

"They've cancelled my flight. What an absolute pain!" Flynn's frustration carried clearly through to Melita.

"But why?"

"The winds are too strong. It's some weird one-in-ten year event. The airport is closed and passengers are lounging and sleeping everywhere."

"Oh, Flynn, I need to talk to you."

"What's up?" She imagined him straightening and raking his hand through his hair. Did he ever rue the day he went looking for his troublesome sister?

Deflated that she couldn't air her suspicions to Flynn, she rolled onto her side and pulled her doona up to her chin. If his flight had taken off on time, he'd be whizzing his way along the Bruce Highway towards Tully right now.

"Look, sorry. You don't need this on top of having to hang around the airport. When do you think they'll reschedule the flight?"

"Mel, don't start that rot, and they're talking a couple of hours. Now, what's up?"

The delay had irritated him. She should've kept her mouth shut and not burdened him with her worries. *Damn.* He'd eventually get it out of her, so it was pointless waiting until he arrived. By then, she would be an absolute mess. *So make it fast.*

"A woman answered Luke's phone at midnight. He should've been sleeping, since he told me they were working long hours during the day." She swallowed. Now that she'd said it, it sounded petty and immature.

"Why the heck did you phone him at midnight? Did you try again at a decent hour?"

"No, and I had some news to share."

"Jeez, what news couldn't wait?"

Now impatience laced his words. This was a bad move on her part. She should've concentrated on Flynn's problems. He had to cancel a couple of meetings with big sponsors tomorrow. The last thing he needed was a bad outcome for his clients because of delays.

"Mel, did you phone him back to get him to explain, because I'm not understanding this. This is not like Luke and we both know it."

"No, but—"

"No, but what?" Flynn's raised voice buzzed down the line and smacked her ear hard.

"*He* phoned back, but I let it go to message bank."

"You did what?"

"Then he sent a message and asked me to call him back."

"And have you?"

"No."

"Mel, I'm getting off this phone so you can call him back right now."

"Flynn, what really happened in Boston, the week after I left?"

"I'm hanging up, Mel. Ring Luke *now*."

Flynn's voice died in her ear.

She should've mentioned it straightaway, her suspicions about Luke lying. She clearly remembered how adamant Luke had been that he was fulfilling some request for Jim. Just before dinner, her patience snapped and she phoned Jim. Either Jim was telling the truth that he knew nothing of it, or he was party to it.

She'd refrained from pressing him further and laughed it off as a misunderstanding. After hanging up, she barely ate any dinner. Her disappointment about Flynn's delayed flight compounded her headache. Once again, family—or Luke in this instance—was lying and keeping secrets from her. Was Flynn an innocent party or did he know something?

Tears threatened. It'd take nothing to unburden herself of them. In fact, she was seriously considering a good sob session. It never resolved anything, but it always made her feel better. A slow trickle had started when the sound of an incoming call filled the room. Luke's number on her phone's screen mocked her.

She sniffled and sat up.

"Hello, Mel."

"Luke." There were few words left in her. Not enough to greet him the way she usually did.

"About last night. You're upset, aren't you? That's why you didn't answer my call or phone back?"

Of course, I am! she wanted to scream. "No, why would I be?"

"Bloody hell, Mel, I was working."

"What's her name?"

He didn't miss a beat. "Carmela, and you've got this all wrong."

"The same way I got it wrong when I asked Jim about your secretive week in Boston and he had no idea what I was talking about? Why the lies, Luke?"

Luke huffed. "Mel, are you seriously having this conversation with me? Do you trust me so little that you'd think I'd dismiss everything between us and start something new this soon?"

She sank to the floor. Her heart swelled with pain and any minute now she'd unleash it all. "It's okay, Luke." No way would she be that girl driven by jealously.

Doing her best to hold it together, she took a deep breath and slowly exhaled. "It's not your fault. It's me."

"What?"

Her face crumpled. She risked dropping the phone her hand was shaking so much. "When your own parents can't find it in themselves to love you, what hope is there?"

"Mel, what the hell are you talking about?"

Luke sounded desperate, but strained silence pierced the airwaves between them because she couldn't get another word out without falling apart. This turn of events further emphasised what was important in her life—her business venture, and all the satisfaction it would eventually bring her. Finding a man to love her was never going to happen. *So move on,* she instructed herself.

In a calmer voice, Luke finally broke the silence. "Mel, I have to go. We need to get on the road and I'm not quite ready. I love you, but it's killing me that you don't trust me. As for the other thing you said, I have no idea what's going on. As for Jim, there's an explanation for that, too. I'm sorry, but I have to hang up. I'll try to ring you soon."

Luke ended the call and she didn't get a chance to reply. Letting the phone drop, she succumbed to the mother of all sob sessions.

Sleep would be impossible.

⚜

"So there you have it, Carmela. My screwed-up life in a nutshell. To make matters worse, Melita thinks I'm playing around here and have already forgotten her. It's my fault, I know, because I told her I can't handle how much money she has. I also don't want to burden her with my nightmares. I need to sort them out. She deserves better."

"Have you asked her what she wants?"

Luke shifted on the wobbly crate and cradled the hot mug of chocolate. The smell of bolognaise sauce still lingered in the air.

He shrugged. "I don't think I have. I just sort of assumed it'd be best if she didn't choose me. We're from two different worlds."

He leaned against Carmela's refrigerated trailer. The constant whir of the generator pulsed along its sides, humming gently in Luke's ears. "Do you think there's any hope for us?"

"Have a cookie. It's better to think with some food." Carmela handed over a plastic container filled with baked goods and he helped himself to a couple. He bit into a crunchy cookie and tasted chocolate and cinnamon.

"If you had seen someone years ago, you might've skipped those nightmares. I see it in my nephew's boy. He ran into bad crime and got hurt. Couldn't sleep at night until my nephew took him to therapy. He never forgot the bashing, but he learned to live with it. Everyone's different, but you can't wait out something like that."

As he demolished half the biscuits and drank another mug of hot chocolate, they talked. Carmela made a lot of sense. His biggest problem was the recurrence of his nightmares, which had been made worse after the shed incident. They never let up. Sometimes they were toned-down versions; other times he woke up in a sweat. They'd been a constant in his life since that one terror-filled night.

Then there was the huge gulf between his life and Melita's and the vast fortune she held in her fingertips. Money was something foreign in the insulated world where he'd been raised. It scared the living daylights out of him. If that wasn't enough to deal with, he couldn't forget the harsh way he'd spoken to Melita only that morning. And he *had* lied to her.

He answered Carmela's questions honestly, and when it was time for bed, she insisted he fit in one last mug of her special herbal drink.

"What's in this stuff, Carmela? I swear you drugged me last night."

She waved him off, clearly insulted by his words. "There are no drugs in what Carmela gives you. You watch your tongue, young man."

Luke chuckled. He drained the sweet-tasting drink before rising to rinse the mug. "Thanks, Carmela. I'll see you tomorrow."

"Same time and place. We gotta lot to get through, you and me."

Boy, was she right! Was this the shove he needed to sort himself out? Had fate put him in Carmela's path for just this reason?

He wandered towards his trailer, waving goodnight to some of the others still out and about. He'd made some good friends, though some he'd met he wouldn't waste time on. It was human nature; everyone responded differently to others. With Carmela, he'd clicked immediately. The germ of an idea began to settle in his mind as he made his way to the men's toilets before calling it a night.

Chapter 30

Adrenalin spiked Melita's heart rate, excitement causing her pulse to buzz. Her tea house, The Silk Scarf, was due to officially open. Unable to sleep, she'd sneaked over to the tea house as the sun was climbing up and over the horizon. She'd used the small self-contained unit tacked onto the south side of the manufacturing shed countless nights in recent weeks, as she and her staff readied for the opening. Last night had been no different.

The number of hours she slept lately would look daunting if written down, but she shrugged and pulled on a thin sweater, the change towards a tropical winter obvious, even for a North American girl. She cared less and less about how many hours of sleep she'd managed and, instead, dwelt on trivial stuff. Like how the temperature at this time of year was to die for. Or how it was looking more and more unlikely that she'd return to Boston. No way was she going to think about Luke and how he'd promised to call her and never did.

Her last conversation with him three weeks ago had filled her with jealousy. She didn't want to admit it, but his mention of Carmela had sent her into a spin. Night after night, visions of what the two could be doing would rival any nightmare Luke was having.

And there lay the truth—her reason for not sleeping. But she wouldn't let it spoil her big day. She pushed on, dealing with everything that needed her attention, plus more. Her entire family had arrived for the opening and she couldn't be prouder of her achievements.

She stepped onto the dewy grass. The coolness on her bare feet sent a tingle up her legs. She loved feeling the chill and couldn't believe she'd never walked on wet grass growing up.

As she zipped up her sweater, she took in the leafless branches of the frangipani trees. They were stark in the off-season, but she would never remove them. At the right time of year, they were spectacular when they filled with leaves and colourful blooms.

She looked up as she approached the tea house and took in the sign-writer's work on the entrance sign. The wording, wrapped around a red scarf, always sent a jolt through her. She pushed back all the memories evoked by the single piece of fabric. Its location was still a mystery.

She dismissed her thoughts of the missing scarf for now and used her key to open the French-style doors. As she stepped inside, every sense was invaded. The new tables and chairs exuded a smell of leather. Their shiny chrome legs were bright, even in the dim morning light. She absorbed the ambiance and enjoyed her greatest achievement to date.

The first thing that would attract a visitor's attention was the display in the small alcove to the left of the entrance. It regaled the history of the house. The posters and photographs told the story of the Black Hand and the deaths that occurred at the property, of Patricia and her family, of the gold bullion's discovery and how the money was spent in the local community. It also explained the story behind the name, The Silk Scarf, and how it was found covering the gold. The end of the presentation detailed Melita's pledge to donate a portion of every sale towards post-polio syndrome research, and visitors were invited to make their own donations electronically or by using the locked box provided. Beside the donation box and available for sale were red silk scarves embroidered with 'The Silk Scarf Tea House, Tully, North Queensland, Australia' around their edges. Again, all proceeds would go towards medical research.

She praised Flynn's marketing skills. Praised everything about him, except for his constant nagging about Luke. He believed Luke had done nothing wrong and it was up to her to make the first move. She couldn't bring herself to do it—not yet.

Melita stood lost for a moment as she twisted her hand in the tangled mess of her morning hair. Each day that she dithered over contacting Luke would make it harder and more awkward when they came face to face again. She loosened her hand and pushed those thoughts away, forcing her legs to move, then took a deep breath and made her way towards the shiny new kitchen.

The commercial fridges hummed. They'd been filled with prepared food for a couple of days now. Melita glanced around at the shiny surfaces and something lurched inside her chest. The responsibility that now rested on her shoulders scared her for a moment. She took a few calming breaths and thanked the day she'd teamed up with Marcus. After he'd set up the charity and had allocated all the money, he'd moved comfortably into the role of manager. She'd needed someone she could trust to oversee the running of the tea house, and he hadn't been hard to convince. Teamed up with a shy, Aussie girl he'd recently met, the charm of the tropical north was working on him too.

As Queensland was moving into its usual mild winter, North America was steamrolling into summer, which meant her swimwear would soon be showcased in the *Sports Illustrated Swimwear Issue*. She'd seen the proofs and couldn't believe how good they all looked. With so much happening in her life, emotion pushed against the constraints of her chest. Pride was not something she indulged in often, but she deserved to feel a little proud about everything she'd achieved.

Melita didn't delude herself as to whether feeling proud was enough, as she left the café and made her way upstairs to the boutique. Her heart ached constantly, but it was still a couple of weeks before Luke returned home. If he came back at all. Some days she wasn't so sure he would and would it be enough to restore her?

She stopped on the staircase and leaned against the wall. Tears built
up behind her eyelids as she thought about him. If he wasn't spending
time with this Carmela, he'd have phoned her. In her private moments she
wasted a lot of tears on him, then always got angry at herself for getting
upset.

Determined to shed the depression threatening to settle around her, she
pushed her shoulders back and continued up the stairs. The smell of Lycra
greeted her and stirred her excitement. Rack upon rack of swimwear in all
shapes, colours, styles and sizes awaited her. It was enough to temporarily
push Luke to the back of her mind. This was her territory. This was
what would carry her for years to come. She loved designing, and yes, she
could be proud. Not a little, but a lot. Despite how low she'd fallen after
her mother's death, she'd pulled herself up and now led a fulfilling life.
Designing swimwear had saved her and the mafia house was her salvation.
She would overcome the Luke thing if things didn't work out between
them. She'd been doing it for years now. It was normal for her.

She ran a hand across the hanging swimwear. The feel of the shiny, cool
lycra instilled her with the confidence she needed to face the day. Everyone
would be there—her father and Flynn, Zane and a very pregnant Ella,
and Patrick and Kelly. Jim and Patricia were a certainty, along with every
local dignitary and politician. Flynn had been very busy contacting local
newspapers and television news reporters.

The transformation of the mafia house was big news. It was a building
with a tragic and turbulent history, so no one wanted to miss out on
its rebirth. The locals hoped that her business would transform the local
economy. It didn't matter what time of year it was in this part of the world,
swimwear was always in demand, and she couldn't have built her first
landmark tea house in a better location. She allowed herself a smile and
shuffled a curtain across one of the changing cubicles.

Flynn had every intention of milking her *Sports Illustrated*
success—any opportunity to espouse why her swimwear and the tea house
should feature in national and international news. It was what every

swimwear designer coveted—to feature in one of the world's most popular swimwear magazines, especially one that had dictated decades of swimwear fashion. She was thrilled to be part of it.

She spun around and, pulling her shoulders back, made a pact with herself to enjoy the final moments of calm. When the limelight settled on her, she would be too busy to worry about inconsequential things, like why Luke had never phoned back.

Oh, yes, she'd achieved all this. Her dream was coming true. She allowed herself a moment to feel proud, then savoured it a little longer before shrugging it off and heading back down the stairs. She had to fit in a hair appointment after breakfast and no way was she going to be late for the opening of her first tea house.

***

Luke parked his hire car a couple of hundred metres away, on the South Johnstone turn-off. He'd never had any intention of missing the tea house opening, but only Flynn knew he was arriving. He'd warned him parking would be scarce.

Luke unbuckled his seatbelt and turned to Carmela. "We're here."

"Good Lord, my boy. You bring me all the way over here to some big cane paddock?" She twisted around and glanced over her shoulder. "And those over there? Bananas?"

He nodded. Sugar cane grew around the tea house, but further down the road to South Johnstone, banana crops took over.

"Come on, Carmela, you have a job to do. I didn't bring you all this way for nothing."

She chuckled and hoisted her generous body out of the car. "Is it always this hot here?"

"It's nearly winter, just so you know."

"You lying to me, my boy?"

He laughed and got out of the car, then taking her arm, he steered her along the rough-edged road. Two weeks he'd wrangled from the advertising crew, stealing their kitchen captain too. Actually, it would only be ten days. Of those, two would be taken up with travelling and a third was the official announcement of the photography competition. All the dates tied in perfectly for him.

He had no idea if Melita had seen anything on the bus photographic competition online. With an announcement of the finalists due to be released on social media in a few days, he had some time up his sleeve. As part of the deal he'd struck with Bianca, Melita wouldn't be sent an official invitation until the very last minute. By then, he hoped to have Melita aboard a Qantas jet, flying to Boston for the gala event.

Could he pull it off? It'd been a long five weeks and the modelling stint was a little behind schedule. His only knowledge of what had been happening in Tully was through Flynn and Jim, but he planned to see the modelling project through until the very end and then run like hell with all his money. He'd worked ridiculous hours for weeks to get this short reprieve.

He stopped short at the front of the tea house and Carmela barrelled into him.

"No way. No frickin' way."

"Is there something wrong, my boy?"

She called him 'my boy' in nearly every sentence she uttered and it had turned out to be his comfort blanket. They'd spent countless hours talking together and delving into his mind. His nightmares had eased and his confidence that he could beat them completely had grown alongside their friendship. But not once, not ever, had he brought up the subject of the silk scarf—and not once had bloody Flynn mentioned the tea house was to be named after it.

He swayed, dizziness obscuring his vision before he cleared his head and looked again at the sign. It was the perfect name. The silk scarf's discovery had been the pivotal moment when everything had meshed together for him and Melita. And the damn thing was still bringing them together. The photography competition was just another chapter in its incredible journey.

"I haven't told you about the silk scarf, have I?" he asked Carmela.

"Is it important?"

He took her hand and squeezed it. "It's important to me, so I think I should tell you. But it'll have to wait." He tugged on her arm. "Come on, let's go meet Melita."

Filled champagne glasses were offered, along with finger food and conversation. Guests laughed and talked in small groups and large, while a man with a video camera slowly wound his way around the café. Adrenaline pumped through Luke's body at the thought of seeing Melita again.

He stopped to get his bearings. Beside him, Carmela freed her hand and reached for nibbles offered by a passing server. They'd spent the night in Cairns to recover from jet lag and had eaten breakfast a few hours ago, but food was the last thing on his mind. He gazed around the room, from left to right, desperate to see only one person. He spotted his grandfather and Patricia and wanted to bolt up to them for a hug, but he held back, refusing to move until he saw Melita.

He gasped. There she stood, being interviewed by a reporter. "Come on, Carmela, I found her. I need you right beside me."

"Coming, my boy." Carmela moved with him but not before reaching for more selections from the passing server.

Luke pressed forward, squeezing past the throng that appeared denser the closer he got to Melita. "Excuse me, could you let us through?"

Two to three hundred visitors must be squeezed inside the tea house. His chest puffed when he saw how many locals were here to support Melita. She'd won them over in the end. Her determination to spend the proceeds from the gold in the local community had eventually squashed the hostile welcome she'd first received.

He was only a couple of metres away from her now. His heart danced a jig when the reporter thanked her for her time and she answered with a smile. It transformed her beautiful face and illuminated her unusual grey eyes. He couldn't quite see the brown specks in her irises, but he'd dreamed about them plenty. Would he get one of her magnificent smiles when she spotted him?

She turned and their gazes locked. Her smile dropped. The last few guests separating them melted away, leaving a metre of space yet to conquer.

"Luke?" Melita's lips quivered.

He wanted nothing more than to still them with his own, but first things first. "Mel, I'd like you to meet someone."

Hope disappeared from her face. *Come on, girl, don't do this to me.* He overlooked the obvious lack of trust he'd sensed all those weeks ago, and before she had a chance to run, he said, "I'd like you to meet Carmela."

Melita glanced to his right, to Carmela standing beside him. Instant confusion marred her beautiful face, then her eyes locked onto his, and after that she looked neither left nor right. Royalty could've been standing beside him and she wouldn't have noticed. She finally dragged her gaze from his when Carmela stepped forward, and the revelation that she'd got it completely wrong was painfully exposed.

"Young lady, I've a heard a lot about you." Carmela grabbed Melita's limp hand and pumped it up and down a few times. "We can talk later. I'll go and find something to drink."

Carmela was gone as fast as her size allowed. Her job was done.

Luke ignored the din of the crowd as he looked into Melita's ashen face. He didn't miss the black rings around her eyes or the general tiredness her expert make-up couldn't quite hide.

"Get over here, girl, and don't you ever do this to me again." His voice came out gruff, his emotion at finally being close to Melita sticking in his throat.

Chapter 31

"Finally, I want to thank everyone in the local community. I couldn't have done it without them." Melita smiled into the camera as the red recording light blinked.

The cameraman turned back to the reporter and Melita released a huge sigh of relief. Her interview was done and she had no more official commitments. She could now relax and enjoy champagne with Flynn and the others. Would she ever get used to being in the limelight? It always left her feeling awkward and exposed. Shrugging objectively, she dismissed the concern. It was no different to her experiences growing up in Boston.

Melita took a deep breath and a moment to gather her bearings. She recalled her final words in the interview. There'd been a point when she'd been close to giving up on the community. If Jim hadn't come north. If Jim hadn't offered to approach Patricia. If Jim and Patricia had never clicked. If, if, if. The pivotal point had been when she secured Patricia's support and friendship. She might've been a long way from Tully right now if her destiny had taken a different road.

She glanced up, hoping for a glimpse of her family, but didn't search for long. Her heart pulsed an almighty beat inside her chest and she gasped.

Luke! Crazy, gorgeous and at her official opening. She couldn't drag her gaze away from his hypnotic hazel eyes. When he moved a few steps closer, the air in her lungs whooshed out.

"Luke." Her lips trembled for the longest three seconds of her life.

Then he said, "Mel, I'd like you to meet someone."

Her hope was dashed. Her legs shook and she was at risk of falling. No way was she going to meet his girlfriend. Not in this life. She and Luke weren't finished yet. They hadn't agreed it was over. Was this why he'd not called her once in three weeks? He couldn't do this; he couldn't show up at her official opening with his latest pick-up.

God, kill me now.

"I'd like you to meet Carmela."

That name again. The same one that had tortured her night after night. The one that sparked the same revolving images of a sensuous body, entwined with Luke's, the exotic accent, the heat. Someone grabbed her hand—all strength long gone from her body—and pumped it up and down. She wanted to yank it free and run away, hide in a corner and bawl.

"Young lady, I've a heard a lot about you."

Slowly, something trickled along her sensory nerves and infused strength back into her limbs. Her hand was released, but it didn't drop to her side. It remained in mid-air, her brain unsure what to do with it. She dragged her gaze away from Luke's accusing stare and noticed the kind and cheerful face beside him.

The second it took for her hand to drop by her side was all the time she needed for the truth to be revealed. For her brain to compute what her jealousy had done. Her immaturity. Guilty as charged; she was so, so ashamed of all the assumptions she'd made. Carmela reached across and patted her shoulder, said something about talking later and finding a drink.

"Get over here, girl, and don't you ever do this to me again."

She swallowed, her tears rapidly making a blurry image of Luke.

She rushed the last few steps and, landing in his waiting embrace, threw her arms firmly around his neck. "I'm so sorry, Luke. So sorry."

She pushed her face against his neck and inhaled all the smells she associated with him. In her imagination, she could still smell the fragrance of freshly cut timber, as if he'd forgotten to wash his hair since leaving Tully all those weeks ago.

"Are you finished here for a bit?" Luke whispered in her ear.

Her only response was to tighten her arms around his neck. He wasn't going anywhere on her watch. And oh, he felt so good. All the way down to his muscled thighs.

"Have you set up the unit in the shed?" Luke asked. He pulled back and she sunk into his gaze.

"Yes," she managed breathlessly, because she knew exactly why he was asking.

"Half an hour. Come on, no one will miss you."

She didn't argue when he took her hand and dragged her past guests who were cheerfully drinking her wine and champagne and eating tray after tray of finger food. No one stopped them on their quest and they exited the front of the tea house without the slightest hiccup.

It barely took a minute to reach the unit. Another thirty seconds to find the key in her purse. Another twenty seconds before Luke took the key from her shaking hands and opened the door. And a final ten seconds for Luke to shut the door and firmly lock it.

Her purse fell to the floor at the same moment Luke took the zipper that ran the length of the back of her dress and opened it. "I suggest you take this off. I can't be responsible for what might happen if it doesn't come off *now*."

The soft lilac dress slipped from her shoulders. Melita stepped out of it, picked it up and draped it over the back of a chair, and kicked off her shoes. Then Luke was there. He found her mouth and kissed her ruthlessly, just the way she wanted. He unclasped her bra expertly and the relief was instant when he pushed the straps off her shoulders.

She fumbled at his shirt buttons and gasped for more air, ever reluctant to part from his mouth. She lost track of what Luke was up to until her thighs touched his flesh and she realised he'd removed his jeans and had stepped out of them. He made short work of her underwear after she'd pushed his shirt off his shoulders.

She wanted to be everywhere; frustrated from the long separation and smarting from the hurt. She started in his hair and roughly massaged his head. Their lips continued to punish each other and their breathing sounded louder with each passing minute. His hand found its way between her legs and she gasped, clinging tighter as she struggled to stand upright. Then Luke had her in his arms and they tumbled together onto the bed.

He wrenched his mouth away from hers. "How dare you not trust me, Mel? How could you think I'd pick up with someone else so soon or at all?" His hands made tracks on her skin and dug into her flesh. Up and down her arms and along her thighs. He couldn't get deep enough for her needs.

"You don't phone me for weeks. How dare *you*!" She bit into his shoulder and then sucked on it for dear life.

"Poor rich man's baby girl. Why didn't *you* phone me?" He rolled onto his back and took her with him.

His ferocious kissing made her push harder against his mouth. "Why are you even here? I have too much money for you, you poor struggling builder."

He wrapped his legs around hers and tightened his hold. She was trapped, just like she wanted to be, but he wasn't playing fair.

He pulled her away, as far as his hold allowed, and his eyes blazed back. "I've changed my mind. I want you and your money. Complete package or nothing."

She gulped. "Oh, really? Well, I say nothing."

"What?" Luke demanded as she took his left nipple in her mouth and sucked on it as hard as she could. His resulting groan was all the satisfaction she needed.

She tore her mouth away. "You lied to me in Boston, that's what."

Luke rolled her onto her back. "Jeez, woman! What the hell are you on about?"

"Your secretive week in Boston. The one you said had something to do with Jim. Remember it?"

"Bloody hell."

They duelled like two combating insects. She dug her hands into his flesh. His frustration was obvious when he cupped her backside and pulled her against his body. The sound of their harsh breathing filled the small unit as they both tried to gain the upper hand.

He rose onto his knees and looked down at her. His glazed eyes overflowed with a thousand emotions. "Okay, so I lied. But I have a darn good reason."

"And that's supposed to make me feel better?" Lying on her back, she reared up and wrapped her legs around his waist. As she hung from his neck she continued to punish him with her mouth, her teeth grinding against his.

"I don't have nightmares anymore," he managed to say when she pulled back to fill her lungs with air.

She stopped, her mouth open, panting liked she'd run a marathon. "You don't?"

"And I sleep better and think clearer."

She dropped her legs. "You do?"

He nodded. "I'm an idiot, Mel. I can't believe I let money come between us."

She twisted her mouth into a wry grimace as she ran her hands blindly along his torso. Oh, yes, he was a deliciously sexy idiot. "You admit to lying. I don't get it."

Luke flopped beside her on the bed and groaned. "Seven days, that's it, and then I can tell you the truth." He rolled to his side and captured her cheek in his large hand before locking gazes with her. "I promise it'll be the one and only white lie I ever tell you. I just need you to be patient until then."

She stewed a little, trying to find the right words. His thumb rotating gently along her jaw line wasn't making it easier. "Luke, if there's one thing you should know about me, it's that I hate secrets."

He snuggled closer and kissed her neck. "But was discovering the truth that bad? Didn't it change your life for the better?"

She mangled his once-combed hair as she considered this. He had a point. Nothing disastrous had happened in her life because of those secrets, but still, she'd hated the unexpectedness of learning the truth. "Is it going to hurt when I find out?"

He captured her face in both hands. "I hope not."

She harrumphed. "Well, that's no consolation."

"I need some trust here, Mel. Please."

She thought about it. Her trust had nose-dived when she'd learned Jim knew nothing of Luke's secret week in Boston. It'd hurt a lot. She'd cried copious tears over it. A person didn't quickly get over being lied to. Being in the dark now wasn't helping.

She turned away and stared up at the ceiling.

"Mel, please."

She turned back and made an effort to look him in the eye, then gritted her teeth and warned, "The only way I'm going to be patient and forget about it for a week is if you do something very amazing about right now. I didn't let you into my room without expecting some reward."

"My God, that's my girl."

Passion ignited swiftly as Luke touched and rubbed her all over. Her lips suffered again, but despite Luke's long absence, they still had the ability to create magic between them. Nothing had changed. She raked her nails down his back and Luke made a beeline to the moisture building between her legs. Then he took hold of her hips and entered her slick opening, answering all her prayers—until he jerked away and fell beside her, breathing heavily.

"I'm sorry, Mel. I'm not prepared. I have nothing on me."

Mel glared at him. "No way. You don't get to stop now." She pulled at his hand and insisted he finish what he started.

"Hey, why me?" he mock-grumbled.

"Because you lied to me." And then she was moaning as he expertly took her where she needed to go. It was the cure she'd needed for many weeks.

When he was done, she flatly refused to feel any remorse for his unsatisfied state. She used a pillow to cover his erection.

He turned towards her, agony etched in every line of his face. "You're a cruel girl. I promise never to lie to you again."

His look of suffering was too much for Melita and helpless laughter erupted from her. Luke tried to look offended until he could no longer hold it in. They clutched each other, with a pillow safely between them, as laughter bubbled into the air and tears coursed down their faces.

Chapter 32

When a knock sounded at the door, Luke stirred. Had they fallen asleep? It wouldn't have taken much, sex or no sex.

"What's the time, Mel?"

Melita had risen and was reaching for a white bathrobe hanging from a hook near the bed. She glanced at the digital clock. "Shoot, I've been gone over an hour."

As she headed for the door, she slipped on the robe and clutched it around her chest.

"Mel, are you in there?" Flynn called before Melita had a chance to open the door.

Alarmed at his nakedness, Luke used the faithful pillow to hide the worst—it was too late to scramble into his clothes.

"Mel, what happened to you?" Flynn exclaimed when he entered. "Everyone's looking for you." He took in the spread of clothes scattered around the room. He wouldn't need to be a rocket scientist to understand the situation immediately.

Taking her chin in his hand, he turned her face towards better lighting. "My God, did he try to kill you?"

Melita chuckled. "Enough of that. Give me ten minutes and I'll resurrect myself."

"Good luck. You look a mess."

Melita grabbed her dress and dashed into the bathroom. Luke eyed Flynn warily. There were few secrets between them, and on many occasions, Flynn had acted as his confidant—but he'd never caught Luke like this with his little sister.

It wasn't until Flynn looked down his nose at him and smiled that Luke relaxed.

"Okay, you can get dressed. You couldn't wait until tonight?"

It was hard to explain the urgency that had driven him and Melita out of the tea house. He'd been desperate to patch things up and make things right between them. And then there'd been the burning need to touch her—he'd needed reassurance that nothing had changed.

"She was mad about the secret week in Boston." Luke rose from the bed still clutching the pillow. He kept his voice to a whisper, not wanting to alert Melita to what they were talking about. "I'd forgotten about using Jim as an excuse and she asked him about it. Trust me, it didn't go down well."

Flynn chuckled. They both loved Melita differently and would walk to the ends of the earth for her. It didn't come easy hurting her.

"By the way, nice scratch marks along your back," Flynn announced.

Luke smiled at the memory of their tussle as he discarded the pillow and began putting on his boxers.

"She's been in frustration mode ever since Carmela answered the phone that night," Flynn added.

"Damn." He'd forgotten about Carmela.

Flynn must've sensed the reason for his alarm. "Don't worry. Thomas is taking care of her, though Carmela's keeping him amused too. And she's under no illusions as to why you both took off. She just didn't realise you were so close."

"Very convenient, I know." Luke chuckled and pulled up his jeans, then tried to pat down his hair. He was oddly reassured that there was no way he could tame it enough to look respectable.

"What are your plans for the week? I assume Mel doesn't know about the trip to Boston?" Flynn kept his voice low.

"No, I haven't mentioned it yet. It'll probably go down like a lead balloon." Luke found his shirt, slipped it on and began buttoning it up. Then he sat and reached for his shoes. He was suffering from jet lag and lack of food wasn't helping. "I'm starving. Any chance there's some food left?"

"I'll rustle something up for you."

Luke rose and adjusted his shirt so it sat neatly. Things like that never used to cross his mind. His modelling stint had changed some things. "I'm going to head to Brisbane and catch up with Mum and the girls. I'd like them to meet Carmela."

Flynn nodded. He knew the impact of Carmela's help. Luke had opened up to him about his terror-filled nightmares and his reluctance to get involved with Melita because of her vast fortune. He'd been another person to unburden his fears onto and doing so had further lightened the load he'd kept close to his chest for so many years. Since he'd started talking about the trauma he'd suffered, it felt less and less significant in his everyday life, when, during all the years since the incident, it had dominated it.

He realised now that it was wrong to go it alone. From the day he'd spilled to his grandfather, he'd grown mentally and had come to respect how much of a difference family and friends could make to a person's wellbeing. Jim was up-to-date on Luke's remarkable turnabout, so now that only left his mother and sisters. His recovery wouldn't be complete until he told them everything.

"I promised to show Carmela a bit of Australia. She's a fanatic about anything Aussie. I only wish we had more time, but as we both need to get back quickly, I'll restrict her stay to Queensland. I'll take her to see some spectacular natural sights."

Flynn sat on the edge of the rumpled bed while they waited for Melita to appear. "When do you plan on leaving for Boston?"

"Flights are booked for Thursday afternoon. Six days to go. Carmela will leave on a flight to California, then Melita and I will head to Boston via New York. I won't have any time to waste in Boston because I need to be back on set the following Tuesday."

"So Saturday's the big night?"

"Even bigger if Bianca wins the competition. It'll throw so much attention Mel's way. I hope you're ready for it and have it under control."

"The competition isn't the only thing sweeping her away with success. She tried to phone you that night to tell you about it."

"What are you talking about?"

Flynn tilted his head and raised his brows. He looked like a man with a secret.

"Flynn, are you keeping something from me? And while I remember, why the bloody hell didn't I know the tea house was being named The Silk Scarf?"

"I wondered what you'd think. With all that's going on with that scrap of material, I finally came around and agreed it was a good choice."

Flynn was the only family member privy to Luke's involvement in the photographic competition and what the final shot entailed.

"I can't believe how one lousy piece of fabric has had such an impact on our lives. Who knows what it's seen?" Luke said.

"After what I think happened here today, I can use my imagination with little effort," Flynn added dryly.

Luke averted his gaze to hide his embarrassment—until he remembered the thread of their earlier conversation. Quietly, he asked, "What else is sweeping Mel away? Should I be worried?"

Melita emerged from the bathroom, looking refreshed. He didn't miss her swollen lips and the restored glint in her eyes. Neither did Flynn by the way he studied her.

He rose from the bed. "Come on Mel, we better head back to the tea house. Before we do though, how about you suck in those lips? They're about triple the size they were an hour ago."

Worry crossed her face.

"You look beautiful, Mel," Luke told her. "For once, ignore your brother. I'll be a few minutes behind you."

Flynn chuckled when Melita punched him playfully on the arm. Then she turned around, put her arms around Luke's neck and squeezed. "Thanks for being here today."

"I was never going to miss it."

"I think you already have," Flynn chided. "Now, can we go? I have TV reporters and newspaper journalists recording everything, and the disappearance of the main star is not likely to go unnoticed."

Melita laughed good-naturedly, her demeanour fully relaxed as she rescued her handbag from the floor and followed Flynn to the door.

"By the way, Mel," Luke called before they had a chance to leave, "be ready to fly to Boston on Thursday afternoon."

She halted. "What?"

"Um ... you and I are flying to Boston at the end of the week."

"Do I get a choice?"

"Not really."

She stared at Luke for a moment, despite Flynn's urgency to leave. "Is that when you'll reveal your secret?"

Smart girl. She missed nothing. "Ah, yep."

He detected a hint of annoyance when her mouth straightened.

"Some warning might've been nice."

"Sorry, couldn't help it."

She turned to Flynn. "I'm going to kill him." But her grimace wobbled and a half-smile fought its way to the surface. Joy speared Luke's chest. If he couldn't get her on that plane, all his planning would be in vain. But it looked as if she'd decided not to make a fuss.

Luke caught Flynn's words before the door shut.

"You should stop smiling and make it sound like you mean it."

Chapter 33

Luke never ended up following Melita back to the tea house. She'd found him sprawled over her bed, asleep and fully dressed, shoes and all, when she'd gone looking for him after the teahouse launch ended. She sneaked out after leaving a note explaining where she was headed, then hitched a ride with Flynn and Carmela for a celebratory dinner with her family. It was a rare event for them all to be together, plus there'd been added excitement, as Ella's baby was due in a couple of months.

Now, six days later, she was frantically gathering clothes, shoes and toiletries and shoving them in her suitcase. It was very unlike her, but the wild pace of the tea house in its opening week meant she was now rushing to pack for Boston. There'd been a hundred teething problems to sort out, the most critical being the shortfall of staff. Melita had been seating customers as often as making cappuccinos and pots of tea. The tea house was in the perfect spot for those travelling the road to take a break.

If you hadn't read about the tea house in the papers, seen it on the news or scrolled past it on social media, you were most likely dead. Flynn had saturated every possible outlet—and all this without the latest *Sports Illustrated Swimwear Issue* released yet!

She stopped packing and took a moment to enjoy the anticipation of what its release would mean for her. But then she envisioned how Flynn would put her through the gruelling mill of television and radio interviews again. Her shoulders dropped and she groaned, then got back to packing, already afraid of the extra limelight that would shine her way. Maybe it wasn't such a bad idea to get out of the country for a few days.

She turned around to locate the shoes she needed and winced when she recalled Flynn's excitement earlier that afternoon. He'd reported that two Australian magazines were keen to feature her business on their glossy pages. He was only waiting until her swimwear spread hit the New York stands.

Her phone pinged and she dropped the shoes to check it.

Just leaving Brisbane now. See you soon. L.

She sent him a quick reply. Their flight out of Cairns International Airport wasn't due to leave for four hours. She would only just make it in time at the rate she was going.

Almost packed. Will be at the airport in time for our flight. Love M.

She smiled when a series of happy face emojis appeared on her screen. How could they have been apart for six days already? She wasn't about to let on that she'd barely had time to miss him, but when her head hit the pillow each night, sleep came immediately, and during daylight hours, she was on the go from the instant she rose.

She recalled their only night together since the tea house opening. After she'd had dinner with her family, she'd left Flynn and Carmela at her rented house in Tully, with bedding sorted and a promise to return Flynn's car the next day. Then she'd grabbed some essentials from her bedroom and had driven back to the tea house. The look of relief on Luke's face when she'd shown him how prepared she was had been priceless. She chuckled at the memory of his eyes widening at the sight of the condom. It was like he'd won the lottery. Despite having just woken, he'd shown incredible restraint and tenderness as he'd built the heat between them with impeccable timing.

God help her, she loved him. A person could feed off a memory like that for years.

Too many lasting memories—that's what they were creating and her body now showed all the signs of wanting more. Heat pooled between her legs and her urgency to get out of the house and to the airport suddenly trebled. They had thirty glorious hours together, between flights and stopovers, with not a care in the world.

All her worries for the tea house she would leave behind for Marcus to handle.

⁂

Luke frantically paced the tiled floor of the airport. Carmela boarded her California-bound plane an hour ago, but where was Melita? She'd told him she was leaving in her last message and that had been three hours ago. Plenty of time to arrive and find a car park.

He peered anxiously at every person that entered the building. Time was ticking away and if she didn't arrive soon, it'd be too late to check-in.

"Luke, I'm here."

He spun around, relief at finding Melita behind him leaving him light-headed for a second. She must've used another entry. "Mel, where—"

"Don't ask. Let's get going."

They dashed to the business class check-in counter and were swept through the usual security checks. Now both seasoned travellers, they had it down to a fine art and weren't held up. They made it to their gate with only minutes to spare before the notice to board was aired over the public address system.

Once seated, Luke stretched his legs and prepared for the long flight. Melita had barely had enough time to catch her breath, so he let her organise her hand luggage and get seated first before he kissed her.

She ran a hand through her hair, which added to her frazzled look. "A road accident and road works. It was a fight to get here today."

He took his fill of her. Her lateness had frightened him. A missed flight could have jeopardised everything.

She gave Luke a pointed look. "And don't ask why I didn't leave earlier."

He leaned in and nuzzled her neck. "You did have me worried."

"I'm sorry, Luke, but it's been one crazy week. You're lucky I'm here at all. I'm sure we experienced every possible problem."

He winced. His plans could've been thwarted before they'd even started. He leaned against his seat with relief. "You didn't let on when we spoke on the phone. Did you manage to get enough sleep?"

"I didn't want to worry you. As for sleep, yes, I was pretty much unconscious all night, every night."

"Really? That doesn't sound so great. Did you find time to dream about me?"

She smiled. "Come here, you big brute."

She tangled her hand in his hair, drawing him closer. He sensed her winding down, her body relaxing against his; it was the best they could manage in aeroplane seats.

"Did Carmela enjoy her time?" Melita asked, using her free hand to loosen her seatbelt before leaning in to rest her face against his.

"She had a fabulous week and will be back again one day."

Luke touched his lips to hers and all the tension of the past couple of hours drained away. It'd been a long journey to get to where they were, but as he kissed her, he knew he wanted to take care of her forever, and the surprise waiting was the start. He could tuck away his anxieties because the time was right.

He pulled back and lost himself in her tear-filled eyes, damning the restrictions of their seatbelts and armrests. "I've missed you so much, Mel."

He understood why she was emotional. They'd been to hell and back a dozen times, but they only had one or two more trips to make before they could finally stay together.

She bit her bottom lip and rested her head against him. "Me too."

He gave her some time, stroking her hair and tucking it behind her ear. When she looked up again, he asked, "Apart from all the problems you experienced, how was the rest of your week?"

"Hectic, frantic, headachy, amazing, incredible, wow."

"So you're tired?"

She smiled that beautiful, radiant smile of hers—the one that lit up everything inside him. "I shouldn't need to sleep the entire flight."

Luke found her mouth again and enjoyed being close to her. He was making up for lost time before the flight attendant bothered them with unimportant things, like checking if they wanted a glass of water or a hot towel.

"We've got two months to catch up on, Luke. I want to hear everything," she whispered.

"Same goes for me." He drew back and unbuckled his seatbelt. "But only if I get a hug. I really need one."

Without hesitation, she complied, and despite the armrest between them, they embraced. He inhaled her scent, breathed it in through his nose, revelled in the familiarity of it. It was intoxicating and sent all sorts of visions through his mind—and to different parts of his body. He laughed out loud. Maybe the hug wasn't such a great idea ...

"Excuse me, you'll need to fasten your seatbelts for take-off."

Luke drew away, though his gaze never left Mel's beautiful face. He loved her so much. He hoped she felt the same way and that the final image of the photographic contest didn't scare her off.

⁂

Thirty hours later, after stopovers in Auckland and Los Angeles, their plane was coming in to land. New York was a long way from home, but they were one flight closer to Boston. Luke raked a hand through his dishevelled hair and stretched his arms above his head. They should've slept for longer, but the chance to kiss Melita for hours had been irresistible and had clouded his brain. He chuckled, enjoying the stretch.

They had so much to talk about—his modelling contract and the people he worked with, Carmela's magical touch and how she'd saved him from his nightmares, the court case and how it was progressing, the work involved in opening the tea house, the community fund and how the money had been allocated ...

Luke rubbed his tired eyes and raised his seat as the flight attendants prepared the cabin for landing. The past two months had been crucial for both their lives.

There'd been so much change.

For their sanity, much had to be aired and discussed. At least they had the night in New York to sleep soundly before flying to Boston tomorrow.

When the seatbelt sign was switched off and the captain announced mobile devices could be used again, Melita quickly reached for hers. "I might check in with Marcus in case there have been any issues."

Luke yawned, relieved the plane had landed in one piece. He doubted he would ever be cured of all the superstitious fears he'd acquired over the years. Flying always left him nervous.

As they waited to disembark, his nosed twitched. Odours from his unwashed body filtered up to his nose, the kind of smell only hours of sitting in a plane could produce. He welcomed the thought of a hot shower and a long sleep after it. As it was already after midnight, he wanted them both—fast.

⁂

Melita dreaded having to tell Luke her plans.

They'd both been beyond exhausted when they arrived at the hotel, but they'd each managed a quick shower before collapsing into bed. She'd managed to get a few hours of sleep—not too bad considering what played on her mind, but to bring it up earlier would've meant neither of them would have got any. This way, at least, Luke got a sound night in. She tapped her screen to check the time and double-check the flight details. It was almost nine o'clock and Luke began to stir beside her. He needed to be back at the airport within ninety minutes. She'd been awake an hour and had used it to change her flight.

"Morning, beautiful." Luke pulled her into his arms and lavished delicious kisses over her face. She couldn't help giggling.

"That's better," he said when he pulled back. "Your face had more worry creases than the number we're going to leave on these sheets by the time I'm finished with you."

"Luke, stop for a second."

He did, unexpectedly fast, and concern crossed his face. "Hey, what's up?"

She hesitated, baulked at what she had to ask. "What, ah … time do you need me in Boston?"

"Why?"

She took a deep breath and crossed her fingers under the quilt. "Well, I received two messages last night. One was an invitation from Bianca to attend the announcement of the results from the photography competition. Does this have anything to do with your secret? It seems very convenient I'm in Boston on the same night."

His mouth twisted wryly. "Yes and no."

She frowned. "Luke Harvey, that doesn't answer my question."

"Hey, did you get enough sleep?"

She sank back onto her pillow and sighed. "I'm sorry, I didn't mean to sound so crabby. I did get enough sleep, it's just that—"

"Forgiven. And just so you know, it'll be a secret right up until the last moment, so I can't give you specifics."

She sagged lower under the covers. This was going to hurt, but unless he gave more details, she had no choice.

Come straight out with it, girl.

"Okay. Well, um ... I changed my flight for later this afternoon because of the second message I received. I have some business to attend to and it's *very* convenient that I happen to be in New York."

"What the—" Luke scrambled from the bed. "You did this without checking with me? What's so important you have to spend the day in New York?"

She thought about the night she'd phoned Luke to tell him about the swimsuit spread and the agony she'd suffered during the weeks that followed because of miscommunication. They'd discussed plenty on the flight, but this was something she wanted to tell him when they weren't so tired. Besides, she couldn't deny that his secrecy had rankled from the beginning, so she decided to keep her secret for a few more days. Surely, he would understand.

"It's a secret. I can only reveal it in a few days."

He stared at her, his mouth a straight line. Gradually, it dropped and his shoulders slumped. He must've recognised the same words he'd used to tell her about his secret.

"So this is tit for tat?"

She hoisted herself up and swung her legs over the side of the bed. "It's why I rang you the night Carmela answered. I was calling to tell you about it."

"So tell me now."

She tilted her head and waggled her finger at him. "All will be revealed soon."

He scrubbed a hand over his face. Defeat was obviously not a place Luke liked to visit. "When do you plan on arriving in Boston?"

"Do I need to be at the photography competition venue, because I have the details in the invitation."

"Yeah."

She rose and put her arms around his neck. "I'll be there, Luke. I promise. But you need to leave soon and so do I."

The forlorn look on his face tore at her heart. He'd been like an excited kid the entire flight over. What the heck was so important about this competition? Sure, it meant more fodder for Flynn to milk if Bianca won, but her swimwear spread in *Sports Illustrated* was more important to the success of her business.

Luke released her and turned towards the bathroom. "I better get ready."

Melita began getting changed. "I promise this'll be the last secret I keep from you, Luke."

He didn't turn back when he answered dejectedly, "Yeah, I said the same thing once."

Chapter 34

The final image of Bianca's entry slid from the gigantic screen and still the seat beside him remained empty. The cheering was loud enough that he could hide from the world for a bit. So far, he'd kept a smile pasted to his face, but now the effort was flagging his spirits. Melita's last message had been to let him know that the plane would be leaving shortly. He worked out she should've been at the venue two hours ago.

The crowd, showing their appreciation for Bianca's team, continued clapping and cheering. Even with his inexperience, Luke could tell it was an outstanding entry. There were two more still to be aired and the final decision would be announced in less than an hour.

A large portion of the audience had risen to their feet. A group of Bianca's supporters jostled the back of his seat. Jubilantly, they wolf-whistled and wound up the crowd using a portable megaphone. It would be minutes before the emcee could continue. When someone clapped him on the shoulder to encourage him to stand up and join them, surprising him in his disillusioned state, it nearly sent him reeling across the table. He managed to steady himself and stabilise the chair.

His sole purpose for doing the photographic spread and keeping it a secret was for the last image. Now he had to acknowledge that his plan was a monumental flop. Would it be up to Bianca to answer the whisperings around him of people asking, 'Who's Mel?'

As soon as Melita had told him about needing to stay in New York, the interrupted conversation he'd been having with Flynn the day of the tea house opening flared up in his mind. Flynn had been on the brink of telling him Melita's secret before she'd returned from the bathroom.

How stupid of me! I should've remembered to ask Mel or Flynn. What had Flynn said? That she would be swept away with some other success? Luke had been bone-tired that day but had never meant to fall asleep, and then he hadn't thought past the reward Melita had presented to him when she had returned from dinner. He'd forgotten about his conversation with Flynn until Melita announced her changed flight plans.

Someone thrust a glass of champagne at him and he gulped it down. He choked on it and coughed to clear his throat, then putting the glass down, he checked and rechecked his phone. There were no new messages since the last one.

Not in the mood to view the remaining entries, he eyed the glassed-in bar on the other side of the function room. He wouldn't be missed if he disappeared for a few minutes of blessed silence. The noisy crowd and music were beginning to jar.

He rose on doughy legs, mentally tallying how many drinks he'd had, and weaved around tables to get to the bar. Once there, he pushed on the glass door with his shoulder. The abrupt quiet once it closed behind him was a balm to his frayed nerves, though the heavy throbbing either side of his brow indicated a headache was on its way.

Small round tables dotted the space. He removed his tuxedo jacket and laid it across one of them before sitting on a stool and loosening his tie.

He turned away from the crowd and instead contemplated the street scene from the ceiling-high glass windows. He registered cars driving past, pedestrians walking in both directions and the occasional couple walking hand in hand. When a couple stopped and kissed, he closed his eyes. Too much love in the air physically hurt.

With his eyes still shut, he considered the possibility that his bad luck hadn't completely deserted him. Was it a lifetime curse? Was a nightmare no longer needed to trigger a run of bad luck? Was this his future?

You've sorted out the nightmares, but sorry, mate, you're still screwed.

"Would you like something to drink, sir?"

Luke's eyes shot open to find the barman standing by him.

"A Scotch, thanks."

He may as well continue drowning his sorrows. Nothing else on the horizon looked promising. If a man's girlfriend couldn't tell him what she was getting up to, it didn't bode well. At least his secret had a purpose that fully involved her. Hell, she would have known all about it by now if she'd turned up. But she hadn't kept her promise to be there.

He sipped his Scotch slowly with his shoulders hunched and glum thoughts passing through his mind. He went back to the night it all started, when Melita called and Carmela answered. Their conversation when he'd returned her call had left him miserable, and he'd made a vow, then and there, not to discuss anything personal over long distance again. That had been his reason for not calling her back. Now he realised he should've told her that because it hurt like crazy that she'd never called him. With grim determination he'd pushed the hurt aside and immersed himself in work, spending countless hours with Carmela and working double-time to allow for this short reprieve.

A dismal waste of time.

He sat with his head fogging over, his eyes unseeing. His brain instructed his hand to move the drink from table to mouth. On repeat.

It took the crunch of an ice cube between his teeth for common sense to finally penetrate. A nerve pinched his back as fear wrapped its way around his chest. *Christ*, how self-absorbed and immature could a person get? What if something bad had happened to Melita? What if another bout of bad luck, that sort that caused someone to get hurt, had already struck?

"Bloody hell!" He jumped off the stool but stood immobile, uncertain how to approach his new concern. Did he ring the police, a hospital or

Flynn? God help him, here he was feeling sorry for himself when Melita was probably hurt, in pain and hoping her idiotic boyfriend would realise that something was wrong and come to her aid. So she wasn't present for the announcement of the competition winner. Big deal. It'd be splashed across the internet within three seconds after it was announced.

He should've known better. Could've shown some maturity. Instead, he'd reacted like a spoiled brat—one who hadn't got his way. *Shit!* He'd never forgive himself if she was hurt. They were in Boston after all, where every Van Der Meeliko was a target. She'd told him as much that night in the shed.

He ran an agitated hand through his hair and yanked on his jacket. It was time to get outside into the open air, where hopefully his alcohol-addled head could come up with a plan. He and Melita were meant to be together. Every damn hurdle they'd climbed over was proof of that. His life was nothing without her and he wanted to be part of hers—whether she had millions or not. He didn't give a damn about her money anymore. Melita wasn't affected by it. It was why she was so easy to love—and he had to tell her that. Her remark about her parents not loving her as a child had snagged a nerve the moment she'd uttered it.

He'd seen the hurt written all over her face when, stupidly, he'd used money as the reason they shouldn't be together. It'd taken him a while to grow up, but good souls like Melita deserved to be loved for who they were, not what they owned.

They made a great team—a bloody awesome team—and he had to find her. He'd insisted she come to this damn charade, but he was *not* going to find her hurt. There had to be a reasonable explanation for why she hadn't turned up.

He pushed open the glass door but, expecting a barrage of noise to hit him squarely in the face, stopped mid-stride as he entered the function room. Besides a few hushed whispers, there was silence. He gazed from left to right, jostling for his phone in his trouser pocket when he realised he hadn't checked for any messages the whole time he'd been in the bar.

"Is Luke Harvey in the room?"

His head shot up. The words spoken over the PA system froze his hand and reverberated around his head. He grabbed onto a nearby chair to steady his shaking legs and gulped painfully. How long had he been in the bar? Thirty minutes? Something must've happened to Melita.

Stop it! he wanted to scream. *Nothing has happened to her.*

She was just running late. The plane was delayed, held up, crashed. *No, no, no.* He was not going down that path. But why else would they be calling for him? How would he move forward after this? He'd dragged her halfway around the world on this stupid whim only to find his bad luck had a stranglehold over her and, if they were looking for him, had either hurt her, or worse, killed her.

Or was he just too drunk to make sense of anything?

"Could Luke Harvey please come to the stage?"

Luke glanced in the direction of the stage—and froze.

Chapter 35

"Thanks, Liz. It looks amazing." Melita sat across from the assistant editor of *Sports Illustrated* with the magazine open between them. They'd meticulously gone through every page, critiquing and making comments, and had been at it since Melita first arrived.

"How about some lunch?" Liz asked.

Melita tapped her screen to check the time. When booking her flight, she'd made certain to allow enough time to freshen up before arriving at the competition venue, where she'd agreed to meet Luke. As it was 'top secret stuff'—Luke had used his fingers to make quotation marks—he had to be at the venue early. She'd shaken her head over his secret week plenty of times; she didn't need to again. 'Go with the flow' had become her motto in handling the entire affair, but the sooner both their secrets were aired, the better. It'd turned into some big conspiracy and her decision to keep her swimwear spread a secret too wasn't her brightest idea.

"I think I can manage a quick bite. Have I told you about Boston's photography competition?"

Liz smiled and began tidying up her desk. "Do I want to know?"

Melita gathered her things and rose. "It's the reason Bianca contacted *Sports Illustrated*. She's featuring my swimwear in her entry."

She'd masked her dismay at Luke's reaction to the news of her changed flight. She had the power to hurt him and it frightened her. That wasn't the person she wanted to be. He'd summed it up perfectly when he'd asked if her decision not to tell him what she was doing was tit for tat. It was hard to admit, but it was. She'd never do it again.

Liz stopped tidying and tapped a finger against her lips. "Now that you mention it, I think they told me something about it. Bianca's a close associate of the senior editor, who passed your swimwear project on to me. I don't actually know Bianca personally."

"Then I think lunch is the perfect time to tell you why I have to be in Boston this afternoon."

Liz hoisted her handbag over her shoulder and headed for the door of her plush, modern office. "Please do."

⸙

With about forty minutes to kill, Melita made herself a herbal tea in the business class lounge. Lunch with Liz had been a refreshing break from all the concentrating she'd had to do that morning. Her restless sleep the night before was catching up with her. With a late night still on the cards, her energy was starting to flag.

She took out her phone and placed it beside her cup. Luke had sent a message that morning to say he'd arrived in Boston and she'd sent a quick reply before the meeting with Liz. With Luke hoping to fit in an afternoon nap, she'd saved her next message for when the plane was due to take off.

With her drink finished and the call for passengers to board announced, Melita made her way to the gate. She hoped the herbal tea would do its job and she could relax enough to sleep during the flight. She carried a mask and earplugs, and if she could manage even half an hour of the seventy-five–minute flight, she would be thankful. Jet lag still lingered in her system and she didn't want to turn into a frightful mess later. It was bad enough she was arriving in her hometown, where the Bostonian paparazzi would recognise her instantly.

She grimaced. That's what she loved about Tully. Things might be different after this week, but she loved the anonymity of living there. A lot of people in Tully knew who she was, but compared to a city of millions, the number of people who recognised her didn't rate a mention on her radar of concern.

She hadn't even arrived in Boston and already she wanted to return home. She smiled at the absurdity of her thoughts. So much had changed during the past three and a half years, but she didn't regret a single day. She'd grown and matured and found a true and meaningful path for her future, which she would've never discovered in Boston. Of that she was certain.

Once she'd handed over her boarding pass, she made her way to the entrance tunnel. In a few minutes she could relax, unwind and hopefully sleep. In a couple of hours, she would be with Luke again and that was enough to put an extra buzz in her stride.

Her relief as she sank into the comfortable business-class seat was what she needed after the long and tiring day. A middle-aged woman sat beside her, next to the window. She rested her hand on her chest and looked a little tense, as if she were nervous of flying.

Melita conveyed a cheery hello as she buckled her belt but didn't expect a response. A few years ago, she wouldn't have tried to be friendly, but after living in Australia for so long, it was second nature to her now.

Melita inserted her earplugs so she could try to sleep. She sent a quick message to Luke telling him the plane would be leaving shortly, then put on her mask. Finally, she let her mind drift to simple things, nice thoughts, ones that helped her unwind.

The drone of the safety instructions barely made a blip to her calm state and the movement of the plane along the tarmac was surprisingly soothing. She was nodding off when a hand clutched her wrist and squeezed hard. Melita gasped and tore off her mask. The woman beside her looked alarmed. Her eyes were wide as she clutched at her chest.

Melita, remembering her earplugs, plucked them out. "What's wrong?"

"My ... my chest. I can't breathe," she wheezed, her voice barely audible. "It started when I boarded. Please get help, please, there's something wrong."

Melita glanced around, hoping to catch the attention of an attendant. The plane was still on the tarmac, waiting to take off, so she unbuckled her belt and jumped up, rushed to the front of the plane where the attendants were busying themselves and flung the curtain aside. Clearly alarmed, they jumped back, bracing for a possible attack.

"I'm so sorry for disturbing you, but the passenger beside me is very unwell. She can't breathe."

This alarmed them further. One attendant pushed past Melita, rushing to the passenger's aid, while the other went in the opposite direction and entered the cockpit.

Melita pulled back the black curtain separating the kitchenette and business class section and made her way back to her seat.

"Could someone give us a hand, please?"

Some of the passengers sitting in business class unbuckled their seatbelts and, together with Melita, assisted the attendant. Others looked on and whispered to each other. In the confined space, they laid the woman in the aisle. When her pale skin took on a blue tinge, Melita's heart began beating erratically. The woman may have already had a heart attack and died. Without thinking, Melita took the woman's wrist and felt for a pulse, though she'd never done first-aid training.

When a little blip pulsed against Melita's fingers, she blurted, "She's alive!"

"Great news. We have an ambulance on the way."

Both the pilots and other attendants gathered around and someone opened a first-aid kit that had an array of equipment and other items.

"Would you like me out of the way?" Melita asked.

At her words, the woman tightened her hold. Melita looked down, surprised by the strength the woman showed in her condition.

"I don't think she's willing to let your hand go," one of the pilots commented.

Melita shifted closer to the woman and stroked her hand. "It's okay. I'm happy to stay until the ambulance arrives."

An oxygen mask was placed over the woman's nose and mouth and some colour crept back into her skin. Melita could see the tension drain from the woman's posture. Knowing paramedics were on the way would be helping.

"Can you hear me?" Melita asked. "Squeeze my hand once if you can."

It took a few seconds but she felt the squeeze.

"Good. You know an ambulance is on its way?"

She squeezed again.

They continued a conversation of sorts as they waited. Melita was unaware of how much time was slipping by, though something nagged at the back of her mind, suggesting that things wouldn't go to plan for her today.

When the paramedics arrived, it took time to stabilise the woman before they could confidently remove her from the aircraft. When it came time to do so, she refused to let Melita's hand go. The paramedic tried to prise the woman's hand off, but her strength defied all odds.

"How about I walk beside her to the ambulance?"

The pilot gave her permission to do so, though it compounded the difficulty of getting the woman off the plane. Melita grabbed her handbag from the seat and began forming a plan to help this woman.

It was a careful walk down the mobile staircase, which they'd urgently wheeled into place because of the location of the plane on the tarmac. No doubt this incident would be interrupting the normal schedule of a very busy airport. With the two paramedics on each end of the stretcher, Melita volunteered to carry the oxygen bag.

All the while, Melita continued talking to the woman, comforting her and reassuring her that she would be taken care of. She promised not to leave her side until she was safely inside the ambulance. When it came time to wheel the stretcher into the vehicle, the woman released Melita's hand willingly.

With both hands now free, Melita retrieved two business cards from her handbag. One she placed into the woman's hand, then leaned closer. "I want you to contact me when you're better. Please, promise me you will? I want to know that you're okay." The woman squeezed her hand around the card and Melita's fingers once.

When they secured the stretcher inside the vehicle, Melita gave the other card to the paramedics. "Could you please give this card to the hospital? I want to cover her medical costs. Tell them to contact me to discuss it."

They nodded. The Van Der Meeliko name wasn't as well-known in New York as it was in Boston. It'd take some time for them to make the connection. Regardless, it was something she wanted to do.

But now it was time to board the plane again so it could take off. Once she was back in her seat, she tapped her phone to check the time, then groaned after she realised the episode had eaten away an hour and a half—and the plane hadn't left yet. With her phone in flight mode, she couldn't contact Luke to explain the delay. She chewed on her bottom lip, worrying about how Luke would take her late arrival after she'd promised to be there.

Chapter 36

S he had to go to the motel first, but a quick message to Luke was in
order. She eyed her crumpled navy skirt suit while tapping into her
phone, her knees twitching nervously in the taxi. There was no way she
could enter Boston society without freshening up first. Poor Luke. He
would be at his wit's end. No point in phoning him at this stage. The
damage was done. Only being there to explain her reasons would let her
off the hook for breaking a promise.

"I need you to wait here for about half an hour. Please don't leave," she
instructed the taxi driver. Warned of her predicament he was happy to wait
with the meter ticking, though that was the least of her worries.

A second key was waiting for her at the motel reception. As she rushed
to the elevator, she thanked her lucky stars that her shimmering ocean-blue
dress was non-crushable. She pumped her fist in the empty elevator,
grateful to have a private moment to herself. Ironing the dress was one less
task to complete before she could dash back to the waiting cab.

In a blink, she'd used up the allotted meagre half-hour. Forgetting about
her booming headache, her parched mouth and the sweaty sheen on her
skin, she rushed down the foyer steps, surprised she didn't twist her ankle
in the ridiculous heels she'd decided to wear. Neither did she trip over the
long shimmering length of her dress that reached past her ankles. That was
two positives to help cancel out the negatives she was about to face. She
looked okay; all she had to do was calm down and put a smile on her face.

Not impossible to achieve if she could be guaranteed of smiles at the other end.

She shrugged as she climbed into the cab. Luke would understand once he knew the reasons she was delayed. But what if her late arrival spoiled the surprise? She grimaced as she tapped impatiently on her thigh. When would their lives return to normal? They'd experienced some semblance of it before the shed incident, before the bottle shop drama, before her living room window had been smashed. Before a lot of things.

It was a lifetime ago.

Within minutes, she would be at the venue and needed to boost her reserves. She'd had no chance at sleeping on the plane the second time around, and her tiredness, while not evident, was there and ready to fell her if she made one wrong move. A strong coffee was what she needed, or a stiff drink.

Melita paid her fare and thanked the driver. Outside the venue, she straightened her dress and attempted to calm down. Making her way to the foyer, she took a deep breath and brought up the invitation on her phone.

Finding the function room was easy. This was a big event in Boston's annual social calendar and journalists and reporters jostled around the closed door of the entrance.

"They're about to announce the winner," one reporter said.

Intent on hearing the coming announcement, no one took any notice of her, and she slipped inside without any drama.

The noise when she entered was like hitting a physical barricade. Reporters pushed her further in and the chaos of the announcement was lost on her. She would never find Luke in this commotion. Whistling and some sort of trumpet or mega-phone blasted around the room. Guests had risen and were clapping and cheering.

Oh, Luke, where are you? She just wanted a bed to rest her weary head on.

After a few minutes, she realised the emcee was trying to talk over the crowd. When everyone quietened, he said, "While Bianca Douglas and her team make their way to the stage, we'll replay the winning entry."

Ooh, so Bianca won.

Nerves assailed her. She would finally get to see her swimwear. Bianca's work had been top-secret, so this was Melita's chance to see what had been achieved with her unique designs. And everyone else would see them too. She swayed but steadied herself. No way was she going to faint now. This was her moment, and just the start. The *Sports Illustrated* spread was the next big thing, her first tea house, the icing on top. Excitement tingled up and down her arms. She breathed in short adrenalin-fuelled bursts.

Come on Luke, where are you?

Desperate to find him, she looked over heads, peered left and right, scanned for anyone she recognised—until the first image was aired on the massive screen and she gasped.

Luke stared back at her.

Everything slotted into place. Her jaw dropped and she couldn't move to save herself as each image remained on the screen for about a minute.

"You have to find the red scarf," she heard someone behind her say.

In the moment that followed she spotted it around the female model's neck. In the next image it was cleverly camouflaged, and like everyone else around her, she wanted to point out where it was hiding.

Doubt, or incredulity, hammered against her brain. No way. This could not be! Not *their* silk scarf? But what other answer was there? It was the red scarf that meant so much to her, to them. The same one that had disappeared without a trace. Oh, good Lord. Did Luke have it all this time?

Melita was so entranced with the love story playing out in front of her, with her Luke, that tears built up behind her lashes. The dilemma of figuring out whether the silk scarf was theirs or not, and the fact Luke was nowhere to be found, added to her distress. How he'd managed to keep this from her was astounding. It was big. Really big. No, it was huge—not only for her swimwear but for Luke's *life*. It was never going to be the same again. *Their* lives were never going to be the same—and his other modelling work hadn't even been released yet.

A final image slid across the massive screen, and like a strong draught, it nearly knocked her sideways. She grabbed the edge of a chair and gaped at the photo. In it, Luke faced the female model, though a large straw hat obscured her head, leaving only the back of her sun dress visible. Luke had his hand stretched towards the girl, the red silk scarf lightly scrunched in it, as though he were offering it to her. The words 'Marry me, Mel' were emblazoned across the top of the image—the only words in the entire series.

Marry me, Mel. Marry me, Mel.

The words danced past her eyes and she tried to permit them entry into her head. But it wasn't working; nothing made sense. It felt like hours—but was probably only seconds—before the bold truth smacked her between the eyes and *everything* made sense.

Luke had planned to propose to her!

Oh, Luke. She loved him like no other and she'd turned up late to his proposal. Tears were threatening to bubble over when she heard mutterings around her.

"Who's Mel?"

"Who is this Mel?"

"Does anyone know?"

She sniffed, blinked back tears and straightened her shoulders. It was time to shine and show Luke she loved him. And only him.

And then she realised something, because how else would Bianca have known about her swimwear? She was unknown, a fledgling designer in Australia. Finally, she had her answer. All this time, Luke had been behind her success. Now it was even more important that he learned about her *Sports Illustrated* spread. God help her, she owed him everything—especially her love.

Now was the time. She hadn't got to this juncture in the road to turn around and give up. She and Luke had faced every obstacle—believing they were connected by a sister, learning she'd been adopted, dealing with Luke's terrorising fear that had him blaming himself for all their problems, their abduction by the Black Hand where either of them could've been hurt or killed, their separation while Luke began his modelling career, the miscommunication and the resulting hurt. No more!

She took her first tentative step towards the stage, mustered all the grace she possessed, hoped her make-up and hair was up to Boston society standards and produced the best smile her haggard body could muster under the circumstances.

She wound her way between tables and chairs, guests drinking and talking, and photographers snapping at everything that moved. Every step she took got her closer to the stage. She climbed the stairs, and amidst all the noise and excitement, no one noticed her.

When she reached the emcee's side, she boldly took the microphone and turned to the crowd. "I'm Mel."

No one heard her, so she repeated it another three times. Finally, the crowd caught on and a hush descended over the room, though some people spoke in fevered whispers. Melita saw dozens of camera flashes; no doubt the reporters were having a field day.

She repeated her words once more. "I'm Mel. Where's Luke?"

She stood on the stage, hoping for a sight of him.

A lady sidled up and gently took the microphone from her. "Is Luke Harvey in the room?"

She hid the microphone behind her back and whispered, "Hi, Melita. I'm Bianca. Great to meet you. Luke's here somewhere, so don't worry. We'll find him."

She spoke into the microphone again. "Could Luke Harvey please come to the stage?"

Melita noticed something glint in her periphery. It beckoned like a lighthouse beacon and so she turned towards it. That was when she saw Luke. His hair was tousled, just how she loved it, and the black tuxedo looked gorgeous on him. She'd never seen him wear one before and didn't doubt he hated being confined in it. Her tiredness vanished at the sight of him. He looked confused and uncomfortable—until the moment he clapped eyes on her.

A look of startled surprise crossed his face, reminding her of an animal trapped in the beam of a light. With purpose, he began to move towards the stage.

Melita wasn't waiting a moment longer. She made her way towards the stairs and gripped the railing leading down for all it was worth. Now was not the time to trip and fall in her silly heels. She didn't know what she looked like from his vantage point or if he'd forgive her for turning up late. But those things didn't matter. When they were only metres apart, she risked all and ran towards him.

She stumbled on the last step but didn't care. His warm and loving arms were open as he waited to catch her and she didn't hesitate to wrap hers around his neck. She had the strength of a drowning sailor, holding on for dear life in very rough conditions. Tears began coursing down her face—great, big sobbing bursts that had her hiding her face in his neck.

"Yes, Luke, of course I will!" she shouted in his ear, over and over again.

He tried to pull her away, but she held on, reluctant to reveal her blotchy, tear-stained face. When she relented and stepped back, he wore a confused expression.

"Yes, to what?" he shouted over the noise.

"Yes, I'll marry you." What was the problem? Had she incorrectly read the message?

"But you haven't seen the entry yet."

"Yes, I did. Just now. They showed the winning entry."

Luke's face transformed, tumbling her stomach and bringing alive every pulse on her body. The biggest smile was spread across his face and his gaze was riveted to hers. Her legs shook and her heart beat faster as the rest of the world faded away.

"I love you, Luke. I'm so sorry I didn't arrive on time."

Whether he could hear her or not, it didn't matter. He closed his eyes briefly, then looked up as though reciting a prayer. Relief poured off him and when his gaze came to rest on hers again, he wrapped his arms around her waist and kissed her long and hard.

When he pulled back, he reached into his jacket pocket and retrieved something red. She gasped when she recognised the silk scarf.

"For you," he mouthed as the first bits of gold glitter rained down over them, then he leaned in and kissed her again.

She held the silk scarf scrunched in her hand between them, so it touched her heart and his at the same time. Sentimental crap, Luke would say, but he wasn't saying it now.

When they finally drew apart, she registered the constant flash of cameras. Glitter confetti continued to rain down. They held hands, slivers of red visible between their entwined fingers. This was her and Luke's story. She would never forget how a scrap of red material made such an impact on it. The absurdity of it caused a bubble of laughter to find its way up her throat. When it burst from her mouth, her tears were long gone and she beamed a radiant smile to the world. It wasn't how she'd expected to greet Boston society after such a long absence, but she wouldn't have changed a thing. Cameras snapped close by and for once she was okay with it. Luke laughed with her and together they connected, like they were meant to.

Extract from the *Boston Herald*

Bianca Douglas and her very skilled team have taken out this year's prestigious Boston Photography Competition. The lavish awards presented last night saw the top ten outstanding entries aired to the audience before the winner was announced. It's her third win in the past ten years and she's thrilled.

"Each win is just as special as the first. I'm so proud of my team for their dedication."

Little is known about the fresh-faced Australian who made his debut in Bianca's winning entry. By all reports we haven't seen the last of him. Contracted to Bluefin Productions, Luke Harvey is at the tail end of a six-week contract. Advertising from that project will be on your screens by the end of the year.

The swimwear worn and promoted in the entry was designed by none other than our darling of Boston society, Melita Van Der Meeliko. Unconfirmed reports suggest she's been spending time in Australia, where she's been busy designing swimwear. Melita hit the jackpot when Bianca chose her swimwear to feature in her entry. Stay tuned, because reliable sources suggest that Melita's swimwear is set to feature in the next *Sports Illustrated Swimwear Issue*, due out in only a couple of days. Melita was unavailable for comment, except to confirm that she is the 'Mel' referred to in Bianca's last image. As to whether she accepted the marriage proposal, she's not saying.

Extract from the *Cassowary Coast Independent News*

Locals in Tully received the outstanding news this week that our very own Melita Van Der Meeliko, owner of The Silk Scarf Tea House, had a win with her swimwear last week when it featured in the winning entry of the annual Boston Photography Competition. This is great news for Australian tourism, as her range of swimwear features popular Australian animals. Melita, when speaking to *Cassowary Coast News*, assures us that the swimwear is available Australia-wide, with plenty of stock at her tea house boutique. Her first combined boutique and tea house in our very own backyard will draw more tourists to the area.

And it doesn't end there for Melita. Her swimwear range also features in this year's *Sports Illustrated Swimwear Issue*.

"I'm thrilled with the whole look and excited to be promoting everything Australian. I've been welcomed with open arms and look forward to expanding my tea house business with other locations along the Queensland coast."

Unconfirmed reports suggest she's recently announced her engagement to Brisbane born Luke Harvey. A well-known tradesman in the area, he's making his mark in both the building and modelling worlds. He featured in the winning photographs in Boston and has nearly completed a six-week modelling project with Bluefin Productions in North America. His recent renovation of the building that is home to The Silk Scarf Tea House has been nominated for Best Eco-Green Refurbishment/Renovation in this year's Queensland Master Builders Awards.

The Cassowary Coast community extends its congratulations to them both.

AUTHOR NOTE

A property does exist at the exact intersection on the Bruce Highway, as mentioned in the story. It has sat abandoned since the 1930s and has always intrigued me. Asking my father if he knew anything about it opened my eyes to the history of the area. The building is known locally as 'the mafia house' and people were allegedly murdered in it. The Black Hand was a very real threat during this time and is an integral part of North Queensland's history. The threat of the Black Hand has long gone, but it still remains a sensitive topic in the area.

Of course, I'm hoping someone will read this story and be inspired to breathe some life back into the house that continues to sit abandoned on this picturesque stretch of road.

THANKS FOR READING

Thank you for reading **The Silk Scarf** and I hope you enjoyed it. If you missed the first two books in **The Australian at Heart Series,** it's not too late to go back and read them. Set mostly in Queensland, you'll recognise town names and places, along with our dusty outback and our refreshing rainforest. Then you can finish the series by reading the fourth book, Rustic Denim Love. This is Flynn's story and is set in and around the fabulous Herberton Historic Village.

Writing a book requires that your mind and body is nourished and taken care of every day. For this I want to thank my father. Thanks Dad! After immigrating to Australia as a young 17-year-old, marrying young and raising a family of six children, it became his mainstay to provide nourishment for all his family. Far from fading in colour, his green thumb has become brighter and greener over the years and he continues to this day to grow the healthiest vegetables and fruits. His generosity knows no boundaries and his family is always the first to sample the goodness of his labours.

As always, I want to thank my critique partner and friend, Lisa Stanbridge. We're still in this together!

My mum always deserves a special mention, as do my three daughters. Always there, always supportive. And my other half who makes me whole.

And lastly, a huge thank you to my readers, who give me purpose every day.

ALSO BY FRANCES DALL'ALBA

The **Australian at Heart Series** tells the stories of four interconnected siblings.

<u>Little Blue Box — Book 1</u>

Regrets, lies, and earth-shattering secrets. When Ella learns the identity of her biological father, nothing will stand in her way. Not even his power. When things don't go to plan, can one little blue box put Ella and Zane back on the same path? This second chance contemporary romance is filled with suspense, emotion and a life-changing sizzling romance.

<u>The Stone In The Road — Book 2</u>

Emotional, passionate and heart-wrenching. This suspense-filled captivating romance will have you dancing in the rain and smiling through your tears. Set in tropical northern Australia, we don't always get to choose our path.

The Silk Scarf – Book 3

An unravelling silken scarf ... mysterious gold ... a breathtaking romance.

An emotional and unforgettable contemporary romance set in Australia.

Rustic Denim Love – Book 4

Forgotten secrets ... blazing fires ... burning love.

She's busy and diligent, doing the best she can to save her crumbling family.

He's funny and witty, with a solution for every problem.

This one may just beat him.

Link to read more and BUY.

https://francesdallalba.wixsite.com/francesdallalba/australianathe artseries

Sway of The Stars Series will share the stories of a group of friends.

<u>The Shooting Star – Book 1</u>

Hidden treasures ... broken spirits ... tangled love. A modern-day treasure hunt where hidden treasures will tangle their love and break their spirits. Duty or love, or can they have both?

<u>The Glittering Star –Book 2</u>

Shimmering waters ... towering giants ... buried mysteries. She's the no filters chick. Funny, full of life and always ready for a good laugh. Until her mother drops a bombshell. He's the environmental warrior. Passionate, driven and determined to save the world. Burnt once before, he's moving on and doing things his way. So how did they end up hand cuffed together on day one?

<u>The Giving Star – Book 3</u>

Endless roads ... timeless discoveries ... unbreakable love. She's packed up her life ready for change, with one regret still hanging over her head. He's working his way back from hell, adamant he's never going there again. But one stumble, one discovery, and one hotbed of attraction ... and the entire game plan changes.

The Priceless Star – Book 4

Forgotten treasures ... a perilous ransom ... shattered hopes

She's chasing answers long buried since the war.

He's content with a steady working life. Until he's not...

Sent to Far North Queensland to research a wartime mystery, Lucia Levorico escapes her privileged life and finds unexpected passion with reserved local, Theo Mather, under an outback sky – until a sudden goodbye and a devastating worksite tragedy tear them apart. When a ruthless ransom plot targets Lucia's wealth, their only reprieve will come from sharing the unravelling of a wartime mystery and its priceless treasure. Unless they're willing to fight for what they have.

Link to read more and BUY.

https://francesdallalba.wixsite.com/francesdallalba/swayof the stars

Eight Seconds, is a standalone story inspired by Australia's first female open bullrider. She pushed past the barriers and succeeded in a male dominated sport, creating a new legend showcased in two Australian halls of fame.

Triumph, hardship, true grit ... and one crazy dream.
An inspirational story about one woman, with one dream, and one almighty driving passion.

Link to read more and BUY.
https://francesdallalba.wixsite.com/francesdalla lba/eightseconds

Jack& Eva, is a standalone contemporary romance set in tropical North Queensland. It showcases our unique and adorable Lumholtz tree kangaroo and the valuable work done by Dr Karen Coombes in her care and continued research of them.

Broody meets bubbly ... and a bunch of cuddly tree kangaroos.
When the tempest blows over, will Jack and Eva be able to find a way forward, or are they destined for a train wreck with a bunch of furry animals caught up in the middle?
Fall in love with our adorable tree kangaroo while reading an emotional and passionate contemporary romance set in Australia.
Link to read more and BUY.
https://francesdallalba.wixsite.com/francesdallalba/jackandeva

ABOUT THE AUTHOR

As a contemporary romance author, Frances loves nothing more than losing herself in a good romance. She's all about helping you forget the housework, or the bus to work you're going to miss, if you don't put the book down now!

She's devoted to giving her readers an emotional, passionate, possibly some ugly-cry, fairly steamy love story, that'll melt your heart and have you fighting for the happy ending right until the end.

Frances sets her books in North Queensland. She makes no excuses if some of her settings include amazing lakes and waterfalls, stunning views from tops of mountains, spectacular outback scenes, or crystal-clear creeks shadowed by tropical rainforest.

When she isn't writing, Frances is climbing mountains, searching for waterfalls and swimming across lakes. She loves to exercise, would prefer it if someone else cooked dinner every night, and never notices dust on the furniture.

She lives with her husband in tropical Far North Queensland, Australia, and uses her great baking skills to tempt her family to visit home often.

Say hello to Frances

Visit her website: https://francesdallalba.wixsite.com/francesdallalba and subscribe to her newsletter. It will keep you up-to-date with everything happening in her author world.

Follow Frances on Facebook, Instagram, Bookbub, TikTok, and Goodreads. To do so, click on this link: https://linktr.ee/francesdallalba

Still have a question?

Ask her at: https://francesdallalba.wixsite.com/francesdallalba/contact

Leave a Review

Did you enjoy this book? The best favour you can do for an author is to leave a **review**. If you'd like to leave a review, go to your place of on-line purchase of the book, or search for the book on **Goodreads** and leave a review. Thank you.